BUTTERFLY

In A Flame

NADIA RED

BUTTERFLY IN A FLAME

iUniverse books may be ordered through booksellers or by contacting:

iUniverse
1663 Liberty Drive
Bloomington, IN 47403
www.iuniverse.com
844-349-9409

ISBN: 978-1-6632-2160-5 (sc)
ISBN: 978-1-6632-2161-2 (e)

Library of Congress Control Number: 2022923634

Print information available on the last page.

iUniverse rev. date: 11/22/2022

Prologue

There's Nothing Wrong with a Little Love and Hate

Ring! Ring! Ring!

Reaching over, I swipe right to answer the phone. "Detective Bates," I groggily say.

"Sorry to wake you, sir, but you're needed out in Santee off Boulder Ave at the Envy Center. There's been a homicide."

"Great," I mutter. "Give me an hour."

I stretch my tired muscles and get out of bed to get dressed. After brushing my teeth and washing my face, I put on jeans and a shirt with a lame dad pun on it: "Becoming a vegetarian is a big missed steak." In fifteen minutes, I am out the door. *No need to dress up for the dead.* I get into my rusted blue 1972 Chevy Cheyenne and head to the location. After parking amid the other cop cars, my partner Pamela meets me with a hot cup of joe.

"What're the stats?" I inquire, taking a tentative sip of the beverage.

She ticks them off on the fingers of her left hand. "Young female, gunshot to the head from behind, suspect on a run driving a silver Dodge Challenger, only witness is unconscious and on her way to the hospital."

As I near the yellow tape, I catch sight of a body covered by a white sheet. The fabric is sticking to the wet ground from the light drizzle of the recent thunderstorm. Bending down as my old knees crack in protest, I lift the corner, examining the corpse.

A once beautiful woman in probably her late twenties lies somewhat on her side, her left cheek pressed against the grass. It seems she was amid a sad smile before the assailant shot from behind at a small distance. A large hole is present in the back of her skull, covered with hair dried in blood and fragments of brain sprinkled throughout. The corner of her lips slightly tilted upward, with high cheekbones causing her eyes to crease. The image frozen upon her face looks like a work of Da Vinci himself.

I hear my partner questioning some guests that are standing around witnessing this tragic event. Murmurs filter through the night air, the onlookers processing that someone they personally knew or laid eyes on that night is dead. A Halloween wedding has gotten its haunted ending. Just as I go to return the sheet, my eyes catch something across the victim's chest peeking out from her torn shirt: *A rainbow-colored butterfly tattoo.*

One

"Move, a-hole! Who taught you how to drive, your blind, decrepit grandma?" I growl as I swerve from behind the brand new, white Ford F-150. The jackass driving seems to have all the time in the world. I am stuck in this Wednesday-morning mayhem trying to get downtown. I'm not sure why I thought I could rush to work on a weekday morning in San Diego. The contractor who believed six lanes would be more efficient in getting drivers to their destinations quicker was smoking something. Instead it caused major confusion to occur among everyone trying to get around the city at once. Now I must scream, dodge, and honk at an excessive number of individuals that have been granted a license. With my horrible road rage, I am the one that would chase you down if you cut me off. I know I should not be doing that in this day in age; it is just that not everyone should be allowed behind a wheel.

I work for Lilac Essences as a marketing coordinator. Mr. Earl Mitchell, a short, stocky man in his late forties, is the CEO. His dark blonde hair is greying at the roots and cut like that of Vincent Vega from *Pulp Fiction*. Like, dude, we are in the twenty-first century! Why does he still have that hairstyle? He started this company out of his basement after his attempt at being a rock star fell through. They are now among the top major marketing corporations in California and in the top five of the United States. It is named after his late wife's favorite flower.

In my last year of business school, she gave a presentation on behalf of her husband, and I fell in love with the company. Their ethics and the expansion of their creativity inspired me the most. I knew on that day I would work here no matter what. When I came for my interview, Mr. Mitchell hired me on the spot. He loved my smart wit and no-BS attitude. However, he did not bargain that having me on his team would blow up in his face. After six months of being here, I became a serious handful. Now, I would not call us hateful, but I will say we do not get along and often throw professional side comments. A lot of the staff are surprised that I have not been fired yet. Do not get me wrong; he has tried his hardest to make me quit by giving me crappy campaigns and challenging clients. I must jump through flaming hoops just to receive the raises I deserve, and my completed proposals are finely combed through before his approval. However, I am still here for three years, proving my worth so I can become one of the big dogs in that corner office.

Running late for my particularly important client can be a major setback. LTW Construct is the number-one typhoon construction company on the West Coast. With a new high-rise built almost every three months, I want this company in my books. I am supposed to persuade them to sign with me in twenty minutes.

However, my eye candy for the month unplugged my phone from the charger sometime during the night, causing it to die and not alert me this morning. I met Clark at the bar about a month ago when I was out with the girls. What attracted me was his bronze-carmel skin that matched mines and his short, curly brown hair. We have been at it like cats and dogs ever since. One thing I can say is I *love sex!* There is no such thing as too much of it and finding a way between some sheets is no issue. I have even experimented with a few females, but nothing can top a long, warm, thick … okay, yeah, you get my point. *I should have just blown Clark off last night.* Cocking my head to the side, I smirk. *Well, I did do that!*

As I pull into the garage of Pacific Gate, I glance down at the dashboard to see it is ten minutes past the hour. *Crap! I am really late.* I park my sleek midnight-black Audi R8 with red chrome rims in an open spot. Grabbing my things from the passenger seat, I slip out of the car, locking it as I straighten my pants suit. I quickly stroll to the elevator, trying not to trip in my red Giuseppe stilettos. I scan my keycard to gain access, taking a deep breath to calm my nerves as I watch the numbers on the panel slowly increase. I step into the lobby, waving to the secretary at the front desk.

"Good morning, Zola! Guess Clark kept you up late," greets Lynn, one of my closest friends from college. She exaggeratedly winks at me as if she is having a seizure in the face. Her mass of natural red curls that have a mind of their own, sensibly tamed for once. And yes, she has the stereotypical fiery redhead attitude.

Her mother moved around a lot since she could not keep a steady job after Lynn's father abandoned them when she was eight. She ended up attending four different schools in six years before she finally settled in Texas to graduate high school in one place. Lynn moved to New Orleans for college after receiving a full athletic scholarship for volleyball. She is currently in nursing school while working part-time at Lilac Essences.

I chuckle. "Girl, I had him tapped out before we even made it to round three."

I swear Lynn's jaw hits the floor before she bursts into laughter at my comment. Along with our other bestie, Kyla, we have been breaking hearts from our hometown of New Orleans across the southern border. Now we are all settled in the breezy community of San Diego. We may not be America's next top models, but we are in the top ranks. Our group is a mix of different personalities, ethnicities, and vibrant styles, making us a triple threat. All the women want to know us and be us, while all the men want to claim us. Real friendships are hard to come by, which is why I lucked out on finding them.

Kyla, our workout guru with Brazilian roots, was the shy one who worked the front desk of the sophomore dorms. One night when my date stood me up, I asked her to join me for drinks when she was getting off work. She tried to refuse, but I convinced her to come. Ever since that night of bonding, we became fast friends. We met Lynn the following year. She was arguing with her boyfriend, Ronnie, at a fratparty. It was a funny sight with the contrast of her short frame to his much taller one. When he went to put his hands on her, we stepped in, and the three of us beat his ass.

"Are the men of LTW Construct here?" I ask.

Lynn sighs and places a hand beneath her chin. Her large baby-blue eyes take on a wistful look that has me snapping my fingers in front of her to get her attention. "Gurrrllll! Those hunks are America's Greek gods." She takes a deep breath, fanning herself. "They are in Boardroom Two, waiting on you. And let me say Mr. Mitchell is not happy now. He has already called up here twice, asking if I knew where you were. Naturally, I played dumb."

"Shit! Well, I know I'ma get a lecture this afternoon." As I mention earlier, I am not one of the boss's favorite people.

"Well, if it isn't the almighty Zola Saunders. Shouldn't you be in a presentation now, or did Mr. Mitchell finally come to his senses and decide you don't deserve this account?" Landon says snidely.

Landon Tate is Mr. Mitchell's *biggest* ass kisser in the firm. If you ever see him, he will remind you of a Pez dispenser with a tall, skinny body; big head; and bulging Adam's apple. He wears his black hair in a long ponytail at the nape of his neck and no matter the temperature outside, he rocks a leather jacket. Like, the idiot does not even know how to ride a motorcycle. Landon is at Mr. Mitchell's beck and call, which works in his favor since he hardly does any work and gets all the major contracts. I'm fairly sure he has been on his knees a couple of times under the boss's desk, if you catch my drift. He is also my mortal enemy and rival because he wants the same corner office I do. I, unfortunately, had to plead with the boss to give me a chance on this account. So now Landon and I are doing a face-off to win LTW Construct's marketing contract.

"Landon." I smile sweetly, brushing my raven-black dreads with electric-blue dyed tips off my shoulders before anazlyzing my nails. "You still overcompensating for your nonexistent penis with the idea that you have adequate marketing skills?"

Lynn roars with laughter in the quiet lobby, causing the door to Boardroom Two to open with an outraged, very red-faced Mr. Mitchell on the threshold. "Zola," he hisses through clenched teeth as he strides toward me, his arms rampart straight against his sides. "So glad you remembered you had a presentation this morning and graced us with your presence." Sarcasm is dripping from his words.

Rolling my eyes at Landon's sardonic look, I paste on a golden smile. "Sorry, sir. Cali traffic shows no mercy. I'm here now."

"Next time try calling to give us a heads-up. Now, let us get things moving before Landon wins by default." He retreats into the boardroom after giving Lynn a glance.

If I did not know any better, I would assume the old buzzard has a thing for her. He seems to always find himself by her desk though his office is three floors above us. I am consistently dropping hints about his crushing attitude, but she denies it and claims they are just friends. Yeah, okay! This chick has daddy issues and has a creepy attraction to old men. Hence Michael, one of the two men she is jugging. He is her sugar daddy, whose wife is battling cancer.

"Good luck," mouths Lynn as I head toward the boardroom. Right as I reach the door, I turn around and flip Landon off. The murderous look he sends me gives me all the confidence I need to dominate this presentation.

Two

I have gathered a great amount of research on LTW Construct. The three partners consist of Traymel and Lincoln Crane, twin brothers, and their childhood best friend Wesley. They started this company from the ground up after graduating from college. It was rough initially, but it came around and is now known all over the West Coast. Lincoln handles the business aspects, Traymel comes up with the designs and locations, and Wesley is all about the financials. There are two other offices up the coastline with the headquarters located in San Diego. LTW Construct is looking to expand into the eastern region, which is why they are here today. With word of mouth from their connections, they have grown so far. However, to get to the heights they anticipate, they need outside help, and Lilac Essences is a major brand.

I hear Mr. Mitchell speak when I open the door. "I apologize! Ms. Saunders has just arrived, and I assure you her presentation will be worth the wait." *He gave me a compliment. Surprising!*

All eyes turn to me as I walk into the boardroom with my head held high. The way I fill out this charcoal-gray pantsuit is sinful. It is like a second skin, putting my hourglass figure on display. The tops of my breasts strain against the fitted jacket. The pants clad my thick thighs and flare out down long legs. The one twin with the fade seems a bit uncomfortable in his chair as I slowly trek to the front. My hips sway with a slight bounce of my apple bottom to a rhythm my body established in my younger days.

After pulling up the PowerPoint on the projector, I set up the canvas board on the stand. My slanted almond-shaped hazel eyes settle on each of them with a smile so bright and allow my presence to capture the audience. Using a soft and alluring yet demanding voice, I go through the presentation. Having come up with a profitable, affordable, and captivating proposal, I point out their business strengths as well as some areas the company should improve on.

"Are there any questions?" I ask, turning off the PowerPoint and facing the group.

"I understand the annual return is fifteen percent over last year's profits. Is this spread throughout the year or as one big chunk?" inquires the one that reminds me of a chubby RuPaul in his forest green suit.

"You should see the first wave of increase after the first three months, and then it'll level out with a minimal difference monthly," I respond.

They glance at one another, smiling and nodding in approval. *With any luck, they will prefer my viewpoints and decide on me.* "Well, gentlemen, thank you for your time, and I apologize for keeping you waiting this morning."

Mr. Mitchell encourages them to take a fifteen-minute break before Landon's presentation. I gather my things and make my way to the door. The twin that has been eyeing me as if I am his last meal grabs my arm just as my hand touches the door handle. He quickly releases it as a physical shiver, barely noticeable, runs down my back. With my hand still on the doorknob, I lift my eyes up his towering frame. He stands a little over six feet with dark chocolate-colored skin and steel-gray eyes. His hair is cut in a fade with no facial hair. His muscle-infused torso looks to have been sculptured through many years of staying on his weights.

"Sir?" I softly speak.

"You did a good job up there," he deadpans, slipping his hands into his pockets.

"I know." I smirk before leaving the room.

Whew! So glad that is over. I am fairly confident I had them hanging on my every word. What can I say; it is a gift. For as long as I can remember, I have been able to get others to do my bidding with just a flash of my pearly whites. Therefore, I decided going into marketing was the right move, because here I can excel up the ranks quickly. Unfortunately, I got stuck with a judging boss who has a chip on his shoulder because I do not always let him be right.

"So, Bish! How ya do?" Lynn half-whispered, half-yelled across the lobby, interrupting my thoughts. "Pretty sure you crushed it even with you being Ms. Late Diva."

Rolling my eyes at her jab, I raise my arms in the air and roll my hips like a slow-motion cyclone. Of course, that is when the hunks decide to step out of the boardroom and catch my little performance.

"All right, Mrs. Baby Bash," the short one states. I facepalm myself as Lynn snickers at my expense.

Landon ambles up to me and leans over to whisper in my ear, quietly enough for only me to hear. "I guess showing off your goods is the only way you'll get this contract over me." I clench my fists at my sides as he walks away toward the boardroom before I can deliver a remark. *Oh, count your days, Mr. Tate!* I turn on my heels and stalk to my office to await the results.

Time seems to drag as I sit at my desk awaiting Mr. Mitchell. I have been rereading the same strategic blueprint for my current client for the last hour. Setting it aside, I lean back in my chair and close my eyes. My thoughts drift to those hunks of LTW Construct—one in particular. The way his eyes analyzed me throughout my presentation had my body warm. It took everything out of me to keep my concentration. *His lips leaving a soft trail of kisses along my neck, those large hands sliding down my back to grip my ass before lifting me up to wrap my legs around his massive frame. Slowly grinding my . . .*

"Zola!"

I jump from my daydreaming upon hearing a screech.

"Gurl, don't make me walk to your office. Did you fall asleep again?"

Quickly grabbing the phone, I hiss through the receiver at my oversharing friend. "Lynn, *seriously!* I thought we were not supposed to talk about that at work."

"Well, hell, I've been paging you for the last three minutes. They have decided and want you and Landon to meet back in the boardroom."

Whew! This is it . . . the moment of truth. I hang up the phone and stroll out of my office. I take steady breaths as I near the boardroom to calm my beating heart. *Why am I freaking out? I have this in the bag. Get it together, Zola.*

Landon is already sitting in the room when I enter. He has a Cheshire cat grin on his face that I immediately want to slap off. Taking the chair across from him, I acknowledge Mr. Mitchell standing at the front of the room.

"Are we doing this or not?" the twin that did not stop me earlier asks, leaning back in his chair. He seems to be bored and losing patience. He shares the same skin tone and eye color as the other one but has dreads like me, yet all black. His face is framed by a full shaggy beard with a big nose and plump lips. The sleeves of his shirt are rolled up, and I notice that his right arm is covered in tattoos of Egyptian symbols. Even from his sitting position, he seems slightly shorter than the other.

"Why? You have a lunchtime romp you need to attend to?" snickers the last of the partners. He is your typical blonde-haired, blue-eyed, pale Caucasian male. He's a little on the chubby side, with big ears, thin lips, and a goatee.

"At least I experience *romps*, as you call them," counters the same twin, air quoting the word "romps." "The only action you've seen this year is your hand." My hand covers my mouth, trying to hold in the inappropriate laugh that wants to bubble out.

"Well, at least my hand is tighter than your loose-as-a-goose fangirls," replies the chubby one, waving one of his hands in the air.

"It feels tight to you because that beefy hand of your swallows your pint-size cock."

"Mr. Mitchell," the twin with few words interjects, cutting off their childish bickering. "Ms. Saunders is here, so we can continue. We are an active enterprise and have other things to attend to."

My boss nods his head. "Let us get the ball rolling. Both presentations were impressive and captivating. Unfortunately, you both cannot take on the project. We have all discussed the highs and lows of each proposal and finally came to a unanimous decision. The LTW Construct marketing contract goes to"—he pauses, glancing at Landon and me in suspense—"Zola."

I shoot up to my feet, slamming my palms on the table. "Ah, suck it, Tate!"

Landon crosses his arms against his chest and leans back, fuming. I can almost see the steam coming out of his ears. This is the first I have seen him at a loss for words. He usually has a retort. Instead he just sends daggers my way as the hunks come and shake my hand in congratulations.

"Zola, let me introduce you to the men you'll be working with," says Mr. Mitchell. "This is Mr. Wesley Dreer." *Chubby Caucasian.* "Mr. Lincoln Crane." *Dreadhead.* "Lastly, his twin brother, Mr. Traymel Crane." *MuscleMan.*

"Gentlemen, it a pleasure to meet you all. I feel there will be great endeavors in the coming years as we take over the eastern region. I shall draw up the contracts over the next few days and have the final copies in your email by Friday, end of day. That way you can review them over the weekend and we can sign first thing Monday morning."

"Sounds like a plan, Mrs. Saunders," says Lincoln.

"It's just Ms.," I correct him.

"A beauty like yourself unspoken for," Traymel comments, leaning near me. "That's surprising."

"When did I say that?" I coyly counter, cocking my head to the side. "Just pointed out I wasn't married."

"Ah, she's feisty, guys, better watch out," jokes Wesley, slapping Traymel on the back.

I snicker. "Well, I'll see you all next week," I say over my shoulder as I turn to head out of the boardroom. *These three are going to be a handful.*

Rushing over to Lynn, I grab the phone out of her hand and hang it up.

"Bitch! That call was important. I am working, you know," she complains.

I roll my eyes at the lie because she hardly ever works. She usually has her nose stuck in her cell phone. "Oh well, they'll call back. I got the contract, and me, you, and Kyla are going out tonight to celebrate at Oynx. Call her and tell her to meet us at the house around seven to pregame." I begin two-stepping back to my office.

Five hours later, I am putting the finishing touches on my outfit. I am rocking a pale-yellow asymmetric crop top with skin-tight black skinny jeans and knee-high black boots. Lynn and I share a condo in a quaint neighborhood on the east side of San Marcos. Expenses are high in California, and if I want to live the bougie life, I need a roommate. Kyla's husband's family has money, so they have a massive villa off the beach. We spend most of our summer weekends at her place. I walk out to the living room, where Lynn is already spilling the tea of today's events to Kyla.

"I know you whores did not open my 1800 Agave without me."

"Girl, hush!" Kyla waves her hand at me as she takes a sip of her drink. "I wanna know more about these hunks. And congrats on the deal!"

I smack my lips as I walk to the kitchen island to pour myself a shot. "There's nothing to say about them except they are hot and off-limits." After taking the liquor in one gulp, I pour another one.

"Off-limits? I know the bed-hopping diva didn't just say that." Kyla jeers, sending me a pointed look.

I flip her off as I take my second shot. "Boo, I don't mix business with pleasure." I head to the couch and flop down next to her. "I did kind of hope Landon would've gotten the contract so I could take the twins on a ride." I grin up at the ceiling, envisioning how that would be. Lynn bursts out laughing, spraying us with the drink she just took a sip of.

"Eww! You're gonna ruin my new dress hubby got for me," whines Kyla. The strapless aqua-blue high-low minidress that stops right below her ass, along with gold pumps looks good on her atletic frame.

"My bad, girl!" Lynn replies, patting down Kyla's chest with some paper towels.

We head out the door fifteen minutes later when the Lyft arrives. They do not know it yet, but I have a surprise stop before making it to the club. Bewildered expressions are on their faces as we ride down the unknown street.

"Um, sir." Lynn begins tapping against the driver's seat. "You're at the wrong location."

"Nah, guh! This right. I'm feeling spontaneous," I say as I step out of the car.

"Oh, okay! Whatcha getting?" Kyla asks, following me.

I turn to them just as I make it to the door. "*We* are getting a friendship tat to symbolize our freedom and beauty." I emphasize "we" to clarify that this includes all of us.

"*What!*" They exclaim simultaneously with bug-eyed looks. I give the girls my famous show-stopping smile.

Rolling her eyes, Kyla grumbles, "And what is this liberating tattoo?"

"A butterfly."

Three

Lynn's boy toy works part-time as a bouncer at Oynx, so, we are able to go right in. *Good thing!* I think. The line outside is ridiculous for a weekday. Kyla immediately heads to the bar for a drink to drown out the throbbing sensation from the fresh tattoo. She is not a fan of the butterfly's placement. Lynn and I chose the top of the breast near the heart. Considering she barely has any breasts, she complained about it feeling like the man was needling her chest bone. Lucky for her, she does not have to deal with the hassle of bras. Ladies, you know when you get home that is the first to go. We all agreed to it being rainbow colored; the array of colors complemented the beauty of the design.

"The pain feels the same you experience after stubbing your big toe on a metal bed rail," she whines to me, downing her drink.

I order one from the bartender. "You will get used to it." This is not my first.

"This my jam!" Lynn screams in our ears as the DJ drops *Wooty* by Edubb. She grabs our hands and drags us between all the sweaty and gyrating couples to the middle of the floor. This is going to be a night for the books. For the next two hours, we get lost in alcohol and music. We either danced among each other or entertain the many men that came up behind us.

"Yo, I'm gonna go pee," Kyla says, fanning herself, her dark-brown hair now up in a ponytail.

"Need me to come with you?" I ask while backing it up on a white boy, my legs burning from all the twerking and dropping like it is hot. *I could use the break.*

"Nah!" She shakes her head. "Guh, I'm good. Do your thang." She walks off wobbling. I guess she is starting to feel the effects of all the shots she had us consume earlier. When you are on the floor with your adrenaline pumping, you feel as if your tolerance is at an ultimate high.

After another song plays, Lynn comes up to me and yells over the music, "Zola, where's Kyla?"

"She went to the bathroom." I stop mid-twerk. "She has been gone for a minute. Let's go check on her." Ignoring my confused dance partner, Lynn and I head off.

We weave our way through the crowd to the back. Stepping into the restroom, we find it empty besides a chick in a leopard catsuit with smudged makeup, sitting on the floor under a sink, looking drugged up. *No point in asking her for our friend's whereabouts.* As we head to check out the bar, Lynn sees the door for the janitor's closet ajar. She moves toward it and peeks inside, finding Kyla sprawled out on the floor, lying in vomit.

"Oh, shit—Kyla!" Lynn rushes to her side to check her vitals and to see that she is still alive. *How much did this girl drink?* She shakes her and smacks her across the face until she regains consciousness. Her eyelids slowly flutter open.

"Is she okay, or do I need to call 911?" I ask, beginning to freak out.

"Kyla, can you stand?" Lynn inquires. She nods and slowly makes her way to her feet with Lynn's help.

Noticing her pale skin and quivering lips, I suggest, "Maybe we should bring her to the hospital."

"*No!* No, I'm okay," responds Kyla. "I just wanna go home." She wraps her arms around herself.

My eyebrows furrow. "Are you sure?" I grab a roll of paper towels from one of the shelves and hand it to Kyla, gesturing to her face. She rips off a sheet and wipes off the vomit.

"Yes," she answers, wearily making her way out of the closet. "If I feel bad tomorrow, I'll have Damien bring me. I'm quite sure it's the alcohol finally catching up with me."

"Okay! I'll call us a Lyft," Lynn replies. "I will inform Jonathan that I will not be going home with him and make it up to him later."

In her second year of nursing school, she met Jonathan, the boy toy and other man. Although he may act like a nerd, she finds him intriguing. He has sandy brown hair with green eyes and big, juicy lips. His complexion reminds me of toasted cinnamon. She would always complain that he would covertly check her out during class but avoid her at all costs when she tried to talk to him. When the teacher paired them together for a project one day, they got close and personal. That night she ranted and raved about how he was a cool guy that she enjoyed spending time with.

"No need! You enjoy your night. I will tend to Kyla."

She graciously thanks me and tells me to let her know if anything comes up, and she gives Kyla a quick hug before rushing off. Kyla and I wait outside, away from the club, for the car to arrive. During the entire ride, she stares out of the window with a pensive expression. It is like a forty-minute drive to get all the way out to her villa. I am exhausted and ready for sleep when we arrive. The liquor is starting to shut my body down.

"Zola, what are you doing here?" asks Damien as I help Kyla stagger through the door.

Damien is her six-foot two husband with brown skin and dark brown eyes. He is as skinny as a reed but solid. His jet-black hair is wavy and cut a little past his ears. They met at Yale Law during their second-year criminal law class. During a mock trial, they battled it out against each other about an abortion case in front of the class. He was against the procedure, and she was for it. Although they both came up with some strong arguments, Kyla came out on top and won. After class, he offered to take her to lunch as a congratulations. They skipped the friendship stage and started dating shortly after.

On the day of graduation, he proposed in front of their entire class, friends, and family. She found out she was pregnant with Jamar, my godchild that I attempt to kidnap often, a week later. They rushed the wedding so he could be born legitimately. It was a summer ceremony on the beach in Destin with a small attendance. They are both partners at Damien's father prestigious law firm, Key High Associates, representing the elite class of society.

"How about you come get your wife out of my hands and bring her to your room." He quickly picks her up bride-style and carries her up the stairs with me trailing behind. "She passed out in the janitor's closet at the club, and I'm staying the night to make sure she is okay in the morning."

"Why was she in the janitor's closet?" he asks over his shoulder.

"Not sure. She didn't talk on the ride over here. Get her cleaned up and put her in bed. I'm going to the guest room to crash."

"I know how to take care of my wife, Zola." He scowls in my direction as he walks into their room.

I scoff, remembering Kyla's recent complaints about him. "Yeah, sure you do."

I go to the guest room and head to the adjoining bathroom to shower, leaving my clothes in my wake. As I stand under the hot water, I think back on Kyla's expression when she woke up. It seemed almost as if she was expecting someone to be ready to harm her before masking the look with calmness when she caught sight of us. *Did she really pass out from the alcohol, or did something else happen in that closet?*

Moving back toward the room, I dig through the drawers for some clothing I left for backup. After slipping on a pajama set, I jump in the bed and snuggle against the thousands of pillows Kyla insists on putting on it. As I drift off to dreamland, my thoughts revolve around a certain owner of my new contract.

The sun shining in from the window I did not close the curtain on last night wakes me up. I groan and throw the covers over my head. Rolling over, I try to fall back to sleep, but a pounding in the back of my skull leads me to search for aspirin. After finding some in the bathroom cabinet, I peek at the clock to see it is after nine. *Seems I will be late to work again.* Stretching as a yawn overcomes me, I slip out of the room to check on my friend. Damien should have left for work by now, so I just barge into her bedroom without knocking. Kyla is sitting against the headboard with an absent look.

I crawl under the covers with her and lay my head against her shoulder. "How are you feeling?"

"Groggy and hungover."

"Wanna talk about what happened?"

She exhales through her nose. "Nothing happened. I accidentally thought it was the bathroom when I rushed in to throw up. Must've passed out in the midst."

15

"Hmm … okay! If you say so. Hand me your phone so I can text Lynn you are fine. I don't want to hear that heifer's mouth later." After I finish sending the text, I spot a blocked number with a weird message at the top of her inbox. "Don't make me find you," it reads. "What is that about?"

Kyla turns and snatches the phone out of my hand, locking it. "N-Nothing! It was the wrong number." I can feel the beats of her heart pick up.

"Well, that's creepy to send someone." I hop out of the bed. "Since you seem okay, I'm going to make us breakfast. After all that liquor last night, I'm hungry." I head to the door, wondering the cause of the tears glistening in her eyes.

Four

"I hope you aren't burning down my kitchen," Kyla remarks, heading to the coffee maker for a cup.

"I am *not* Lynn." She did that a lot in college.

"True! She was the reason I started dating that fireman because of the number of times his team came to our apartment. The landlord almost kicked us out before he weirdly changed his mind."

After removing the eggs from the skillet, I turn to her, pointing the spatula in her direction. "That was because she visited his apartment and gave him one of her, and I quote, *signature blowjobs*."

"*Zola!*" She sputters out the coffee she has yet to swallow. "That man was like sixty."

"Exactly what I said when she told me. I mean, I guess he was getting no action, so I'm sure he nutted in like two minutes."

She shakes her head. "Bish, you are too much."

I set our plates of bacon, eggs, grits, waffles, and fruit on the table.

"Are you preggo? This is a lot of food." Kyla slides into a chair, eyeing the mountainous feast in front of her.

"Girl, don't jinx me." I join her at the table. "No, I'm hungover, and you know how we get the munchies." During college, after our crazy Saturday nights, we would make a big brunch Sunday morning to recuperate for the week.

However, I notice Kyla is not that interested in her food. She unconsciously moves it around on her plate as if her mind is occupied. I choose not to comment. She will let me know if it is serious. We happily chat about past adventures and current events for the next thirty minutes until it is time for me to leave so I can at least make an appearance at work before lunch. Kyla drops me off at home, and I rush to get dressed. It is a plus that I do not wear makeup and have dreads. It cuts the getting-ready routine by at least thirty minutes. I hop into my car and speed down the freeway. There is less traffic at this time, since a majority of the residents have already made it to work.

Stepping off the elevator, I wave to the secretary that works on the days Lynn is not at the desk. She is an older woman with graying hair and small glasses with a chain. She always brings us donuts in the morning.

Walking the path through many cubicles, I make my way to my office. I am blessed with an office because I climbed the ranks and showed my worth, despite the agitation of my coworkers and the downplaying of my boss. I am happy that I have made it this far, but I know there are larger heights I still must achieve. I am always willing to grow.

I slip into my leather chair as I power up my computer so I can check my emails. With obtaining the LTW Construct contract, I have been given a lessened load of other clients. This is a major deal for Mr. Mitchell, and he does not want me to mess this up. Even though I have proved my capability, his belief in me is hardly present. I know he was rooting for Landon to land the account and believes it would be in safer hands with him. I will once again have to fight to show value when it is already apparent to everyone else.

Fortunately, the day flies by with ease, and I am soon welcome to return to my car to enjoy the offers of life. Praying the interstate is clear of obstruction, I turn up my tunes, speeding in the middle lane. I think back to the actions of Kyla this morning and wonder why she seemed so wired up. My gut tells me there is something she is hiding. The question that plagues is why. Since college, the three of us have been practically inseparable. Having secrets is not something we do. We tell each other everything, to the very last funny, nasty, or disturbing detail.

Arriving home, I head to my bedroom to change into comfortable clothes. After slipping on my slippers, I proceed to the kitchen for some tea. Settling on the sofa, I put on Netflix and turn to *Orange Is the New Black* to catch up on the latest season. Now that the prison takeover fell through,

I am curious what the girls are up to with their extended sentences. Cindy was wrong for not having Taystee's back. I guess their friendship was not as real as it seemed. Do not get me started on Piper's whining and annoying ass. I've been wishing she had died.

I am on the fourth episode when my phone buzzes. Opening the text, I see it is Kyla complaining in our group message. She and Damien just got in another argument about the topic of having a second baby. He insinuated that she felt Jamar was an accident. I wonder what the real reason she is so against having a second child is. Is her vision of opening her own firm to assist the less fortunate the full story? Is she beginning to doubt the life that she built over these past few years?

Glancing down at my chest, I touch the healing tattoo—the friendship token my trio got last night—with the pads of my fingers. It symbolizes the strength of our bond and stakes our connection in skin. Meeting new people to have time to build a relationship is worth remembering. I am lucky to have found these two and to be a part of a group of girls that travel, bicker, and experience life. They have made me float out of my lows that I felt would drag me into the depths of despair. They have also lifted me among the clouds in my times of joy and accomplishments. There are few people one can meet and build an unbreakable link with, in the midst of turmoil.

Monday morning comes around quickly. I am excited about seeing Mr. Traymel Crane again—that tall, muscular, yummy goodness. I have always been one to steer clear of dipping my pen in company ink. Even with him being off-limits, there is nothing wrong with some flirtatious fun—some entertainment to help the days go by. I dress in a high-collared peach dress with long sleeves that tapers to my curves with the hem stopping right above the knees. My locks are piled upon my head in a messy bun.

I leave the condo before Lynn to make sure I am on time and prepared for the arrival of the men of LTW Construct. I booked the SkyWay room for the contract signing. It has one of the most beautiful views of the San Diego skyline. Three of the four walls of the room are made completely of floor-length windows. The floor is covered in lush hunter-green carpet that allows my feet to sink in. Two black leather sofas lie parallel to one another, centering a large, thick glass table with a bronze frame. When they enter, I turn from my gaze out the center window to face them, sporting a flawless pearly white smile that would mesmerize any person.

"Wow! You are gorgeous," Lincoln compliments from behind Traymel, craning his neck to look over his shoulder.

"You are not so bad yourself," I respond with a wink. "Good morning, gentlemen! I hope you enjoyed your weekend." I walk to one of the couches and sit down. "Have a seat. I assume you are not afraid of heights, given your profession." I pull a file from a bag by the couch. They move to the couch across from me and sit down just as Wesley rushes through the door.

"Sorry I'm … Whoa! This room is niiiiice. Understand the name now." He glances at us. "I'm going to sit by the lovely lady—if you don't mind, miss. There is too much testosterone over there."

I stifle a giggle. "Of course, Mr. Dreer. Have a seat." As Wesley settles down, he sticks his tongue out at their scowls.

I place a contract in front of each of them. "Are there any lingering questions?"

"I believe we are all set on our end," Traymel responds.

"Great! These contracts are standard. Lilac Essences will have sole marketing rights for the next two years with me as the head coordinator. We guaranteed a fifteen percent increase with our methods the first year and five percent every year following. If you choose to go your separate way after the two years but still want to keep our technique, we will require a two-hundred-fifty-thousand-dollar payout immediately upon completion. If you would like, do a quick scan of all the fine print, and then sign your names on the bottom of the last page. Since the three of you are a unit, I will need all to agree to move forward. We don't need any legal battles in the future."

They briefly scan the contract before agreeing and signing their names. I gather them up and return them back to my bag before grabbing a bottle of champagne and four glasses.

Turning to Lincoln, I hand him the bottle. "Would you like to do the honors, Mr. Crane?" My hand lingers a little longer when it encounters his. He smiles and then pops the cork with ease. "Someone has had practice."

"With the number of ladies he entertains, I would suspect so," Traymel remarks snidely, his shoulders tense.

I arch an eyebrow. He seems a little jealous. *Good!* Lincoln sends Traymel a murderous look as he pours his drink. Looks like brotherly rivalry. *This could be fun.*

"Well! I'm sure you've mastered other qualities as well with the experience," I say, stirring up more tension. I smile coyly as he fills up my glass.

"I don't know. Maybe I should try it out on you," Lincoln responds, wagging his eyebrows.

Wesley roars in laughter, spilling some of his drink on his hands. "Let's get this toast in to cool off the hormones burning in the room."

"Well of course," I agree. "Here's to a great beginning and exciting experiences. The eastern region better get ready for LTW Construct to dominate." We clink glasses and down the drinks. I stand to my feet, setting the glass on the table. "Gentlemen, I must get going. I have some paperwork to handle. You are welcome to finish off the bottle and enjoy the view."

About an hour later, Lincoln stops by my office to invite me for a tour of their current project. They are adding a wing to the Scripps MD Anderson Cancer Center. I agree to meet him after I grab something to eat.

The cancer center is where Lynn met Michael one day while going to clinicals as he was leaving the hospital. She was on her way in when he did a 360 to catch up with her. Michael is a light-skinned, five-foot-ten-inch teddy bear with a bald head in his late forties. He was charming and seemed sweet, and she saw nothing wrong with exchanging numbers. They chatted over the phone some nights and texted throughout the day, but as time progressed, she felt he became a bit controlling. He told her he worked at the city office but never went into detail. However, when she told us about him, Kyla informed her he was the mayor of San Diego and that he had a wife with lung cancer. Lynn was livid and cut ties for a few months.

During this time, she begun messing around with Jonathan. Nonetheless, after Michael spent weeks of trying to win her back, she allowed him back into her life. According to her, if the wife got a clean bill of health, she would leave him alone. I do not understand how she juggles the attentions of two men.

I follow the directions of my GPS to the site. I am surprised I have never actually visited the hospital. Driving around the back of the building, I notice the gravel road leading to a trailer. I park next to a royal-blue Silverado.

As I step out of my Audi, I remove my sunglasses and toss them on the dash. My step falters when I turn and see a familiar man who is staring at me in complete shock. "Clark?" I squeak.

"Zola, what are you doing here?" he asks, crossing his arms across his chest.

I arch an eyebrow at his gesture before responding. "I'm here to meet Mr. Crane to tour the site." Not that I owed him an explanation. I'm not sure why I gave him one either.

"Wait! You two know each other?" Traymel speculates as he and Lincoln stride over.

"Um, yes." I bite my bottom lip. *Talk about awkward.* I have been thinking about the boss of my current fling. I try not to get acquainted with my companions to avoid catching feelings, since I am against the whole relationship thing. "He … Clark is a friend of mine."

"What a small world," says Lincoln, smacking Clark on his back. A frown forms on Clark's sour face. "Ms. Saunders, if you just come inside while I get you in some safety gear for our tour." I follow Lincoln into the trailer, not glancing back at Clark.

We enter the trailer, and Lincoln leads me to the closet by an office. Opening the door, he mutters to himself, "Hard hat, glasses, vest." His eyes sweep to my hair when he turns toward me. "Ms. Saunders, as much as I love that messy bun, I don't think a hard hat will sit right on it."

I snort before reaching into my hair and unraveling the bun. My dreadlocks slowly cascade down my back from their binding. I reach out my hand for the hat after securing the hair tie on my wrist. Instead of handing it to me, he steps closer, keeping up that intense eye contact, and places the hat on my head. I wet my lips, peering at him through my eyelashes. Just then, Traymel and Clark walk into the trailer, causing me to jump back, quickly donning the vest and glasses.

"Zola, you look good today," Clark says, his eyes raking over me.

"Thanks," I mumble, straightening the glasses on my face.

"So, seriously! How do you know each other? I am feeling some tension between the two of you." Lincoln interrupts. "I hope Clark isn't competition."

I smile at him. "What makes you think you are in the running?"

He rubs his hands together. "Ah, Ms. Saunders, I do love a good chase."

"I think it's time for that tour. I do have other things on my agenda," I reply, heading back outside.

Laughing, he grabs some keys, following me out the door. I stand by one of the golf carts. "We are taking this, ma'am." He walks toward the green-and-silver four-wheeler.

I eye it skeptically. "How are we both going to fit on that?"

"You will sit behind me and wrap your arms around my waist."

Crossing my arms across my chest, I roll my eyes. "You are not slick, Mr. Crane."

He drags his eyes from my breasts, which are being lifted by my arms, and meets mine. "Well, considering you are in heels, you can't walk around certain areas of the site. So, to prevent you from not getting a proper tour, the four-wheeler can get us places those golf carts can't."

I chew on my bottom lip as I muddle over what he just said. "Fine!" Walking over to the four-wheeler, I gesture for him to get on. He straddles the seat and starts the engine. "However, I am not putting my arms around your waist, so don't drive fast," I warn before hopping on behind. My nipples harden instantly as my breasts rub against his back. As he pulls off, I catch a glimpse of a scowling Clark in the trailer's doorway. *What is his problem?*

The tour takes about an hour as we go through the site and meet some of the workers. Some give Lincoln a thumbs-up as we ride away. I am quite interested in the ins and outs of the project. I never knew much about construction, and this was the perfect opportunity to broaden my knowledge, so I asked a lot of questions that he had no problem in answering—which is kind of surprising to me, since I got a vibe that he was a little chauvinistic. At one point, he took the four-wheeler over a big pile of dirt, causing it to tip back a little. I quickly wrapped my arms around his waist and squeezed my outer thighs around his to keep from falling off.

When we returned to the trailer, Traymel was standing by the truck I was parked next to. "Lincoln, can you drop me off at my house?" he says, looking up from his phone.

"Sure!" Lincoln responds, hopping off the four-wheeler after me. "Lemme just finish up here."

"It's okay. I must stop by the office before I head home, and I want to avoid that rush-hour traffic. Thanks for the tour; it was enlightening."

With that, I head to my car. "Nice seeing you Mr. Crane," I add, waving at Traymel.

Through the rearview mirror, I see them watching as I drive down the gravel road until disappearing on the highway. They seem to be saying something to each other. I wonder whether Clark said anything to Traymel about us knowing each other as a little more than friends.

As I head down the highway to the office, I think back to this morning. *I know it was wrong to play that game. They are brothers, for goodness' sake. I shouldn't be leading Lincoln on just to make Traymel jealous. Lincoln is too much of a player for my taste. He screams commitment issues. Besides, there is a pull I have with Traymel. I can see myself settling down with him. Wait! Did I just think that? I barely know him! I am going to have to get laid tonight. I am having crazy thoughts.*

"Call from … Clark," says Bixby.

Great! I did not want to have to deal with this can of worms already. I press the button on the steering wheel to answer.

"Yes?"

"Wow, you answered this time." Clark's voice filters from the speaker, a hint of contempt in his tone.

I roll my eyes. *Didn't I just talk to this fool earlier?* "I've been busy with work. I had a major deal to close, as you now know."

He snorts. "I see you and Lincoln have been really busy."

Is he serious right now? "Clark, you know we aren't dating, correct?"

"I'm trying to make us exclusive," he tries to explain.

"I don't want any relationship drama right now. Just trying to make sure my career is set."

"There are no problems with us. We work well together."

Well, right now you are being extra clingy. "That's because it's just sex. We know what to expect. I assumed this was good."

"Yes, but I don't appreciate Lincoln and Traymel drooling over you." He sighs. "I want to make my claim."

Traymel was drooling over me. *Yes!* I slam my hand against the steering wheel in excitement. "Well, I belong to no one. So if you can't accept that, then this can end." I hang up. I do not have time for this. There goes my sex appointment.

"Call from … Clark."

I send him to voicemail. Pulling up in the garage, I head to Lilac Essences.

"Zola! Can you take me home when you leave? My car is in the shop," Lynn asks, bombarding me as I step out of the elevator.

"Sure. Let me send some emails and drop off the contracts to Mr. Mitchell, and then we'll head out."

"I'll take the contracts to Mr. Mitchell for you," she responds, overly excited.

"Sounds like a plan—a trip I don't have to take." Avoiding Mr. Mitchell is a major plus in my day.

I take the contracts out of my bag and hand them to her. She heads to the elevator as I proceed to my office. I stop short when I walk through the door and see Landon sitting in my chair with his feet on my desk. His hands are clasped against his chest as he looks out of the window, appearing entirely too comfortable.

I walk in, stopping right in front of my desk. I put my hands on my hips to stop myself from smacking him. "I know you better have a damn good reason to be in my office *uninvited*." My voice rises at the end.

He turns and smirks at me as he drops his feet to the ground. "Trying to get into the mind of Ms. Saunders. Wondering why anyone would think your ideas are better than mine."

I feign sympathy. "Awww! The poor baby still salty." Pointing toward the door, I continue. "*Too bad!* Get the hell out, Landon."

He stands up and walks around the desk toward me, putting his hand on my shoulder before I instantly shrug it off. "Your reign is coming to an end." He then saunters out, slamming the door behind him. The frames on my wall rock from the impact.

"Pompous prick!" I mumble to myself before sitting in front of my computer to compose the emails.

The day is at its end, and I meet Lynn in the lobby. On the way to the house, she turns on the radio and we sing off-key to all the latest hits the station plays. When we pull up to the apartment, Jonathan is waiting by the door. "Is there some for me?" I ask as I step out of the car, eyeing the takeout bag.

"Sorry, Zola. Just feeding my baby today."

"Rude!" I unlock the front door and head to the kitchen, leaving Lynn to deal with her boy toy. I drop my purse on the counter and look in the fridge. *Guess I'll fry a porkchop.* I pull out the ingredients and turn the fryer on.

Glancing at my phone, I see there is a text from Clark asking for me to come over. I ignore it and go to the sunroom with my food and turn on *Criminal Minds. Guess I will just have dirty thoughts about Morgan.* After binging and drinking wine for a few hours, I head to my room to get ready for the night. I turn on my reggae and hop in the shower, swirling my hips to the beat as I scrub down with the loofah. I handle my other nightly duties before getting into bed and falling fast asleep.

Five

The next few weeks fly by as I start the preliminary work for the LTW Construct proposal. I avoid the Crane brothers like the plague, since I am still a bit conflicted about them. They both shamelessly flirt with me, Lincoln more than Traymel, and it is hard to control my urges of wanting to jump their bones. Even though I am intrigued by Traymel, I would not mind fucking Lincoln just once. Especially since I cut Clark off and have not had a lay in over a month. I never have been a person to use a vibrator, but that one in my bottom drawer I got from my sister last year as a gag gift is looking mighty tempting.

Clark has already moved on to some white girl and avoids me when I am at the site. It is a little clingy how the girl is always stopping by to see him and to bring him food. *No, I am not jealous!*

It is finally Friday, and I cannot wait to meet with the girls for our weekly happy hour at our favorite bar. Wesley and I are finishing up the spreadsheet for next month's budget. We have become cool recently since I spend most of my time with him. He is neutral ground. He moved from Michigan in junior high as the youngest of five siblings, being the only boy. His sisters would always dress him up in dresses and practice makeup on his face. That's probably what helped him come out of the closet so young.

I stand from the chair, stretching my body. "Wesley, you should come out with me after work."

"What did you have in mind?" he asks, still typing on his computer.

"I'm meeting my besties for happy hour at Newtopia off of Main."

"Are they as cute as you?" Lincoln asks, interrupting as he walks into the office.

I roll my eyes and ignore him, returning my attention to Wesley. "Our bartender makes bomb-ass drinks."

"Yeah! I'll come," Wesley replies, looking up at us.

"Count me in!" Lincoln answers with a broad smile.

I smack my lips. "No one invited you."

He shrugs his shoulders. Walking up behind me, he leans over. "It's okay! Free country. I can go anywhere."

"Where are you going?" Traymel inquires, joining us in the office with a box in his arms.

"Is there a reason everyone is in my office?" Cries Wesley, throwing his arms in the air.

Lincoln shoots him a crazy look, pointing at me. "The lady, *duh!*" He turns to Traymel. "I'm going on a date with Zola."

Traymel turns to me with a comical hurt expression. I shake my head, hitting Lincoln on the arm. "Wesley is coming out to happy hour with me and my friends. Lincoln invited himself, so I guess you can come too."

"Do you want me to come?" he asks, setting the box on the ground in front of him.

"Yes." I hesitate, not sure of my answer. I mean, I want him to come, but I don't want to be obvious about it.

Lincoln scoffs, throwing his arm over my shoulders. "You have no problem with him joining. He's my twin, so what makes him better?"

I shrug before shyly smiling at Traymel. "Y'all only share the looks. Everything else is opposites."

"I agree with the lady," Wesley chuckles. "I would pick Traymel over you too."

We joke some more before I leave. *The girls are going to crack up over them. Lynn is already infatuated with the twins.* I hop in the car, turning on some of the oldies. As Lauryn Hill spits out "Ex-Factor," I merge onto Pacific Coast Highway.

Bixby comes through the speakers: "Call from ... Sis."

"Heyyyy Nikki," I excitedly screech.

"Hey, guh! Y'all still coming down in two weeks for Jazz Fest?"

"You know it. Lynn won't miss that for nothing." It is her favorite, and she forces us to go every year. She claims we can really learn and enjoy the raw culture and music of Louisiana there. It is not tainted to appeal to the many tourists, which often happens during the carnival season.

She sighs. "Good! I want to finalize the dresses for the wedding, and I need my maid of honor down. Also I want to do some cake tasting."

"That works for me. I'll be down for a week. How's the fam?"

"They are good! I didn't call to have no dragged-out conversation with you. I need to get back to work."

"Um, rude much?" I mutter, rolling my eyes.

"You'll be okay."

"Bye, bish," laughing, I hang up.

My baby sister Nicole is marrying her high school sweetheart Ethan. They have been on and off for years but always seem to find their way back to each other. For a minute there, I thought the door was closed for good when he got another girl pregnant on one of their breaks.

Nevertheless, three years later they are back together, and the wedding is around the corner. They are getting married on Halloween weekend. Like, what person gets married on Halloween? That is the perfect holiday for when evil comes knocking in the darkness to find where secrets are kept hidden. To have a supposedly joyous occasion at that time sounds like a setup for failure. And with their track record, I can only hope for the best. I am still trying to decide what to do for her bachelorette party. I have been thinking of a Caribbean cruise in the late summer—not too expensive, and yet we can have all the fun we want in one spot.

I pull into the parking lot of Newtopia just as Kyla gets there. Lynn is standing by her Camry, talking on her phone. We pull into the spots she held down for us. We have a rule that whoever arrives first must find three spots together and guard them until the others arrive. As we are walking to the entrance, I tell them that I invited the owners of LTW Construct to join us.

"Yummy! I can stare at the Crane brothers *all day*," Lynn gushes, fluttering her eyelashes.

"I can't wait to see these *hunks* y'all told me about," states Kyla.

We get a large table with high-top chairs on the patio and chat until the boys arrive. I see Wesley walk in, and I stand up and wave to him. He makes his way to the table. "Wesley, this is Kyla, and you already know Lynn."

"Hi, ladies. Traymel and Lincoln just parked and should be in soon," he explains, sliding into a chair.

When the Crane twins walk in, a few of the females turn and stare them down. They are a formidable pair of sexiness after all. The way those jeans fit, and with their shirts stretched across chiseled chests, they seem to tower over the tables as they make their way to us.

"The yumminess has arrived!" Lynn rejoices, drumming the table with her pointer fingers in excitement.

I laugh. Kyla is sipping on her drink as she turns around to see them. The next thing I know, her drink slips out of her hand, crashing onto the ground as she stares at the twins. A shocked expression covers her face, and her mouth gapes open. Her hand that was holding the fallen drink is shaking.

"Kyla, you okay?" I reach out for her.

"Excuse me," she whimpers before getting up from her seat and running away, dodging the tables as she rushes across the bar. She crashes into a woman making her way through the door and stumbles to catch herself from falling before quickly apologizing and exiting.

The boys look in my direction with confused expressions. I quickly stand to my feet and follow behind. Once I make it outside, I see Kyla pacing in the parking lot. She is taking labored breaths as she constantly wipes her hands on her slacks.

"Kyla." I hesitate as I walk toward her. "What was that about? Is something wrong? Do you know the twins?"

"Twins?" She tucks some strands of dark-brown hair behind her ear, casting her eyes that match to the ground. "No, I don't know them."

My eyebrows furrow. *She is lying.* "Why did you rush out?"

"One of them reminded me of someone from my past. It wasn't a positive memory, and I just needed some fresh air."

"Um, okay." *Maybe not lying.* "Do you want to talk about it?"

"No, I'm okay." She claps her hands together. "Let's get back inside. I want to know everything about these twins."

I look at her a little longer, contemplating whether I should keep pushing the matter. She gives me a forced smile and urges me inside. Deciding to grill her later, I turn and head back through the front door with her following me. When we reach the table, Lynn stands and meets

30

us before whispering in Kyla's ear to ask whether she is all right. She nods before slipping into the chair across from Lincoln. He glances at her with a smirk. I notice her give him a cold stare, which just causes the corners of his lips to tilt upward more. *That is weird.*

"So, Kyla, these are the twins, Traymel and Lincoln," I trumpet, pointing to each as I say his name. "Guys, this is Kyla."

"Nice to meet you both," she says, her eyes lingering a little longer on Lincoln than on Traymel. I glimpse at Lynn, who is watching the interaction also.

"Yup! She's just as beautiful as you, Zola," remarks Lincoln, his eyes raking over her face.

I scoff. "Watch out for him, guh. He's a flirtatious type."

Lincoln shrugs. "Hey! I just love the women."

"Too bad they don't love you," heckles Wesley.

Lynn swirls her finger in her drink before popping it into her mouth. "I'll give him a chance," she assures.

"Yeah!" Traymel mocks, rolling his eyes. "Until you have to deal with him on a long-term basis."

"Lynn, you would give any sexy man a chance," Kyla teases with a smirk.

"Ah, all three think I'm sexy, Mel." Lincoln snickers, poking out his chest. "Seems I am beating you with these ladies."

"As I said earlier ..." I pause. "Traymel is better."

Wesley leans over the table, laughing. "Burn, Lin!"

"Zola, you hurt me," Lincoln says scornfully, looking at me with puppy eyes.

"I'm sure you'll be okay." Kyla remarks with an eye roll.

Traymel shakes his head. "Bro! Now you are getting double-teamed. Stop while you are ahead."

The conversation and the laughs continue for the next hour or so. Rounds of shots are consumed. I covertly admire Traymel. I cannot deny how good he looks. His broad shoulders and wide chest are covered by a fitted red polo exposing strong arms that end at his large hands gripping the neck of his beer.

Kyla abruptly stands from her chair once again. "I'm going to run to the ladies' room." Turning on her heel, she scurries away before anyone responds.

"I am going to go order us another round of shots," Lincoln communicates before leaving the table also.

"Um, he does know the waitress can just bring it to us?" Lynn says.

I notice Lincoln completely passing up the bar and heading to the back. Letting my curiosity get the best of me, I finish my drink and stand from the table. "I'm going to visit the ladies' room too."

Winding through the tables, I head down the hallway. I hear muffled voices ahead. Pressing my back against the wall, I peek around the corner to see Kyla pushing against Lincoln's chest.

He steps back. "I think you know my name by now."

"Doesn't mean I'll give you the gratification of saying it."

Wait! They do *know each other.*

"I see you didn't tell your friends about us."

Us?

Her arms cross her chest. "What makes you believe that?"

"Because I'm pretty sure Zola would have my ass by now."

Err ... why would I have his ass?

I stand there so confused as to what is going on.

"So! You agree you crossed the line, and I should call the police?"

He smirks, stepping closer. "But you won't."

"Don't be so sure." Kyla raises her chin, showing she is not one to back down.

"You would have already done it after that night in the club."

Night at the club? Oh my! When we found her in the janitor's closet.

She gapes at him. "I didn't even know your name."

"Doesn't matter." He shrugs. "You still could have made a report or told your friends. Besides, you like me more than you want to admit." His hand reaches up to graze her cheek.

She smacks it away. "Yeah, sure! The hot, crazy man that used chloroform on me."

WTF! Hell no.

"I want to apologize for that." He rubs the back of his neck. "It wasn't supposed to go down like that; I just had a bad night."

"Yeah, I don't care. Just say away from me, and we will be fine." She goes to walk past him before he sidesteps in front of her. I take a step toward them, ready to have my friend's back in case Mr. Crane wants to get physical.

"Could you move?" she says in exasperation. "I'm fairly sure they are wondering where we are."

"My brother is keeping Zola occupied, and Lynn and Wesley are having some type of debate. I just need a minute."

No, no sir. Zola is right here listening.

"Minute has long been over."

"Kyla!" he utters, rubbing his hand down his face.

She rolls her eyes with a grunt. "What do you need, sir?"

He leans closer. "This."

Oh my god! I was completely caught off guard when his lips pressed against hers. *What is going on? I cannot believe she hid this secret, especially with Lincoln. Traymel told me his twin is not a one-woman man.*

I quickly rush back to the table, hoping they do not catch sight of me. Just as I sit down, Lincoln comes into view. After he is settled, Kyla joins. Her lipstick is smudged at the corner of her mouth—evidence of what I just witnessed. I sip on my new drink, eyeing them both over the rim. *I will have to get to the bottom of their conversation. I see he is the reason she ran out earlier.*

It is not much longer before the night comes to an end and Lincoln pays the tab. He loves being flashy with his money. As we are walking out, Lincoln walks super close behind Kyla, brushing against her every so often. She practically falls out the door to get away from him.

"Do you ladies need us to walk y'all to your cars?" Traymel requests.

"No!" Kyla interjects a little loudly before Lynn or I can answer. I am sure she is trying to get away from Lincoln. "We will be fine. We parked by each other for this exact reason."

"Well, I hope you gorgeous women have a great night," responds Lincoln, rubbing his jaw in a sensual way. He sends me a wink. I squint at him. I see his game now. Whatever he did to my friend, I will make him pay.

We walk to our cars giggling about the night. Kyla stays quiet. We hug and promise to let each other know when we make it home before piling into our cars and driving off.

Six

I lie across my bed with my legs bent at the knees, swinging my feet in the air. I'm working on my laptop to finish the final touches on the ads I made to advertise LTW Construct. They came to us to grow their business in the eastern region and become a countrywide entity. Many companies are seeking assistance in building up their corporations, but they need the right persuasion to see us as the top pick.

My phone vibrates with a message from Kyla asking me to watch Jamar for a few hours. I scroll through my work before deciding it is at a good stopping point so I can spare some quality time with my little man. I hop up to change into some light denim skinny jeans and a purple crop top. After I tie up my Chucks, I head to Lynn's room, peeking my head through her ajar door.

"I am going to entertain Jamar. Wanna join?"

She is sitting at her vanity with her hair wrapped in a towel, wearing only a bra and panties. Sweeping a makeup brush against her cheek, she says, "I wish, but I have to entertain Michael. He has this idea I have been avoiding him." She pauses, picking up the eyeliner. "I guess I am since he is acting like a lovesick teen. I thought messing with a married man meant enjoying the pleasures of the skin without commitment or consequences. Instead, I have been experiencing a bit of suffocation."

I tilt my head to the side in thought. "Maybe he is starting to fall for you more than you would like. He probably is that lovesick teen these days."

Her jaw slightly drops as she gapes at me through her mirror. "Let's not joke about that."

I shrug before walking out of the room. I grab a water bottle from the fridge before heading out the door to my car. With it being the weekend, I make it to the waterfront in a short time.

After picking Jamar up, I take him to Central Park to enjoy the sunny afternoon and give his active stamina something to exert itself on. I scroll through my social media, reading posts from my classmates and family back at home in the lower ward in the city of New Orleans, Louisiana.

Many fall in love with the different stories of the southern city that never sleeps, wanting to experience it themselves. My city is known for its jazz music, Cajun cuisine, nonstop alcohol consumption, and inherited French culture. Let us not forget the many festivals, the main one being Mardi Gras. It has a homey ambience that one feels no matter where in the city one is. It is a place that embraces its heritage and bloom in its culture.

Seeing the sun set, I call for Jamar to let him know it is time to go, but he is not happy to leave his new friend. After stopping to get ice cream to calm his grumblings, we head back to the house. Jamar tells me about some girl who rubbed paint on his cheek during art time. I smile. *Early stages of opposite-sex flirtation.* He insists on eating in front of the television, being a big fan of *Paw Patrol*. Kyla has considered getting a dog for the house. It would be much easier to take care of than another baby.

The following day, I go to Bath and Body Works to pick up some more candles. It is a beautiful afternoon as I drive through the city in thought. I normally would have ordered online but I let it slip my mind, and now I am completely out. Now I am stuck dealing with the horrific parking and the crowds that are impossible to navigate through.

After twenty minutes of searching for a spot, I walk through the entrance on a mission. I know what I am looking for, and this is in and out. I am too engrossed in smelling a candle to notice a presence walking up behind me. Arms wrap around my bare waist before the figure behind me bends down to whisper in my ear. "Surprise."

I freeze as a gasp escapes before turning my head to look over my shoulder and into the person's eyes. We stare at each other for a split second before I place the candle back on the shelf and remove his arms from around my waist.

I turn toward him with a hostile expression. "What the fuck, Clark? We are, like, over."

"I miss you," he mumbles, rubbing through his curls.

"Well, I don't! You do not have permission to put your hands on me, and next time I will break your fingers." Turning on the heels of my kicks, I head for the entrance, forgetting my task of buying a candle as anger boils in my veins.

I head home filled with aggravation. I am unsure of what was going through Clark's head just a half hour ago, but that totally threw me for a loop. It was a possessive move that I would have normally found appealing if it was not from someone I truly felt nothing for. Even I began to bore of his sexual escapades toward the end. I tend to get distracted easily, which is another reason why I feel I am not the right person for a relationship.

"Shit, shit, shit!" I hear hollered out from the direction of the kitchen as I step into the condo.

I jog toward the sound, thinking something is happening to Lynn. As I round the corner, I see that it is. However, it's just another one of Lynn's moments. I should not have to witness so many instances of my friend's sexual experiences.

Michael's head is between her thighs, eating her out with gusto. Her hips jerk toward the edge of the counter to meet his mouth. Her head rocks from side to side against the cabinet as she bites down on her bottom lip.

My eyes quickly snap shut, and I slap my hands over my ears to unsuccessfully block out her moans of pleasure, right at the point which I can only assume, by her volume, she is brought to bliss.

"You have to be fucking kidding me!" I shout, my eyes and ears still closed and covered. I hear some things that were most likely on the counter crashing to the ground.

Hands cover mine against my ears before yanking them off. "I am so sorry, honey," Lynn says, shaking me by my hands. "Stop acting like a prude. You have seen worse."

I slightly open my left eye. "Are you decent?" She nods before I open the rest of that eye and the other. I glance down her body to see her wearing one of Michael's button-down shirts, which barely conceals her generous chest since the buttons are not all done. "Lynn! In the kitchen." I shake off her hands and gesture to the counter. "You'd better bleach that shit before you go to sleep."

"I gotchu! But first I have to handle that rod waiting for me in my bed."
I grimace at the mental picture my mind conjures. "OMG! Shut up."
She giggles, running out of the kitchen.

Deciding on not eating now or even at all, I head to my room, closing
the door so I will not have to subject my ears to their lovemaking—even
though she has told me about the times I have gotten out of control. It
helps that our rooms are on opposite sides of the condo and we do not
have to share a bathroom.

I plop on my bed and kick my shoes off my feet after using my toes
to push them off my heels. I flex my toes, stretching on my back. *Lynn
just had her pussy eaten in our kitchen. Talk about a hot prepared meal.* The
way Michael was going to town in between her thighs, I could tell he was
sucking up every drop of juice.

Still on a sex drought, I have not found a replacement for Clark, and
now my hormones are in overdrive. I consider going out to find a one-night
stand. My mind is beginning to get cloudy with thoughts of jumping
Traymel's bones, knowing it would be inappropriate. He, unfortunately,
seems to be the only one I am yearning for these days.

Two days later, I spend time at the trailer site, wrapping up some
spreadsheets with Wesley. The project is almost complete, which is good
if we get this gig in the east we are working on. LTW Construct have
been picked as one of the final three companies up for the contract of the
major company.

I lean across the couch in the main area when a view in the corner
of my eye captures my focus. Standing in front of the windows by the
front door is Traymel, talking to some of the workers. I notice the way
those jeans, worn from many washes, fit his muscular legs. His gray
T-shirt stretches snugly across his broad shoulders and rippling torso. Sweat
coats his forehead under the hard hat in the beating sun of the hot early
afternoon. His Adam's apple bobs in the thick column of his throat as he
gulps down half the contents of the bottle of water he just opened. As if
sensing my gaze, his eyes lock with mine, water coating his lips. I quickly
glance back at my tablet, trying to feign being busy. Even though I was
caught red-handed, blatantly eyeing him, I do not have even an ounce of
shame.

The door to the trailer opens, and heavy boots pound against the wood floor. Steps make their way in my direction, stopping right in front of me. I continue to pretend to be engrossed with my tablet, not acknowledging the presence standing above me. The tablet is plucked out of my grasp, causing me to peer up into the gray eyes I should be avoiding. The sweat is still running down his forehead and onto the skin exposed by the shirt. A smirk covers his face as he looks down on me from that towering height of his.

"So now you can look my way." His gruff voice fills my ears. "You are not really into this." He waves the tablet in his hand.

"I have no idea what you are talking about." I flash him a smile. "I was doing some work."

He arches an eyebrow. "Is that so?"

"That is what you pay me for."

He leans down to my eye level, his gaze flicking over my lips before returning to my eyes. "What if there is something else I need that is not actually paid for?"

I lick my lips, aware of the tension in the air now. The meaning behind his words is flashing on a neon sign at how subtle he failed to be. "It depends on the need."

His smirk deepens before he returns to his height and heads back to his office. I rub my sweaty palms against my slacks, noticing he took my tablet with him. *Do I dare follow him to retrieve it?* I am unaware whether this is a game for him. *I could be reading the signals wrong.* A cough interrupts my thoughts, and I see Wesley standing outside his office, looking at me. I send him a shy smile, deciding to avoid Traymel and finish up my business here as soon as possible. It seems our flirting is rising to a new level.

Seven

I am so ready to make it through this day. The girls and I travel home tomorrow for Jazz Fest. I get to see my family again since I last visited for Christmas. I am all about family values, and I miss mine with a passion. It is always a party when we link up. My Aunt Linda's house is located downtown amid all the festivals. Everyone ends up there sometime throughout the weekend for an old-fashioned kickback where the liquor is flowing and the food selection is unlimited and tasty. My mom and her sisters get together and cook all morning so we young ones can eat as they chill out in the yard drinking and playing cards. I am only looking forward to the pounds upon pounds of crawfish. Those spicy critters originated and were perfected in Louisiana, no matter what anyone tells you. Of course, I will be washing them down with a daiquiri, one of those slushies of alcohol-infused goodness that give an instant brain freeze.

"ACME Corp approved your preliminary sketches and wants to meet next week to finalize the deal and make plans for starting construction," I inform Traymel as I walk into his office while looking at the tablet in my hands. It was returned to my office the next day following that incident. After two months of running ads and promoting presentations to the big businesses in the eastern region, someone is finally taking a chance on LTW Construct. This could be the break they need.

ACME is a major oil production company in the southeastern region. Their business has been booming for the past five years, and they are building a new facility in Tennessee. Their previous contractors made a fatal mistake in their past site that resulted in three deaths. They are currently on the lookout for a replacement. With my persuasive marketing plan and Traymel's building design, we came out on top in their decision.

"Are you serious? ACME wants us!" He stands up from his desk and walks around it to the stand in front of me.

"Serious as a heart attack." I laugh as I smack his shoulder.

He takes a step closer to me. "Thanks for this, Zola."

I lick my lips as my eyes flicker to the floor to avoid his intense gaze. It seems to be getting a little hot in here suddenly. I rub my left hand down my right arm. "This wasn't just me. The three of you sold your business with the skills you all bring to the table."

"Still." He reaches out and places his hand on my chin, lifting it so he can look into my eyes. My hand drops to my side; the other holds the tablet against my chest. "You are the brains in this operation and keep us in check." Traymel slightly bends from his tall frame. His lips hover above mine as puffs of air leave his mouth to cool my feverish skin. "Tell me to stop." I close my eyes on instinct as his lips brush across mine. "Don't allow this." I feel his tongue run along my bottom lip, causing me to involuntarily gasp at the sensation.

It is only a second before I feel the pressure of his mouth against mine as his tongue slips past my parted lips. I moan as tingles explode throughout my body. He thoroughly explores my mouth, tasting every hidden crevice. My free hand moves to his neck as he grips my waist, pressing my body against his. The tablet bites into my chest through the fabric of my blouse. It feels as if the kiss lasts forever before we come up for air.

"I've wanted to do that since you walked into that boardroom for your presentation," he rasped.

"Uh … um! I-I have to go," I stutter before stepping back from him and spinning around, my flustered nerves going haywire. I quickly make my way toward the door, grabbing for the handle right as Traymel places his palm on the door, keeping it close. *How did he make it over here so fast? I did not notice he was even following me.* I can feel his chest close behind me, but I refuse to turn around. "Lemme go." I lean my head toward the door, tucking my chin.

"No, Zola." He leans closer, pressing against my back. "I am done with the games. Why deny this chemistry?"

"I don't mix business with pleasure." I squeeze my eyes tight, trying to hold a stance on the situation. I cannot get lost in that whirlwind I just experienced. "We need to stay professional."

He slams his palm against the door above my head, causing me to jolt, and making my eyes snap open wide. "Fuck professional! You want me just as badly as I want you." I continually stare at the door, not responding. "Look at me!"

I slowly shake my head.

He leans closer to me before running his tongue against my earlobe and softly whispering, "Look at me." My back flexes as I slowly turn toward him, finding him way too close. I lift my eyes to his, where I see determination and a hint of lust. He raises his other palm against the door, and I am caged between his body, those large arms, and the oak door with nowhere to run. "Tell me you don't want me."

I bite my bottom lip to find the courage to say what I must say. I do not need to go down this road no matter how bad my body aches for him. "I don't …" I begin to confirm, only to be cut off when his lips capture mine a second time in a bruising kiss.

His tongue plows through my open mouth, showing his dominance. His hands slide down the door to grip my ass, pulling me hard against him, smashing my breasts against his chest. My body betrays my mind during this fierce onslaught upon my lips. My nipples harden as he grinds his hips against me where I feel his rather noticeable and rather large bulge in his pants. My panties dampen in anticipation of what might happen next. I am engulfed in him and these feelings I have been trying to bury. The tablet is slowly slipping from my fingers, which are pressed against the door beside me, holding me in an arched position to push my heavy breasts against his wall of muscle, cradling his rod of lust in the apex of my thighs.

He pulls away. "Why lie, Zola?" he challenges as he plants kisses along my collarbone.

I press the back of my head against the door to try to clear my thoughts. My fingers tighten on the tablet. A moan slips from my throat as he rubs my hardened nipples through my shirt. "Please," I whimper. To tell the

41

truth, I am not sure whether I am begging for him to stop or to soothe the ache between my thighs.

"In due time, *cheri.*"

He steps back, walks to his desk, and sits down, returning to the work on his computer. *WTF!* Staring slack-jawed in his direction, I wait for him to acknowledge what just happened and explain what made him decide to cross the line we have been tiptoeing around. When I am still ignored after another minute, I turn around and open the door. Slipping out, I run smack into Wesley on the other side.

"Whoa, Zola!" His hands clasp my shoulders. "Where are you rushing to?"

"Um." I pause as I try to collect my thoughts. "To find you and Lincoln to share the good news." He stares at me as if he is waiting for me to say something. I step back, looking at him quizzically.

"You were looking for me." He removes his hands from my shoulder and places them palms down against his chest. "I am here. You sure you're okay?'

Right, crap! Traymel has my mind messed up right now. That damn kissing session got my lips tingling for more attention. I glance down at my tablet, hoping to keep attention off the obvious. "LTW Construct got the ACME project, and they want to meet next week."

Wesley grabs me in his arms. *What is up with these men and hugging?* "That is great news!" My feet dangle as he squeezes me tight, lifting me in the air.

"Yes, I know. Well, let me go tell Lincoln."

He sets me down. "You can't; he left early for the day. He had something to tend to."

"Useless!" I roll my eyes. "I guess I will just give him a call."

"You girls be safe on the trip home and bring me back something."

"I gotcha," I reply, sending him a thumbs-up.

I grab my purse from the office I use when I am here. Riding the elevator to the lobby in silence, my fingers press against my swollen lips. I envision the warmth and feel of having his pressed against mine. How good it felt. Once I am on the highway, I open the sunroof for some much-needed fresh air. I really need to handle my itch.

I send Kyla a text to let her know I am on the way. She is staying with us tonight since our flight leaves early tomorrow and we are all leaving from the condo. I still have not asked her about the Lincoln situation I witnessed the week before last. She has not mentioned it to either me or Lynn, so she must want to keep it a secret—which is peculiar, since we share pretty much everything.

As I drive, my mind recounts that interaction with Traymel. Why would he cross the line and get me riled up only to leave me hanging? Did he regret it? *Ugh! This is why business stays business. I do not need this confusion. I have been too horny since I have not gotten a fix in months. I need to get my lust under control.* From what I felt through those slacks, Mr. Crane promises to be a ride worthy of anticipation—one I was almost willing to give just prior. But I know I cannot allow myself to indulge in thoughts of what it would feel like to be in his arms as he brings me to bliss. Putting on an audio book, I let Dan Brown drown out my naughty thoughts with his famous *The Da Vinci Code.*

I pull into Kyla's driveway and park before heading in through her garage. They have a habit of leaving the inside door unlocked yet not closing the garage door. I walk into the living room to see Damien and Jamar watching *Transformers* while devouring a pizza.

"Nanny!" Jamar beams up at me with sauce all over his cheeks when he sees me. I smile and blow him a kiss.

Damien whips his head in my direction. "Really, Zola! You can't just walk in people's houses."

"Well"—I look behind me—"I just did!"

Kyla comes down the stairs. "You be a good boy for Daddy this week," she says before leaning over to kiss Jamar on the forehead. Damien smacks her ass. I roll my eyes, heading back out to my car to wait on her.

"Whew, Guh! The head game Damien laid on me last night," Kyla says as she joins me in the car. "We got in a big argument about the second child again. I don't understand why he is so intent on knocking me up."

I turn out of her neighborhood. "Y'all have that argument a lot, huh?"

"We did before, but he laid off of it for a while."

"Kyla." I look her way at the stoplight. "Are you happy in your marriage?"

"What kind of question is that?" She pulls a piece of gum out of her purse and puts it in her mouth.

"One I'm asking."

She stares through the windshield, chewing her gum. "I mean, we have our ups and downs, but overall I'm happy."

"Did you know Lincoln before you met him at the happy hour?" I am not working my way up to the elephant in the room anymore.

She chokes on the gum. I pat her back as she erupts in a fit of coughs. "Talk about left field. Zola, are you implying something?"

I rub my hands along the steering wheel to collect my thoughts. *Maybe I should not have brought this up.* I peek at her from the corner of my eye to see she is waiting for the ball to drop. "Um, I kind of overheard you and Lincoln at Newtopia that Friday the boys came."

"Overheard what?" She squints, probably aware of what I am going to say next.

I look back at the traffic. "Something about him drugging you?"

Her eyes enlarge as her lips part before she turns her gaze out the passenger window. We sit in silence as I drive down the boulevard along the water. I start to regret bringing the topic up. Kyla seems pretty shaken up, as I can tell by the nervous bouncing of her left leg.

I try to retract the awkwardness. "I didn't mean t—"

"No," she interrupts. "I need to get this off my chest. I made a horrible decision that I constantly reprimand myself for. If Damien were to find out, it would be the end of us. Like, I haven't done something this reckless since my college days." She takes a deep breath, leaning back against the seat. "I am a wife now, a mother."

I grip the wheel tighter, anticipating her meaning. "Kyla, what happened?"

"A few months back, after one of our happy hour rendezvous, I stayed a little longer after y'all left. I wanted to indulge a little more because of the stress I was dealing with that week. Damien was on a business trip, and I was slightly happy since we needed some space. We had been arguing over his favorite subject of having that second baby." She looks my way. "I am finally in a place in my career where I do not need a baby to distract me; Jamar was a handful on his own."

There is that reasoning again that I do not feel is one hundred.

Returning her gaze out the windshield, she continues. "As I was settling my tab, this yummy dark chocolate man with stunning gray eyes slid into the chair next to me."

"Not Lincoln!" I blurt, swerving out of my lane as an oncoming car honks at me.

She nods, not even fazed that I almost wrecked. "I told him I was married and wasn't interested, but he just wouldn't let up."

I snort. "Definitely sounds like his ass." Lincoln is such a ladies' man and believes he is a gift to women.

"So I let him walk me to my car, hoping he would leave me be. Unfortunately, he took it upon himself to kiss me and was rough with it, which excited me. I don't know why, but I responded. One thing led to the next, and I fucked him in my backseat in Newtopia's parking lot."

"*Nooooo!*" I gasp, glancing her way, once again swerving into the lane next to me. "Why? Why? Why?" I shake my head.

Her eyes mist with tears, which makes me frown. It bothers me to see my friend sad. "I don't know, Zola! I hate myself. Like, I *love* Damien."

"Don't hate yourself. Are you going to tell him?"

"O gosh no!" She looks at me with watery eyes. "I just want to forget it. I didn't know his name or anything about him until I saw him that day."

"What about the drugging?"

"Oh, I was just referring to the alcohol we both consumed that night."

I take the exit to my condo. "Wow, Ky! That is extreme. I never thought you would be a cheater. You have always been the Goody Two-shoes."

Silence fills the interior of the car, and for a moment I find I may have been a bit harsh. "I am not sure what came over me that night, but I have learned my lesson and will make it up to my husband." She clenched a fist against her chest. "Lincoln was a mistake."

"Lincoln is a player, so definitely try to steer clear from him from now on."

"You don't have to worry about that." Kyla sits up in the seat. "Can we keep this between you and me and not tell Lynn?"

I give her an incredulous look as I park in my spot. "Say what now! How do you expect me to accomplish that?"

"Pleaseee, Zola!" She places her palms together with her fingers pointed upward. "Just for now."

I roll my eyes with an overexaggerated sigh. "Fine!"

As we walk inside, she explains the meeting she was in all day with a local politician that is on trial for money laundering. Seems the egotistic prick is difficult to work with and another reminder why she is ready to branch off and open her own practice to help the less fortunate. She believes they at least do not feel entitled to be above the law because of their status.

Eight

I was excited to finally land in New Orleans after a long layover. I never understand why Southwest makes its customers get up super early just to get to their destinations late in the afternoon. Flights are supposed to be convenient. Instead, we were sent in the opposite direction to spend three hours in a freezing airport just to head back south. Next time I am paying the extra $150 and flying Delta so I can land before lunch.

We head to baggage claim to gather our stuff before meeting my sister outside. We are staying with my mom tonight before we check into our Airbnb tomorrow. We wanted to be smack in the middle of the festivities so we will not have to worry about our well-being after these intoxicated nights.

Lynn yawns as we load into the car. "I am so tired."

"How? You slept the whole flight," chimes Kyla.

"And?" She stretches her entire body. "Sleeping in an uncomfortable plane seat is not considered real sleep." Her muscles pop in distress.

"I agree with Lynn; I could use a nap," I say, cracking my neck from side to side.

"Well, good luck on getting some rest," my sister responds, pulling away from the curb. "Lamar is having a barbecue at the house for one of his frat brothers, and it's chaos."

"Ugh!" I slam my head against the seat. Those Greek affairs always seem to get wild. I used to enjoy attending them, strolling across the floor with my line sisters and meeting new fuck buddies on the road. Now I am tired and not in the mood. "Why is he doing it there?"

"Because Mom is staying with Aunt Linda this weekend for the festival, and he lives in an apartment."

Rolling my eyes, I glance out the window. "Don't care! Now I have to be bothered with his friends and folks I don't miss." I fell into drama with the tail of my line, and she spread rumors about me that many believed since I had a reputation of being "loose."

"Well, keep that same energy when you see Travis," she retorts. I swing my head in her direction, my face scrunched in displeasure.

Travis is the knucklehead that took my virginity. I had a huge crush on him for so many years, yet he saw me only as his best friend's little sister. However, that day he was at the house with Lamar for my senior prom, I got the impression he saw me in a new light. My lime-green dress accented my curves, my hair piled on top in some updo. His eyes seemed to strip me naked, leaving me bare in front of his penetrating gaze.

When my date came to pick me up, Travis was overprotective of me, questioning and threatening the poor guy. His hostile stare made me feel a tad uncomfortable as I posed for my pictures. It seemed as if he was a little jealous that I was in the arms of someone else. He made a comment that his little LaLa had grown up into a gorgeous woman. He did not verbally say it, but his eyes alluded: he wanted me.

When I was in college, I crossed as a Delta Sigma Theta. After the show, there was a large party to celebrate. I allowed myself to indulge in large amounts of shots that soon muddled my thoughts and erased my inhibitions.

The hands of Jamal, Travis's brother, became a little too adventurous as we danced near a corner. I was unable to step away from him. He had other plans for me and used my intoxicated state to persuade me. Travis came from out of nowhere as I was pinned up against a pillar in Jamal's embrace. He yanked me away from his brother and dragged me out of the party. He insisted it was time for me to go back to my dorm.

The cold, clear air triggered my senses, which gave me some control of my actions. On the elevator ride to my floor, I leaned on Travis for support. I was fully aware as I rubbed my hand against his chest that I could feel the panes of his muscles through his shirt. When we reached my room, I opened it with my key. He pushed me against the door with his unyielding body when I turned his way to say good-bye. My lips were never allowed to utter a word. His lips crashed atop mine and swallowed up my questioning. He kissed my soft, innocent lips bruisingly as I shoved my palms against his chest. He bit my bottom lip when I tried to deny his tongue entrance. It caused me to gasp in pain and a slight hunger, which allowed him to plunge his tongue into my mouth. I became a prisoner of his.

So many thoughts ran through my head that night as Travis seemed to try to cure his thirst with the taste of me. He showed me no mercy as he dominated. I dripped from the onslaught. This was a new delight that I had not been aware of—something I had only heard of from Lynn and a few of my line sisters during rush. He made me mush in his malleable hands as they rubbed against me. We allowed air to enter our lungs only when he gripped my ass and picked me up as he opened my door with his foot. We tumbled onto the bed among my collection of stuffed animals, and our hands ran frantically over each other.

We were consumed by the cloud of sexual haze that put us in that state of euphoria. I had never thought I would get the chance to sleep or even make out with Travis. He filled a void I was unaware existed. A lock clicked perfectly in place. Desire raged through my senses. I lost my innocence with the one that had bewitched me from my childhood days. He made me believe we would be together.

Boy was I wrong. He avoided me afterward, leaving me used and heartbroken. I locked myself in my dorm for over a week and cried in despair the whole time. None of my friends convinced me to leave. I guess you could say he ruined the whole relationship idea for me, and that is why I am the "fuck them and leave them" type of woman.

"Uh oh! Travis is there," Kyla interjects. "Zola was finally over him after being broken up over his engagement with that whore Bianca"

"That marriage never happened, since he caught her cheating with his brother," Nikki replies with a chuckle.

Well, that is not something to laugh about.

"Seriously! Jamal is dirty for that," I say, shaking my head. "Besides, Travis doesn't even cross my mind anymore. He can do what he pleases." I have finally rid myself of my obsession with him.

"Uh huh! Sure, Zola," responds Lynn while rolling her eyes.

As Nicole pulls up to the house, I see the party is still in full swing. The yard is filled with gyrating couples and people drinking and eating.

I consider that maybe I can rush through the door and lock myself in a room so I can avoid stumbling upon anyone I know.

As I step out of the car, I am lifted into the air by strong arms. "Ugh! Let me down, you buffoon."

Lamar, my older brother, laughs as he hugs me tightly. "I miss my baby sis, and you haven't called in months."

I wiggle out of his grasp. Pulling down my skirt that rose in the attack, I turn to look up at him. We share the same hazel eyes that we inherited from our mom, whereas Nicole inherited our dad's dark brown ones. Lamar towers over me at six foot three, about the same height as Traymel. His hair is pulled back into a puff on top of his head, his beard trimmed short against his jaw.

"One, I am not the baby. Two, I have been busy with my current client and tend to lose track of time. Three, we still text frequently." I tick the items off, holding my fingers in front of him. Lynn snickers beside me. "But"—I dramatically drag out the word—"I miss you, Marly."

He rolls his eyes at my nickname as he goes and talks to Kyla, who just stepped out of the car. They used to date when we were in college before she broke up with him when she went off to law school. When she returned to town engaged to Damien, he was kind of heartbroken. I guess he believed they would get back together when she finished her studies. However, they are now good friends.

"LaLa."

I freeze as I hear his deep tone voicing his pet name for me. A shiver tickles my back and goosebumps creep down my arms as I heave a deep exhalation. I slowly turn around as my eyes land on Travis—the man that had my heart and destroyed it, damaging me for others. He has not changed much since I saw him, which was right before I moved to San Diego after finding out he was engaged to Bianca. He is about six feet, light-skinned with red-dyed dreads. His muscular torso is still lean, with both his arms covered in tattoos. *The man is still fine!* "Hey, Travis."

"You are a sight for sore eyes." His eyes squint in the bright sunlight.

I laugh as I head to the trunk to grab my luggage. Travis meets me and takes my suitcase from my hands. "Really?" I turn to him with my right fist on my hip.

He shrugs. "Just trying to help."

"I don't need your help. How about you go back to avoiding me. You are good at that." I try to snatch the suitcase back from him, but he just holds it out of my reach.

He snorts. "Are you still being salty about the past?"

I glance at him before I roll my eyes and stomp off. If he wants to carry my luggage, then so be it. Nevertheless, I do not have to talk to him while he does it. He can drop it off in my room. As I make my way through the crowd, familiar faces stop and speak to me to try to catch up on what they missed. Of course, most are mainly wondering about my love life. I am baffled as to why many classmates are so interested in what is going on in another person's home. *How does that adversely affect them?* I politely smile and respond to none. These people are irrelevant to me, which is why they do not know any of my business. Many of them paid attention to me only because I was one of Lamar's sisters or to get details on the rumor. He and Nicole were the popular kids, whereas I was the shy, smart one. I grab a drink from the table before going into the house. The red punch at Greek parties is sure to put you on your ass. Large amounts of white liquor are mixed in that cherry-flavored concoction.

"You can't just ignore me," comments Travis behind me just as I cross the doorway.

Dammit! I had assumed I lost him in that crowd. *Why can he not catch the hint and leave me alone?* Still tuning him out, I climb the stairs to my room, slamming my entire foot on each step before stepping up to the next one, repeating the process over and over. I peek over my shoulder halfway up to see he is just standing at the bottom of the stairs, observing my tantrum.

As I make it to my room, I wait for Travis as he reaches the second floor with my suitcase in his hand. "You can leave it on the floor on your way out," I finally say. I gulp down half the contents of the drink prior to setting the cup on my nightstand. I collapse face-first on the bed as I feel the exhaustion take over.

When the door closes, I am relieved to finally be alone. However, that is short-lived, as I soon feel my bed by my legs sink. I quickly turn over and jolt up to see Travis still in my room and intently looking at me. "Get out!"

"Zola, we need to talk." His hands are on his thighs.

I scoot to the edge of the bed, as if my body is a caterpillar, and place my feet firmly on the floor. I begin to stand up to leave the room myself when arms wrap around my waist and toss me back on the bed. My body bounces against the mattress on my back twice. Tatted arms bracket my hips among the bunched-up blankets. Travis lowers his weight on my body to keep me from moving. The contact is thrilling, and I try my hardest to compose my features so he does not see how unnerved he has me. *I really do need to get laid.*

"What are you doing?" I breathe in short puffs. He brushes a few dreads from my face that have found their way out of my ponytail at the nape of my neck before running the pads of his fingertips lightly against my lips.

"God, I miss you!" He leans down to kiss me, but I turn my head at the last second and his lips connect with my left cheek.

"Is Bianca not living up to your expectations?" I say in a snappy tone, knowing she is not in the picture but wanting to be petty.

"We aren't together." His lips are still brushing against my skin.

"Pity!" My sullen gaze returns to his face. Alluring green eyes stare blissfully into mine. "I am not your fallback girl."

"Zola, you are always number one." A frown pulls on the corners of his mouth. "It's just complicated when it comes to you."

I furrow my eyebrows. "Why is that?"

"You are Lamar's baby sister, and I don't want to lose my best friend and ruin our relationship because I can't keep it in my pants. Nevertheless, when I did finally have you, I knew it wasn't just sex between us, and I was too young to deal with the consequences of taking your virginity. I did not want the commitment of what you would expect from me after. However, I have done a lot of growing up and want to build that connection between us again. Just give me a chance to prove to you I'm different."

I just stare at him with a blank expression, not knowing whether I should believe him. *It is not wise to open that emotional floodgate again.* I could never really think when he was around, and I tended to make irrational decisions. For example, in this proximity, I want him to claim me against these sheets. Being in his reach makes it clear to me that those emotions I believed I had extracted were only buried. I miss everything about him, and I do not want to admit to myself that he is still in the back of my head. He, unfortunately, has a hook in my heart I cannot rid myself of.

"Zola! Are you coming back downstairs?" asks Nicole as she bursts into my childhood room. "The par—" She stops midsentence when her eyes land on me lying in an uncompromising position with Travis. They squint even smaller at the spectacle. "Really, Travis! You could not wait ten minutes before you pulled it out on her. Lamar is *so* gonna beat your ass." She abruptly turns to stalk out of the room, most likely to start some mess with our older brother, since she dislikes Travis.

"Nikki, wait! It's not what you think."

Coming to my senses, I shove Travis off me and chase behind my angry sister to stop her mission. This is not how my visit home was supposed to go. I just left one problem for another. "Seriously, Nicole!" I holler behind her, rushing down the hallway. She does not slow down her stride but quickens it. "You know I wasn't getting down with Travis like that."

I see her jogging down the stairs. I have been after Travis since high school. When he pulled that stunt after sleeping with me, I begged her not to tell Lamar about it, because our overprotective brother would have lost it. I am considered the angel in the family, and she sometimes felt he paid a little more attention to me than her. My family knows Nicole can handle her own, and most of the time she keeps to herself. They all believe I am too trusting and allow anyone in.

"You believed it was nothing, but Travis had something else on his mind," she responds as she turns around to me, standing near the bottom of the stairs. "You lack the common sense to identify those that try to take advantage. Travis is one of those people. He knew you had a crush on him all those years, and he entertained your fantasy until he got scared and broke your heart."

I stop at the stair above her, one of my hands propped on the railing. "Aren't you the younger one?" I ask, a little annoyed by once again being treated like a child. "Stop making it seem like I cannot take care of myself. You and Lamar have been babying me most of my life."

"Oh please, Zola!" She throws her hands into the air. "That is not how it is."

"Really? Then why are you going to tell Marly about Travis?" I send her a quizzical expression before sighing. "They are friends, and there's no need to cause tension over a little misunderstanding. Come on, sis! I'm over Travis, and no fucking will be happening between us."

"Whatever, La! You keep telling yourself that." She points the index finger of her right hand at my chest. "Do not forget I know you. Now, your friends are at the party, so are you coming to join or not doing anything with Travis?" She says that last part with air quotes because she believes I am full of it.

Travis leans over the rail at the top to address us down the stairs. "Nicole, you are still putting your nose in business that's not yours. Where is Ethan?"

Speaking of the topic of discussion.

"I was talking to my sister, jackass, and it's none of your business where my man is."

"Oh, he is your man today?" Travis taunts with a sneer. His hands are clasped together, hanging over the railing.

"Travis, *shut up!*" I scold, briefly looking in his direction. My fingers enclose her bicep and drag her outside away from him. He is going to make her come back up those stairs and beat his ass. She has no problem throwing some hands.

Ethan and Nicole have been together off and on for much of school. Their main problem was he would always be a little too friendly with the opposite sex. He claims to have cheated on her only twice, but the women in school sing a different tune. Travis and Jamal are Ethan's half-brothers, so Travis would always have her back when she was left in tears over his brother. However, after the third time of Nicole taking him back, Travis and my sister had a big argument about her stupidity, and since then there has been bad blood. That is the past though, according to her. Ethan supposedly has grown up and stopped his childish ways. The family, of course, is not happy about their engagement, but at the end of the day, she loves him, and he makes her happy.

"Hey, baby! I'm sorry I'm late," Ethan apologizes as he takes Nicole in his arms when we step onto the porch. After kissing her on the lips, he turns to me. "Zola, you back for Jazz Fest, I'm guessing."

"Your guess is correct," I confirm, nodding at her fiancé.

He returns his attention to Nicole. "How was your day?"

"It was good!" She wraps her arms around his waist. "Are we still going to the movies?"

"Yes! Let me go say hi to some of the fellas, and then we can go." He kisses her again before he starts off to his friends.

I glance at the door just as Travis walks out and connects his eyes with mine. I quickly turn my head and hop off the porch, walking off into the crowd with Nicole in tow.

The Jazz Fest was phenomenal this year, just like every other year. The oldies concert on Saturday night was my favorite. Earth, Wind, and Fire lit that stage up, and the collaboration with Gladys Knight and Chaka Khan for the closer was something else. I am currently on the way to Aunt Linda's house for a kickback to celebrate the conclusion of the fest. Everyone flies back home tomorrow, and we must do one last family shindig.

Nicole and I did the cake tasting this morning and she settled on a three-tier red velvet cake with a sweet raspberry cream cheese icing even though I hated it. She allowed me to pick the cupcakes that will sit around the cake, since I was adamant that no one would eat her choice. Considering it is their wedding and nobody else's, it complements their taste, raspberry being Ethan's favorite and red velvet cake hers.

As Ethan pulls up in the lot next to the house, Nicole slips out of the car and skips toward Lamar and Travis, who are out by the road talking. "Hey, big bro!" she acknowledges, jumping on his back.

"Nik! How's my munchkin?"

"Ready for this food!" She hops back to the ground.

"The girls here?" I ask Lamar, joining them.

Lamar nods, pointing over his shoulder. "Yeah, out back."

"Ethan"—she turns to him as he joins the group—"come and speak to my mom."

"One minute bae, I'ma hang out here for a minute."

Ignoring Travis, Nicole strolls into the house. I follow behind her, giving him a shy smile. The day after my arrival, as we were getting ready to head to the Airbnb, Travis cornered me in the bathroom. I did not want to cause a scene and alert the others; so I allowed him to talk, and he convinced me to give us another chance and try to forget everything that has happened in the past. I do need to learn to stop holding grudges. *That is easier said than done.* However, as we have been getting acquainted with one another, I am finding it easier to let him back in.

Randomly stopping to speak to a few people moving about inside, we make our way to the kitchen for a plate. There is so much to choose from, such as mac and cheese, yams, dirty rice, meatballs, fried drumettes, Rotel dip, potato salad, seafood pasta, red beans with sausage, and buttery corn cobs. I can see the crawfish boiling out back in the yard. We missed the first round, so I pile everything on my plate and head outside. I have not eaten all day besides the cake samples, saving room for all these goodies. Giving my mom a kiss on the cheek, I sit at the table with her, Nicole, and Aunt Linda.

"Look who finally brought her ass over. Where is that man of yours?" comments Aunt Linda.

"Auntie! I made it, didn't I?" Nikki rolls her eyes, taking a bite of the chicken. "He's outside with Lamar."

"He better come in here and speak, ol' good-for-nothing fella," she retorts, fixing her wig.

"Linda, leave that man alone," my mom chides. "If my daughter is happy with him, let them be."

I start laughing, choking on my drink. "I brought my quarters. I heard Aunt Johnell doing all the whooping and hollering because Devin's kids made a mess in the kitchen." They are quick to cause a ruckus.

"I can't stand you," Mom shares, looking at me.

I swallow the mouthful of dirty rice. "What did I do this time?"

Ignoring me, she looks at Nikki. "Gimme some money." My sister rolls her eyes before checking her purse and giving our mom a handful of quarters.

"I'ma need that back. You know I'm broke."

"Hey, Mama Anne!" exclaims Ethan as he walks outside, the sun bouncing off a fake gold chain around his neck. He takes my mom in a big hug before she pushes him away and pops him across the head.

She is so abusive.

"Boy, if you don't get off me." She stands from the chair and heads inside.

"They 'bout to play poda, and you know how that gets." Nicole informs him, still smacking on her food.

"I heard Neek in there making a racket. Bae, can you make me a plate?" He pleads, taking the seat my mom recently vacated. "Aunt Linda."

"Boy, I am not your family, even when you marry my niece!" she scoffs as she gets up and follows the crowd into the house.

"She still dislikes me?"

Nicole gives him a kiss before getting up.

"She's crazy with everyone," I assure him. "Well shit!" I stand as the older crowd moves inside. "I'm tryna steal up all they change," I whisper to Nikki as she passes me.

The rest of the night is filled with laughs and arguing and alcohol. I ended up playing a few rounds of cards before Aunt Mary runs me off. Every time someone follows her, she seems to always need the card the follower is searching for. The younger folks are all out enjoying the crisp, spring breeze. Nicole is stretched out on a lawn chaise like a stuffed cow between Ethan's legs. He, Kyla, and Lamar are watching the Lakers game on the big screen my Uncle Jeff has outside.

Travis and I are out by the fence, chatting. My hand keeps finding its way to his chest as I lean near him to laugh at whatever he is saying. It is still as taut as I remember. Lynn told me his eyes seemed to follow me around the whole night.

Interrupting our conversation, Nicole grabs my arm and drags me away. I could have sworn I just saw her across the way. "WTF, Nikki!" I exclaim, tripping over my feet to keep up.

She stops and cross her arms across her chest. "I'm not gonna ask why y'all seem so chummy, but just know … don't call me when he brings that BS again."

"Okay, sis! We were just talking." I roll my eyes. *Here she goes, being dramatic.* "What happened was the past, and we have decided to look past that. Travis is a cool guy, and you used to believe that too."

"I guess! Just don't let him pull you back into his web. Well, I am going to miss you!" She squeezes me in a big hug. "It was great to see you, and I can't wait for my fantastic bachelorette party you're throwing for me."

My famous smile graces my face. "It will be a bash to remember!"

Nine

"Finally! Off that plane." Lynn raises her hands above her head as we walk into the San Diego airport. "Next year we are driving."

"Um, no. That will be even longer," indicates Kyla, her eyes focused on her phone.

Lynn rolls her eyes. "Well, then let's teleport."

"Lynn, the crazy shit you say." I shake my head as I laugh.

We head to the baggage claim as Lynn sends Jonathan a text to let him know we landed. "Zola, are you riding with me or Kyla?"

"Kyla," I answer, checking out the signs hanging over the carousels to find the one our things are on. "I'm babysitting Jamar tonight for their date night."

"A date night!" She gasps is an astonishment, stopping in her tracks. Not paying attention, I walk into her, dropping my purse to the ground. "That sounds cheesy. Married couples do that?"

Kyla grabs her bag from the belt. "It keeps a relationship alive, guh!"

Lynn looks at me before returning her attention to Kyla. "Aren't you still mad about the whole second baby issue?"

"Yes, but I still love him," Kyla explains with a quick shake of her head, her left hand waving off to the side. "It is not going to break us."

As we walk out of the airport, I see Johnathan conversing with Damien by their vehicles. He looks up when Lynn approaches. "Sweetcakes!" he croons before kissing her cheek and bringing her luggage to the trunk of his Mustang.

I wave to Lynn before hopping into Damien's Avalanche, sitting next to Jamar. He is munching on a fruit cup, using his fingers as utensils. I lean over and blow raspberries on each of his cheeks as he squeals, pushing me away with his sticky hands. As we head to their villa, I close my eyes and relax. I am so happy we took the trip home and I was able to spend time with my family. Lynn's mother even drove down from Texas to spend a day with her. However, even with the mild feeling of being homesick, San Diego is beginning to grow on me. I am glad to be back right now.

"Do you want to grab something to eat before we get to the house?" proposes Kyla, ruffling her fingers through her husband's hair.

"Can we just order in?" Eyes still closed as my head lays against the headrest. "I'm ready to just chill out."

"Yes, pizza!" Jamar exclaims, clapping his hands.

I smack my hand against my head, opening one eye to peek at him. "No! What is up with you and pizza?" He just smiles up at me before returning his attention to his iPad. Leaning forward, I tap Damien's seat. "I changed my mind. Bring me to Canes."

I do not realize how hungry I am until I demolish a box combo with extra sauce before we even make it to the house. I take a quick shower and then assist Kyla in getting dressed for her date. I am hoping this will help her out with that spark they have been missing in their marriage. I know she regrets the infidelity, but I feel she did that only because there is more going on between them. She has never been one for one-night stands. Also, that drug comment she made does not sit right with me. I feel she is not giving me the whole story with him.

Once the married couple leave on their date, Jamar and I watch a movie with popcorn, and then I bathe and put him to bed. He insists on me reading him a Dr. Suess story, which I gladly oblige. Kyla did not even know about these books until I got Jamar his first one when he turned three. Talk about the surprise I felt that day; I had to educate her on a childhood icon. Dr. Suess stories were my favorite growing up. I feel nostalgic while reading the words, long after Jamar is fast asleep. Whenever I have my own little one, he or she will know all the books, front to back.

I head to the guest room after tucking him in, and I lie across the bed, watching TV. My phone lights up with Travis's picture flashing across my screen for a DUO call.

"Hey punk!" I answer, smiling into the camera. He looks as if he is fresh out of the shower. Water is dripping from his dreads onto his bare chest. *Talk about yummy!* My hormones kick in.

"Punk?" He arches his eyebrow, leaning into the screen. "If you were here, I would *show* you your punk."

I giggle, rolling on my back, holding the phone in the air with my arms extended. "Yeah, yeah, yeah! Ya know you are not going to touch me." I stick my tongue out at him.

"Zola." His hand slips to the waistband of his pajama pants. "If you knew how hard I am for you right now, you would not torture me with that view of your boobs." I glance down at my chest and see that my tank has shifted, exposing the side of my naked breast, the nipple barely hidden. Yet its presence in the thin fabric is noticeably prominent. "I like that tat, by the way. Is it new?"

"Yeah, me and the girls got it a few months back. So!" I smirk through my eyelashes, taking my free hand and pulling up my shirt. "I got you hard, huh?" I know I should not be teasing him like this since we just started fresh, but I am horny. We are states away, so nothing should come of it.

Travis grimaces, and his teeth clench. "La, don't do it."

I sit up and lean my back against the headboard, pulling my tank over my neck, fully exposing my upper torso. My plump melons sit perky in the camera, the brown buds on their tips shimmering with my "bite me" piercings. Setting the phone between my thighs, I knead them in my hands, flicking my tongue against each jewel at different intervals.

"*Fuck!*" He sets the phone down on the couch and I see a flash of his very large erection.

"*Travis!* What are you doing?" I stop my tease as I gape at the phone.

His face comes back into view. "I told you I was hard. And I am about to handle it with you on the phone right now."

"Noooo! Don't do that." I pull my shirt back over my head. "I am babysitting Jamar, and we are not like that."

"You did this, Zola!" His thick, throbbing manhood is present on my screen. I involuntarily lick my lips, mesmerized by its glory. "I am not about to get blue balls."

"Go jack off to one of your other hoes," I snap, getting a little jealous.

I am sure he is getting something down there. The women have always thrown themselves at his feet.

His eyebrows furrow as the screen is back on his face. "Other hoes? Nah, I am good with you." He angles the phone again to show his hand sliding up and down his length, his gaze focused on my face.

It seems to enlarge more in his hand as he grips it tightly. I rub my thighs together, wishing I could feel it in my honeypot. *Snap out of it, Zola!* I quickly hang up the phone, laying it next to my thigh as I calm my breathing. I'm fighting the urge to touch myself. My cell rings next to me; it's Travis trying to finish what I started. Removing my pajamas, I head to the bathroom for another shower—a cold one.

I am awakened around two in the morning by the constant ringing of my phone. I try to ignore it, but when the fourth shrill fills the room, I assume it is an important matter. Seeing a random number, I cautiously answer it.

I release a sigh when I find it is Lynn calling me from Johnathan's phone, sounding extremely annoyed. She needs me to pick her up ASAP. After agreeing, I slip on some pants and grab Kyla's keys for her Jeep. I see Damien's car parked beside hers in the garage, which means they finally made it home. Thank goodness their guest room is down the hall so I did not have to hear their late-night dessert. I key in Johnathan's address in my GPS and speed off to pick up Lynn, disregarding all traffic laws. I wonder what happened for her to contact me. I call once I arrive outside, not wanting to get out of the car. I see Johnathan standing on the patio, staring out into space. She walks out the door to the Jeep with her suitcase from the trip.

"Talk about a great night ending so badly," she sighs, leaning her head against the passenger window as I pull out of the driveway. "It is not as if I am cheating on him. I understand he wants to be in a relationship, but I thought we were clear that I wanted to wait."

"Lynn, what happened?" I ask as she pauses in her rant.

Sitting up, she shifts in her seat, facing me. "So, like, thirty minutes before I called you, Michael called my phone while I was wrapped in Johnathan's arms, talking about he outside the condo and I told him I was at a friend's house. Well, of course, Johnathan overhears the conversation." She exaggeratedly rolls her eyes, slapping her hands on her thighs. "He starts questioning me about him and then getting all angry, smashes my damn phone against the wall. I finally told him that I am messing around with another man. Then he kicked me out." She shrugs, waiting for my response.

I agree that he overreacted, but at the same time, Lynn should have seen the signs he was giving. The pampering, the all-day hangouts, the sleepovers. "I think it is time for you to decide if you want to date Johnathan or let him find someone else who can give him the relationship thing. Michael is a married man, so it is not like leaving him will be that big of a deal."

"I don't know if Johnathan even still wants to be with me after that commotion."

I give her no response, because even I do not know what may come from it. This is something she is going to have to sort out on her own. We ride in silence, with Lynn in her thoughts about her ordeal on what action she wants to take next.

She skips school the next day, claiming she was extremely exhausted that morning, having tossed and turned the rest of the night after we returned. When I arrive home that afternoon after work, I find her in bed, wrapped in covers, with a bottle of wine. A dismal expression is on her face. Her swollen red cheeks are a telltale sign she has been crying nonstop. I am surprised this is bothering her as much as it is. She has let her mind roam all over the place because of him. I let her use my backup phone until her insurance sends a replacement. Unfortunately, Michael has been blowing it up. It seems he has some big news to share with her.

Lynn talks my head off almost all that night. I have to walk out on her midsentence after my head does a 360 on my neck at least three times in the course of fifteen minutes, the sandman adamantly knocking at my eyelids. She returned to school the next day. Reaching out to Johnathan was futile. He ignores her during the following days after their incident, even with her going out of her way to get his attention.

By Friday, Lynn is a wreck. She is missing their quality time, conversations, and, of course, the sex. Michael is a far-off thought from her mind. She is starting to realize Johnathan's importance in her life.

During our weekly happy hour, she talks nonstop about Johnathan and how she messed up. But she then blames him for overreacting and then puts the blame back on her for having issues. And on and on and on, to the point where Kyla and I tell her to go be with him. *Clearly her mind has decided that he is the one she wants.* The quicker they reunite, the better it will be for us. Finally, she calls Michael and breaks things off with him for good. She then rushes out, leaving us to cover her tab, to beg Johnathan for his forgiveness. Let's just say it goes well.

The weekend flies by hectically. I am unable to rest for having to immerse myself in work. Come Sunday, even I am over this stressful week with everything going on. My mind is a rave event where the colorful strobe lights, pinging about, are the endless thoughts.

I try to allow myself some relaxation as I settle deeper into the tub, letting the jets pound against my tight muscles. Lynn's way has rubbed off on me, as now I am stuck between two men. I reconnected with an old love when I visited home for the festival. We had an abrupt and toxic ending, but with the discussion between us last weekend, we decided to wipe the slate clean and start anew. However, the feelings I once had did not get the memo. Travis took my virginity, and for many that is a token that should be earned through love and care.

Throughout the years we spent together, Travis had always shown me attention and made me feel beautiful. He was there for my tears, had my back when boys disrespected me, and supported my accomplishments. It was like having another brother, minus the fact that I did not feel platonic toward him. He ignored all the suggestions I hinted at and never crossed the line.

That night I became a part of his frat's sisterhood became the best night of my existence, which quickly changed to the worst morning I had lived. A depression took over my mindset when I learned he ran from my innocence. I blamed myself for the inexperience and doubted whether I was even good, afraid that he hated me. I did not ask Lamar about him to avoid suspicion about what had transpired between us. I knew my overprotective brother would have gone ballistic on his best friend, and I did not want a rift caused by me.

I took that hurt and forced myself to forget him, which turned me into a broken girl no one even recognized. It is sad to say, but I became a loose female. I bed-hopped throughout campus and perfected the art of sex while I soothed a heart that ached. That lasted about five months until Lamar got wind and threatened every male not to touch me. I was also subjected to an intervention from my besties and sister. That was when I told them all that had happened, since up to that point it had been a secret. I calmed down during the rest of my senior year. However, the pain lingered, and my relationships then were slim to none—as they are even now. I did not trust men and still to this day have not found one to change my mind.

Still, Traymel is another that I yearn for—a first since Travis. The things he makes me feel I thought were long forgotten. Not knowing how he feels is bothersome. There is a nagging pull wanting me to investigate, to tempt. He has not made a move on me since that day in his office before traveling home—before my rekindling with Travis. He has taken me from my comfort bubble that lacked feelings with those I involve myself with and knocked me off course. I am now being tugged in two different directions, tempting fate on both ends.

One morning in the office, I went to bring up the kiss to Traymel but he interrupted and changed the subject. In one way, I was glad he was not trying to pursue the option of something happening with us working together. But on the other hand, I am curious about how it could be with him. He is making me feel an unusual way.

I get out of the tub and dry myself off before wrapping the towel around me while walking out of the bathroom to sit on the bed to lotion my body.

"Zola! I'm in *love!*" Lynn rejoices as she bursts into my room before falling across my bed. "Johnathan and I made it official, and I'm ecstatic about it. He may be the one." She hugs herself while grinning up at my ceiling.

"Ick! Don't bring that lovey-dovey mushy shit in here."

"Don't be a prude."

"Prude?" I scoff. "Bish, I'm far from that."

"Anyway!" She rolls onto her stomach to look up at me. "What's up with you and Travis?"

I swallow hard, looking away from her. "What do you mean by that?"

"Let's not play stupid." Lynn props her chin in her hands, her elbows holding her head up. "I heard you Duoing him last night, and when we were home, he sure was around a lot."

"We are just working on being friends again." I pull at the threads on the end of my towel.

She smacks her lips. "Then why do you have this big-ass giddy smile on your face now that I brought him up?"

I place my hand over my mouth to hide the smile, now blushing like a tomato. She is right that I got excited thinking about Travis. Our video chats have gotten a little dirty, and I am starting to ache for him. "Lynn, I don't know what's wrong with me. I know I should not think about him, but I do." Gray eyes flash before me. "Then there's Traymel. I'm just conflicted."

"My opinion? Screw Travis because he messed up his chance and jump on that Mel horse." She smacks her ass, waving her other hand in the air as if she were spinning a lasso.

We burst out laughing, both clutching our stomachs. I go back and forth with her about my pros and cons with both men, hoping for some insight. Unfortunately, Lynn is just like Nicole and holds a grudge against Travis for what happened in college. I am normally a grudge holder too, but I cannot seem to stick with it when it comes to Travis. It was so easy allowing him back in my life. We picked up as if we never fell off four years ago.

Tired of discussing the logic of the situation for the night, I kick Lynn out of my room for some alone time. I snuggle deep in my blankets, clicking on the TV. As I flip through the channels, a commercial about ACME products is playing. I stop to watch, thinking of the work the fellas have put in to even be considered by this company. Now they have a contract and will start the groundwork soon. At the end of the commercial, the owners come on the screen for some sales pitch, and I am shocked still as I stare at the familiar face. The creases throughout his face have deepened with age, but the genetic makeup is the same. It's a blast from the past.

Mr. Sinclair?

Ten

I open the door to see Kyla on the threshold. In her arms is an etched crystal vase containing a large bouquet of an assortment of flowers. There are a dozen white roses in the middle, surrounded by a mixture of chrysanthemums and baby's breath. The sunlight illuminates the vase, giving the flowers a beautiful and alluring look.

"Kyla! These are gorgeous, and this vase looks expensive. I'm not big on flowers, but I can appreciate a lovely arrangement!" I exclaim as she hands me the flowers at the door. I head to the fireplace and place them on the mantle above it. The room is immediately overcome by their fragrance. She follows behind and collapses on the couch, exhausted.

"Lincoln sent them *to my job!*" Kyla shouts, staring at the ceiling with her palms pressed against the sides of her head. "Where my husband works! Becca is under the impression Damien sent it to me, talking about 'I'm so lucky to have a man like him.'" She rolls her eyes, mocking her at the end of her rant.

Becca is her assistant at the office, and Kyla believes she has it out for her husband. She cannot fire her for fear of a lawsuit, but she does make it hard on her, hoping she will mess up. Unfortunately, Becca is good at her job and rarely makes mistakes.

"The last time Damien brought me flowers was right before Jamar was born," she notes.

I remember that. Kyla had been feeling moody and bloated with the pregnancy symptoms and called him crying for no apparent reason. We had just finished watching a documentary on giving birth that spooked her from delivering. Damien came home from work that afternoon with an arrangement of sunflowers to cheer her up. Her fear turned to anger at the sight of him. She claimed that since he was the one to knock her up, he was to blame, so she beat him with the bouquet. Have you ever seen a grown man being hit with some flowers by a pregnant woman? *Hilarious!* After the once beautiful array was in broken bits, she went into a fit of tears because the flowers were all destroyed.

"I couldn't have them sitting on my desk when Damien gets back from San Francisco." He is at a trial for one of his dad's law school buddies. "The questions he would ask and lies I would have to come up with …"

"Well, don't lie!" I walk away from the mantle. "Marriages in general have problems all the time, and working through them makes the couple stronger in the end."

She glances my way, blinking. "Says the girl who is against marriage."

I give her the hand. "Guh, whateva! Gonna make us a drink. I *know* you can use it." I head to the mini bar station set up in the sunroom with everything one could possibly need. I worked at Razoos off Bourbon Street during our college years, which in the long run made me an expert bartender. After making my specialty blue motorcycles for us, I join her on the sofa. "Travis's dad is one of the owners of ACME."

Kyla perplexedly peeks at me over the rim of her glass. "The major oil company in Louisiana?"

"Not just Louisiana, most of the south. A new plant is gonna be built in Tennessee during the summer by LTW Construct." I pause for emphasis. "The contract I helped them land."

"Whaaat!" She chokes on the drink she was just swallowing. "Talk about a coincidence."

I sigh. "Should I mention something to Travis or Traymel?"

"For what? It is not that serious."

"You may be right." I blow out an exaggerated gust of air. "I saw him in a commercial the other night and just found it crazy."

"Have you kissed Traymel again?"

"No." My bottom lip pokes out in forlornness.

Her eyes bulge as she takes another sip. "Why not?"

66

I gesture with my empty hand before her, palm facing upward. "Because he hasn't made a move." *Like, duh!*

"So? You make one." She rolls her eyes. "Never stopped you before when you wanted a man."

"I want more than sex with him though." I swirl the liquid in my glass. "And I'm not gonna put myself out there to get rejected if he doesn't feel the same way."

"Hmm. Zola catching feelings." She smirks in my direction. "I'ma have Lynn drop some hints."

I sit up straight on the couch, sloshing the drink over my hand. *"Don't you dare!"*

Kyla playfully smiles at me as she reaches into her purse for her ringing phone. Without peeking at the ID, she answers. When the caller says something, her happy facial expression drops. Wiping my hand on my sweats, I lean a little closer toward her to listen in. I hear a muffled deep chuckle.

"Did you come up with your condition?" she asks the caller, leaning away from me.

A scowl covers her face after a pause. I do not catch their response. "Then do not contact me." She hangs up and turns off the phone.

"Who was that?" I inquire.

She finishes off the rest of her drink in one gulp. "Lincoln."

"I am going to refill these drinks, and you are going to go into more detail." I stand and head back over to the bar to make another round.

"Don't make it too strong. I need to stop by Damien's parents' house and pick up Jamar."

I stride back to the couch, sitting down and throwing my feet on the table as I lean back to get comfortable. "So! I'ma get straight to the point. Why is Lincoln still in the picture? I assumed that one-night stand was the end of the communication besides y'all recently meeting at happy hour."

She grips the bottom of the glass with both hands as it sits atop her lap. "That's what I thought, too, until a blocked number contacted me a month later."

Blocked number? "Wait, you mean that one I saw the morning after the club?"

She nods. "I didn't tell you the full story. He had been harassing me for days before tracking me to the club and dragging me into that janitor's closet."

"*Say what?*" My feet drop from the table. "I'm going to beat Lincoln's *ass!*"

"No, Zola." She places her hand on my arm. "That was so long ago; it is not even that serious."

"Not that serious?" I gape at her. "Are you delusional? Why have you not called the cops? Hell, tell Damien!"

"Because then Damien will find out about me cheating on him. It has not been the best these past few months in my marriage, and I am not one hundred percent certain we would survive infidelity."

"But what about your safety?"

"I don't believe Lincoln is going to endanger my safety."

I scoff.

"Seriously! It is hard to explain, but when he comes around, my body yearns for his touch. Don't get me wrong; I love my husband. However, my thoughts keep creeping in those cheating waters. I am just struggling."

"You sound like Lynn, and you saw how that entanglement ended up."

Her right hand connects with her thigh. "You are no saint! What about Travis and Traymel?"

"We are *not* talking about me now, are we?" I roll my eyes. *Here she goes, trying to pinpoint the drama somewhere else so she does not have to be under the scope when she knows she is in the wrong.* "Yes! It seems we all have a two-men entanglement. Well, not Lynn anymore." *At least neither of mine are married.* We sip our drinks in silence.

"Jamar's last day of school is Friday, and we are taking a family vacation for the weekend. Damien believes it is a good way for us to bond together. Lynn believes we should go to a marriage counselor, but I do not feel we are that bad off at this point. I feel this getaway from the stresses of life will bring our spark back. I know Damien is the right one for me. Temptation is the work of the devil, and I rebuke it."

"Kyla. I just hope you have this under control. I don't want to see you hurt in the end."

We leave the men subject alone and chat about work before she takes her leave to pick up Jamar. After she is gone, I think about what she told me. I knew she was holding out on that story. I still cannot shake what

Lincoln did. Why would he do something like that? I know he does not commit to one woman and likes to be flashy with the opposite sex, but to be a crazed stalker is pushing the line. I know I will not keep quiet. I have a bad habit when something is bothering me; getting to the bottom of it becomes a mission. Lincoln will be getting a piece of my mind the next time I see him. He was right that night when he told Kyla that I would have his ass. She may be sweet and kindhearted, but Ms. Zola Saunders will rain down the heat on him. *I hope Traymel is not like his twin.*

"Speak of the devil," I mutter, glancing at my smartwatch to see a text: "I would love to spend quality time with you outside the office."

Is Traymel asking me out? Crap ... Crap! So he does want to pursue this thing between us. Let me not freak out. I decide to take the leap, considering he is one of the main reasons for my nonstop mind.

"Yes," I text back. My legs jump with excitement. "What do you have in mind?"

"Dinner and Movies?"

I snort. That is boring and so unoriginal.

"What about the fair that is in town for the weekend? I have always been a kid at heart."

"Fair? Haven't been to one of those in a while. How about Saturday?"

"Works for me."

I press the phone against my chest with an enormous smile encompassing my face. Like, I am just so excited. This could be the next step in our relationship. I'm hoping it goes well; otherwise, work may end up as a real disaster. Saturday is just two days away.

How am I nervous to go on a date? *I really lost my touch.* These two days took their time coming around, and it is finally Saturday. As I get ready, I think about the last time I went on a date, coming up blank. Clark was my last fling, and we just met up for sex and a few times shared takeout. Dates allow room for feelings to develop—something you experience when you want to build a foundation for a future instead of using the other person as a placeholder. As I mentioned before, that foundation has not been of interest since Travis. *Travis.* I have not spoken to him in a few days. I ignored his call this morning, feeling a little wrong about going out on a date, as if I am betraying him. *Which is weird!*

The steam from my recent shower fills the confines of my bathroom as I shave my legs while I stand at the vanity. I check the clock on my nightstand to see I have an hour until I need to meet up with Traymel, since I thought it would be best if we took our own cars. I may need a quick escape if this date goes to shit.

A baby-blue linen halter romper accents my hourglass figure with all-black Nike Airs. My dreads are in two pompoms atop my head, resembling Mickey Mouse ears. I apply light makeup and sunscreen. Large gold hoops decorate my ears, and I have gold bangles up both my wrists.

Pulling into the crowded parking lot when I arrive at the fair, I find a spot near the back, since the place is packed with families and teens. I slip on my large sunglasses hanging from my rearview mirror, which almost completely swallow up my face, before heading to the gate. I see him walking to the entrance, blocking the glare from his eyes as he scans the crowd. He stops in his tracks when he catches sight of me. I flash him my trademark smile, and he quickly covers the rest of the distance, taking me into a hug. I stiffen for a second, as I'm not into hugging.

"You look gorgeous!" he breathes above my head.

"Thanks!" I step back from his encircling arms. My eyes rove up his attire. He is wearing white jean shorts with a burgundy V-neck and black Jordans. "You clean up well yourself. Ready to be a kid?"

He chuckles. "You are serious about that huh?"

"Yup!" My eyes light up in sheer joy. "I cannot wait to ride every ride here."

"Wait … ride?" He sucks in air, his eyes ricocheting from side to side. "I thought we were just going to play the games and eat junk food."

I cast him a smirk. "Is someone scared?"

"Of course not!"

I deem he is totally scared. "Good!" I send him a mischievous smile. He pays for our tickets, and I grab his hand and pull him through the turnstile, practically dragging him to a ride toward the back, by the ocean. "We are riding this first. It's my favorite!"

The sign above it reads, "Ring of Fire." It is a six-car roller coaster on a track in the shape of a ring. It goes on a forward loop about three times before pausing at the top, causing riders to hang upside down for about five seconds before going on a backward loop another three times.

"They meant to call it 'Circle of Doom' or 'Unending Disaster,'" Traymel remarks, eyeing the contraption as we stand in line waiting for our group to get aboard. I laugh in response, rushing to the front car. "Maybe we should grab a middle seat," he suggests, looking hopefully behind us.

"Nah! You get the full experience either here or in the back, but that is already taken by those teens." Two goth females, covered in piercings and tattoos, are sitting in the last car.

He settles in next to me and pulls down the handrail, locking us in the shared seat. I bang on the front of the car with my hands in an alternating repetitive motion, yelling with the others getting excited for the ride to begin.

"This is a new side of you I have never seen, with us only interacting in a professional setting."

The joy of being at the fair has me hyped. I hear the loud sound of the engine as this bad boy revs up. He tenses beside me. Peeking over, I see him sweating profusely and taking slow, steady breaths to calm his beating heart. *He is scared, yet he still got on the ride for me.* I am touched.

During the entire ride, he tightly grips the rail with his eyes shut tight, his knuckles nearly white. I lay my head on his shoulder, trying to give him some courage as laughter bubbles out of my chest. The wind from the movement of the ride whips across my face, causing water to leak from the corners of my eyes as I strain to look forward. Once the ride completely stops, Traymel runs off, raising his hands in the air to thank the heavens.

I happily skip toward him to tease. "Want to do it again?"

"Um, no, I'll sit out on this round." He taps his fingers against his throat. "Feeling kind of parched."

Sure, you are. "Oh, okay! Well, let's go to the concession."

"Ride it one more time. I can wait."

I beam up at him before rushing back to the line. After finishing up my third go-round, I head over to Traymel, who is sitting on the bench, texting on his phone. I was not kidding about "Ring of Fire" being my favorite.

"So, you going to continue being macho or admit rides aren't your thing?"

He smirks, returning his phone to his pocket. "My dad took Lincoln and me on a ride called the Spider when I was fifteen, which traumatized me. The way it continuously spun and twirled as the speed rapidly increased ... I screamed the entire five minutes we were on there and even peed my pants." I bend over in an eruption of laughter, holding my stomach. "I gave *that*"—he points at the ride—"a try. Surprised I did not scream for dear life. That was the longest eight minutes of my life in that ring. Confirms I'm still terrified of rides."

I decide not to force him on any more and we head to the games. I am sure I can get Lynn to join me another day to ride the other rides I want to go on. Besides, Traymel claims the games are more his style, which I guess is true, since he soon wins me a big bear from the basketball shot.

"I learned the trick to this back in high school. I wanted to impress my girlfriend at the time, since she was a big fan of the stuffed dogs. You must aim in a high arch, so it goes directly through the center of the hoop."

I enjoy the balloon game—the one where you throw darts to pop the colorful balloons on a wooden board and get the prizes underneath. However, I feel nothing is really on the paper behind the balloons. The worker just makes up the prizes so you can spend excessive amounts of money while being teased with those so-called "big wins." Now, of course the workers must let a few people win so they can walk around the fair with their prize, making others believe it is a possible task to accomplish.

After the games, we get some junk food and relax on the benches by the ocean and chat. I have no qualms sucking my fingers clean of the white powder and chocolate drizzle that coats my funnel cake. Traymel dips his chicken on a stick into a cup of ranch.

It is a little cliché to end the fair date with a ride on the Ferris wheel just as the sun is beginning to set. Still, it is romantic. At the top, while I am mesmerized by the view, he leans closer and presses his lips firmly against mine, catching me off guard. I melt under him as his arms wrap around me, bringing me closer as we fight for dominance. Traymel eventually wins, invading my mouth. He sucks on my bottom lip as the capsule lightly rocks in the cool breeze. My body gradually heats up with desire. I moan as my back arches, pushing my pouting breasts against his chest. Just then, the wheel begins its descent.

We are silent as we walk back to the parking lot, slightly brushing each other as our bodies bump every now and again. Our gaits slow, we enjoy the last of our time together. *Am I ready for this to end?* At the gate, he turns to say something, but I beat him to the punch.

"I actually had a great time."

He arches his eyebrows in an amused expression. "You didn't think you would?"

"It is debatable." I rock my body from side to side. "You are sexy and all but seem uptight a lot."

He raises his arms in the air, looking around. "Wow! Way to make me sound like a delight."

I cover my mouth as a giggle escapes my throat. He had me laughing the entire date. "Well, until next time."

"So there will be a date two?"

Well yeah! Can't fuck you on the first one. I roll my eyes and begin walking to my car, glancing at him over my shoulder. "We shall see." He watches with a leer across his face as I drive off. The date was a success.

Eleven

I am all smiles the following day. Traymel and I texted nonstop. He told me my beauty, personality, and drive are what make me so captivating to him.

Being at work on this cold, rainy Monday morning, I wish I could turn back the hands of time to repeat that date. The way we interacted felt right and not forced. My cheeks were in light pain when I arrived home after all the smiling and laughing I did. He is such a clown and down to earth. The way his body looked was spellbinding. His image is imprinted in my mind. Feeling his lips against mine once again did nothing to quench the thirst I have been feeling for him since my trip home. Thinking of it now has me clenching my legs together at that dull ache between.

There is a light knock at my doorframe. "Zola, do you have a moment?" Mr. Mitchell inquires, walking further in the room. His appearance is rough, with exhaustion apparent upon his features.

"Sure." I gesture to the chairs before my desk, sitting up straighter in my own. When he closes the door behind him, my smile falters. My heart beats a little faster. *This is signifying a bad visit.*

He sits in one of the chairs, leaning back and propping his clasped hands upon his protruding belly. The buttons of his suit jacket strain against the pressure of how small it is compared to his large frame. "I have been meaning to touch base with you on the LTW Construct account. Again, congratulations on winning the rights, and I have been hearing nothing but good things from all three partners. Mr. Dreer was opposed to you in the beginning, but it seems all is well these days."

My forehead creases in slight confusion. *I did not know Wesley was against me being their marketing coordinator.*

"I want to discuss the plan moving forward. The board and I have reviewed your past accounts and spoken with a few." He pauses, heightening the anticipation of what he is about to say. "From their raving admiration of you, we have decided to look into promoting you as the next executive." My eyes bulge at his statement as a large smile takes over my face. "A decision will be made by the end of the month. Keep up the good work!" He slaps his right hand on the edge of my desk, returning to his feet.

O ... M ... G! "Thank you, sir." He gives me a quick nod before opening my door and leaving.

My arms shoot up in a Y shape as my chair leans back, spinning in a circle. This is what I have been working on for the last three years, and it is right there in my grasp. If I get this promotion, I will be one step closer to being at the top of my career. Keep striving no matter the struggles, and results can be accomplished. *Finally!* After all those late hours and hard work, reigning in this major account has worked in my favor.

"What has you so excited in here?" says the voice of my archenemy, Landon. Dropping my arms to my sides, I swing my chair in his direction as he leans against my doorjamb. "I just saw Mr. Mitchell leaving. Are you finally getting canned?"

I do not give him the satisfaction of a response. "Do you need something?"

Pushing his shoulder against the wood, he saunters over to me. "The files on the Mahogany account."

I sit up in my chair. "Why? I closed that out last week."

"The sister called, and she wants me to have a second look at it. Seems there are some discrepancies in the numbers." His innocent look does not fail to raise my suspicion.

"Is that so? Well, I'll give her a call."

"No. No need. She is a real good friend of mine and trusts my judgement a little more than yours."

Of course she does. "I am *sure* you won't find any mistakes." I stand from my chair and walk over to my filing cabinet, searching for the file. Pulling it out, I turn back in his direction. "Unlike you, who needs to be stuck up the boss's ass, I"—I smack the folder against his chest—"know how to do my job." I flip my hair off my shoulder and return to my seat.

Landon squints at me with a murderous glare. "We shall see, Zola." He storms off, leaving the scent of his cheap aftershave in the air. I swear I cannot wait to rub my promotion in his face.

The next day, I head to LTW Construct's headquarters to drop off some paperwork and, I hope, to see Traymel. We barely spoke yesterday, and I kind of miss him. As I walk past the front desk, waving to the secretary, I see Lincoln walking to his office. *That bastard!*

"Mr. Crane. Can I have a word?" I pick up my pace as I sashay over toward him.

He glimpses over his shoulder, smiling, his eyes raking down my body. "Zola. So formal are we today?"

I smack my lips. "This isn't a pleasant visit." He gestures for me to precede him into his office, barely giving me enough room to squeeze by without brushing against him. He follows me in before closing the door.

Setting his coffee cup on the desk, he opens his suit jacket. "What seems to be the issue?" His tall frame folds up into the massive chair behind his oak desk. The furniture alone commands attention in the large room. His forearms press against the wood, his dreads freely hanging across his shoulders.

Not being deterred by his stance, I waste no time firmly stating the point. "Leave my friend alone!"

One of his eyebrows arches. "I am sure Lynn has not been bothered by me."

"That's not the friend I am speaking of, and you know that, so don't try to play with my intelligence," I snap, crossing my arms across my chest, my right foot tapping against the floor. I see he wants to play games and work my nerves. Kyla may not be able to stand up because she is too nice for her own good, but I have no problem defending my friend. Throughout school, I was always the one that had to do the dirty work.

A knowing expression appears on his face. "So she told you. I would be lying to say I am not surprised. She has been so intent on keeping us a secret."

"She is happy in her marriage and would appreciate if you would stop harassing her."

He leans back, propping his left foot atop his right knee, his palms pressed together from the tips of his fingertips to the heels of his hands. His elbows rest on his thighs. "Harassing, eh?" Lincoln tilts his head to the side, closing his left eye. "The woman that has set off a stink bomb in my office at the trailer, causing me to hire a professional to clean and air it out for three days before I could return. The same woman who slashed the tires of, busted the windows of, and vandalized, with pink spray paint, the front of my precious brand-new electric-blue Chevy Silverado, all in two weeks." He points his clasped hands in my direction. "Not to mention the latest attack in the front yard of my townhome: An 'RIP' Halloween tombstone decoration with my name spray-painted on top in big red block letters was stuck in the back of a pile of what smelled like cow dung." He smirks at my surprised expression. "Ah ha! Didn't know that, huh? Seems your *friend* hasn't told you everything."

I lick my lips, trying to come up with a retort. I am appalled Kyla has me coming in here making a fool of myself. I agree I am trying to have her back, but it seems she and Lincoln have their own game going on. The way she explained it the other night made me believe she was helpless against him—unable to ward off his advances because of his overpowering nature. She does not need my help. I feel maybe she is enjoying what is going on between them. It's time to get to the bottom of it. Before I can comment, Wesley walks into the office.

"Lin, I need you to look over this spreadsheet," he says as he makes his way in, peering at some papers in his hand. When he glances up, his feet stumble upon seeing me. "Oh, hey Zola, didn't know you were here."

My head slightly tilts to the side. It is not his comment but his expression that takes me a little off guard. The clench of his jaw is pulling his lips into a thin line. His grip is flexing just a bit on the papers. He almost seems a little upset by my presence, which is weird considering I assume we are cool.

"Yeah. I just came to drop off some paperwork and discuss some things with Lincoln."

"Ah, okay. Well, hopefully you are not looking for Mel. He had to fly out to Tennessee last night."

My lips tilt slightly downward. *I wonder why he did not tell me about it.*

"I heard your date went well."

"Date?" Lincoln looks at me with an amused expression, dropping his foot to the floor. "You and my brother dating? What happened with being so against mixing business with pleasure?" His hands smack the arms of the chair. "I could have played my hand."

"You wouldn't have had a chance. I just tolerate your antics. Besides"—I pause with a cheeky expression—"I am too *single* for your type of woman."

I quickly spin on my heels and leave the room before he can respond or ask further questions about me and his brother. I am surprised Traymel even told Wesley in the first place. It was just a date. Well, a fantastic date. But still, I did not want everyone to know about it. We are still working on a project, and with this promotion so close, I do not need anything ruining it. Our affiliations need to be strictly between us for the time being.

Two weeks later, Lincoln finally finishes finalizing and processing the permits and agreements. Also, the hiring process of the new additions is completed. LTW Construct can now start the groundwork on the new building in Tennessee.

Clark was given a promotion to move out there for the duration of the construction to make sure things run smoothly. I heard his little girlfriend cheated on him with one of the other workers.

I just cannot believe that after all this time and hard work LTW Construct are finally able to test the waters of the eastern region. Their dream to be a countrywide company is finally in their grasp. I played a big part in there with my brilliant ideas; they did not choose wrong when selecting me over Landon.

Because of this, Traymel has been spending a lot of time traveling, getting the new recruits acquainted with the ways they run their company. I hear the training is rough through the few phone conversations we have. He always seems tired and overworked. I guess it is because he is also doing the job of his brother, since Lincoln is handling things on this end.

We are going on our second date tonight. There is a reggae show on the boardwalk I have been wanting to see. It will be a perfect setting: cool night breeze, twinkling stars in the sky, vibing tunes, and a calm atmosphere created by it being so close to the water. I decide to dress up a little more this time and slip into a lavender chiffon bell-sleeve tiered ruffle dress with wedges (since heels tend to kill my feet quickly). I allow my dreads to fall freely down my back and put quarter-size silver hoops in my ears. After spritzing a light perfume and completing the look with a pearl-white lip gloss, I wait for Traymel's arrival. I have agreed to allow him to pick me up this round, taking a leap of faith in what can grow from this.

I open the front door at his knock, and my mouth instantly dries at the masterpiece before me. Black slacks hang from his trim hips—not to tight, yet not too loose. His gray, silk button down shirt is stretched across his torso. A gold cross hangs from a chain around his neck. Black alligator shoes finish off his sharp style.

Traymel lets off a low whistle as his eyes rove up my body from head to toe. The lust pooling in those darkened gray depths is burning away, leaving a path of goosebumps in their wake. My body trembles beneath the intensity of his gaze. "I am sure I will not be able to concentrate tonight."

I blush, casting my eyes downward. "Sure you will be fine."

He leans over and gives a quick peck to my cheek. "I miss you."

My hand rises to my face, my fingertips lightly touching the spot where I can still feel the warmth of his lips. I am caught off guard by the sweet gesture.

"Same here!" Dropping my arm, I step onto the porch. "Ready to go?"

He nods and grabs my hand, leading me to his car: a sleek lime-green Chevy Camaro with a black stripe down the center and all-black rims. As he maneuvers the roads, avoiding any slowdowns by taking back roads, I can tell he is a local resident. I would have been lost in this maze. Just this past year, I finally learned the ins and outs of the freeway, mastering different routes to get to my main locations.

He parks on a side street under a large tree right near the pavilion where the concert is being held. I can already hear the rhythmic beat of the Jamaican dance music. There is an incorporation of musical elements, including rhythm and blues, jazz, mento, and ska.

My hips begin to swirl in a fast-paced motion as we close in. I let the euphoric feeling encompass me. As we round the tent, I see the many people gyrating among each other. Everyone is feeling the high of the melodic ambience. After Traymel pays for our admission, my pace quickens as I move to the bar for a drink.

"Let's do a shot." I suggest, waving at the bartender for his attention. The sizeable number of people congregated along the edge of the bar all need help to fulfill their orders for alcoholic delights.

We both get tequilas, and we salute to a great night. I lick the salt from the crook of my hand where the thumb and pointer finger meet and gulp the strong liquor. The liquid burns a path down my throat to the pit of my stomach. Traymel's face contorts from the taste, and I stifle a giggle.

A classic, "Buffalo Solider," by Bob Marley issues from the speakers as the crowd's energy increases. Bright lights flash throughout the tent, illuminating the sight. Forgetting about my date, I rush into the throng of bodies and sway to the beat with everyone else.

A blunt is passed my way, and feeling aloof, I take a deep inhalation. After a few moments, the smoke clouds my airways, causing me to erupt in a fit of coughing. I return it to the woman who passed it to me as my eyes water, trying to overcome the pain. I have a burning sensation within my throat. Traymel, seeing my discomfort, brings me a cup of water, which I down immediately, thanking him.

After another hour or two of dancing, we leave to proceed along the boardwalk. Sweat glistens on our bodies, cooled by the wind coming from the raging water. A buzzing sensation from the alcohol calms my mind, letting me enjoy every moment. Few words are spoken between us as we walk side by side, holding hands along the sidewalk that runs along the ocean, stopping ever so often to just appreciate the backdrop.

Traymel returns me to my apartment soon after, only to leave me with another one of his toe-curling kisses in front of my door. Though I am yearning for a different fulfillment, I am trying to refrain from jumping his bones and complicating the situation. With everything at stake, riding the wave and seeing how the pieces fall together may prove to be devastating.

Twelve

"Lincoln!" Vanessa, LTW's HR director, calls out.

Lincoln groans before looking up from the permit we are discussing, pasting a false smile across his face. "Vanessa, so nice to see you. To what do I owe the pleasure?"

"We need to talk," she snaps, glancing at me. I go to move away, but his hand shoots out and grabs my wrist, stalling me. He gestures to the chairs in front of us as Vanessa sits. "So?" he invites, leaning forward on his arms.

Her eyes flicker to me again as she straightens her glasses. "Someone filed a complaint on you."

"Excuse me?" he says.

"A Ms. Hillary Steadman." She opens a manila folder in her hand. "She is a head nurse on the day shift at the hospital we just finished."

I snicker, quickly quieting the noise when they both glimpse in my direction. Ms. Hillary Steadman is the nurse that Lynn dislikes doing her clinicals with. She says the nurse resembles a female version of Goofy with trifocals that allow her to see the tiny hairs of one's chin. She always gives her the demeaning tasks instead of letting her get hands-on experience with the real stuff. Lynn says she is just jealous because all the doctors hit on her and not Ms. Steadman.

"About what?"

"Sexual harassment."

He leans back in his chair, laughing. "How is that, considering she does not work for me?"

"By work association." Vanessa flicks through the contents of the folder. "You hit on her many times while on the hospital premises and made her feel uncomfortable."

"What the fuck!" Lincoln curses. "Why would I flirt with anyone that looks an ounce like Ms. Steadman."

"Well, that was rude," I mutter, rolling my eyes.

"Because you are an egotistical, arrogant, sleazy man-whore." Vanessa retorts.

I cock an eyebrow at her. *Seems they have some history.*

"Anyway!" She inhales a breath, straightening her blazer. "I just came to verify or deny her accusations. I am sure I can have this handled before the hospital tries to make it a lawsuit."

"I only called her beautiful when I passed her in the parking lot as a nice gesture. I know she does not hear that often," he says, defending himself.

Still rude!

"Okay, good! That is all." Vanessa stands up and leaves without another word.

"Um." My eyes are still staring at the closed door. "What is up with you two?" That tension was thick enough to cut through with a knife.

"That woman hates my guts."

Not surprising.

"I wish I could fire her if it wouldn't cost us a lawsuit. About six months after she was hired, we had a little casual fun that went south when she caught me out with another woman. She had it in her head that we were exclusive. It was a nasty argument that had both women leaving me high and dry. She refused to quit but makes my life hell."

I shake my head. "You really use women like tissue—a disposable commodity that is available whenever you are in need to show your ass."

"I am a man." He says this with such confidence, as if that should explain everything. I smack him across the head.

We finish up the paperwork to send off to ACME before I head back to Lilac to work on another contract. I am helping a young entrepreneur advance his casino. San Diego just made it legal to gamble within city limits. This is an easy task, considering he will be the first and there are many Californians that want a spin at their luck. I am pretty much just spreading the word throughout the state and to a few surrounding areas for more travel from outside residents.

The following day, Wesley texts me asking to meet up at the mall. I agree, as I need to accomplish some last-minute shopping for the bachelorette cruise I am hosting next month, and he does have an eye for fashion. With the drama Kyla is dealing with and Lynn being smitten with Johnathan, there has not been much time for us all to hang out.

I jump into my Audi and head to Tanger Outlets. It is a beautiful Saturday afternoon as I drive through the city. Normally I would take a jog through the park or sip and relax in the hammock on the balcony, where I could have peace and enjoy the solitude. Enclosed public places seem to erupt in business during days like this, which I find a conundrum, considering one might expect folks to enjoy the outside air. Why would anyone go to the mall? The parking is horrific, and the crowds are impossible to navigate through.

As I park in front of Nike, Wesley texts me that he is running a little late. I head to the food court to wait for his arrival, and I order an Oreo milkshake. Travis sends me an incoming video call, which tilts my lips in a smile. It has been a while since we have spoken.

"Hey, stranger," I sweetly coo as I admire his face, noticing the lingering fatigue he must be feeling. Lines fan from the corners of his eyes with heavy bags seated below the bottom lids. An indented crease runs along the center of his forehead.

"Zola! It is great to see your face." His gruff voice echoes through the speaker, his weariness apparent. "Sorry for being MIA. My dad is out of town, and I have been filling in."

Well, that explains it. "I saw Mr. Sinclair on the TV awhile back."

"Hey! Who is that?" He questions with a scowl, his eyes trained on a point above my right shoulder.

I look over and see Wesley before turning back to the screen. "This is a client of mine." My hand gestures to him as if Travis is unaware of whom I am speaking of since he has not stopped eyeing him with distaste.

"He looks familiar," Travis states.

Wesley leans over my shoulder, taking a closer look at the screen. "You are the man my friends and I met with to finalize the paperwork for construction. Your father is one of the owners of ACME."

Recognition covers Travis's features. "Oh yes! How are you, sir?"

"I am good. Didn't know you knew Zola," Wesley remarks, pointing at me, standing back up.

"Yeah, she and I go way back. I am best friends with her brother." Travis returns his gaze to me. "I thought you said you worked in marketing."

"I do! I am helping LTW Construct expand into the eastern region. ACME is their first contract. Let me letcha go; Wesley here is going to help me shop for the bachelorette cruise." Travis has a confused expression before it quickly changes to one of comprehension. We say our good-byes before hanging up, and I pocket my phone in my jean shorts as I stand to my feet. Grabbing my purse off the back of the chair, I discard the empty shake cup in the trash. "Where to first?"

"I guess we can check out H&M." Wesley suggests as I pivot on my heels and head in the direction of the store. "So you and that dude a thing?"

My steps falter as a frown comes across my mouth. "No. He is the lost love I told you about, and we reconnected when I went home for the festival."

The corners of his mouth slightly tilt upward. "Do you still have feelings for him?"

Yes! But I cannot tell Wesley that, with him being friends with Traymel. I do not even want to admit that out loud. "It's complicated."

"First loves are tough." His eyes gaze downward, slightly glistening in the light. "I never was able to tell mine how I felt." I can tell how much this person means to him.

"Dang!" I bite my lip. "Is he still around?"

We enter H&M, proceeding to the women's department. "Yes, but he is fresh out of a bad relationship." He shrugs, looking back up at me with a wobbly smile. "I did not have the courage in the past, but now I am ready to break that barrier."

I nod. "Well, hopefully you can get a chance. You should not hold back."

"That I will not."

We hit up different stores, and I am surprised to find everything I need. I even get Jamar a cute outfit, and the girls matching sunglasses. Wesley believes I have good style choices, which is a compliment coming from him.

"This is the quickest shopping experience I have ever done with a woman," he says, taking a seat at the table. We decided to grab a bite at the burger joint in the mall. "My sisters would drag me around for hours and second-guess everything they chose."

"I am not big on shopping, so I try to do it as quickly as possible." I pause as the waitress brings us waters and takes our order. "What made you get into accounting?"

"Since I was little, I had a love for numbers. As I grew older, I researched ways to put them to good use. I took an accounting class in high school and fell in love."

"Sounds almost like myself. I always had a knack for promoting." I take a sip of water before leaning back against the booth, peering up at the ceiling as I conjure up a childhood memory. "I remember selling cold cups in my neighborhood when I was, like, ten. My mother wanted me to go to law school like Kyla. She did not believe there was much money being made in marketing, which is crazy considering society itself is based on different marketing schemes."

"Parents, right?" He shakes his head as the waitress sets our food before us. "My dad runs a security company. He expected me to take over when I graduated. However, when the twins decided to start a company, they asked me to run the finances. I agreed without a second thought, resulting in my father not speaking to me for over a year. To this day, I still do not regret that decision of taking a chance with them. It has been great watching our prize baby grow."

"I bet!" I mumble as I finish off the few fries I just ate. "Building a company up is a big accomplishment."

We chat as we finish our burgers. Wesley enlightens me on more information about Traymel's younger days. It seems Mr. Crane has his own set of secrets, including an ex-fiancée that he just broke up with a month before I met them in that boardroom—a detail he failed to tell me. A breakup of that magnitude takes some time to get over. Here I am starting to fall for Travis again after everything that we have been through.

That Monday was the day my dream came true. I was on a conference call with a client when Lynn came barreling into my office. She was jumping up and down in front of me with a Cheshire cat grin on her face. I mouthed "one second" while holding up my pointer finger on my right hand. I was just about to wrap this call up.

"What is your issue?" I ask, hanging up the phone. I lean over my calendar on my desk and write in a lunch appointment I just set up.

"You did it! You did it! You did it!" She exclaims over and over, still hopping up and down in front of me. I wave my hand for her to continue. Finally she stops and takes in a breath.

I guess that was a workout for her.

"Mr. Mitchell needs to see you upstairs in fifteen minutes." She looks at her watch. "Well, ten now."

I shot out of my chair. "Upstairs? Crap! That is not good."

She rolls her eyes. "Stop being dramatic. All the board members are in the meeting. Which means ..." She breaks off, waiting for me to finish the sentence. The problem is that I have no idea what she is talking about. Once she realizes I am completely lost on the matter, she delivers the punchline: "You are getting the promotion."

My jaw drops to the floor. "Run that by me 'gain?" I round my desk and stand before her. "Promotion?" I point at my chest. "Me?"

I start jumping up and down like she was when she entered my office. Not soon after, she joins in, grabbing my hands, as we both jump up and down on an invisible indoor trampoline. I quickly halt, knowing I need to hurry up and get upstairs before they change their minds.

I drop Lynn's hands and rush out of the room, heading to the elevator. My thumb repeatedly presses the button, urging the car to hurry to me. I barely allow the doors to open completely before slipping in and repeating my task of being the fastest button pusher on the button that reads "25"— the executive floor. As the elevator moves upward, I straighten my clothing and run my fingers through my ponytail. Then, deciding my hair would be better down, I slip the scrunchie out, shaking out my dreads.

Just then the doors open to the twenty-fifth floor—the highest floor before the peaked roof of Pacific Gate. I step out onto the shiny hardwood floor, my heels clicking against the wood as I make my way to the secretary in the middle of the room. A glass barrier stands behind her with "The Board" etched in large white writing. A headpiece is connected to her ear as she types away on the keys of her computer. When I step before her, she immediately stops, looking up at me with a smile. *Lynn could take some lessons from her.*

"Ms. Saunders. They are waiting for you just around the corner. Third door on your left." Her right hand points out the directions as she explains. *How did she know who I was?* I nod and go along the route.

As I close in on the door, I hear men talking in the room. Taking one last deep breath, I turn the knob and walk in. Silence takes over instantly as the murmurs cease. Four sets of eyes turn my way in unison. I feel like a deer in headlights. I awkwardly wave as I step further into the room. Seeing only one empty seat, I move in that direction to sit down. I glance up at Mr. Mitchell, who stares at me with expressionless eyes from the head of the table.

He clears his throat. "Ms. Saunders. Thank you for joining us on short notice."

Like I had a choice in the matter.

"The board has been overviewing your work history for the last three years and are very impressed with what you have accomplished in such a short time."

OMG! Did he just give me a compliment?

"As you may know, Mr. Dan Jackson retired last year. He was an integral part of this company, and his shoes will be hard to fill." I nod, anticipating the outcome. "So it has taken the four of us a while to decide on who is the best candidate. After long deliberation, Ms. Zola Saunders, you are that candidate."

I squeeze my hands into tight fists and tap my toes together to stop myself from jumping from the chair in joy. Surely that would be a bit unprofessional. *They just promoted me.* Instead, I plaster my famous smile across my face and eye each of them before speaking. "This is an honor, and I just want to let you know I appreciate this. I have worked hard to get to this point."

"You will be taking over Dan's duties as chief marking officer, a partner of the board. This promotion goes into effect in two weeks, giving you enough time for you to wrap up your current clients and pass any that need longer assistance to another coordinator. You will remain in charge of the LTW Construct contract until the completion of the ACME building in Tennessee. Your new office, located on this floor, is being cleaned, and the carpet will be replaced with your color choice. Come by my office in the morning to discuss the legals and sign the paperwork. Any questions?"

My eyes rapidly blink as I take in all that he said. I am still shell-shocked at this. Getting the promotion has been my goal since I chose to follow the path of marketing at this company, which I have always respected and wanted to work for. This is a major milestone, and I cannot wait to shout it to the world. Outside. Away from them.

Smiling again, I nod. "Yes. Will I still be able to take my two vacations this year that have already been approved months before?" I know I cannot miss the cruise, and definitely not the wedding. My sister would kill me, literally.

"Your vacations are still approved. We will reverify the dates tomorrow and make sure your workload is handled while you are gone," Mr. Mitchell confirms.

"Well, that's all for me." I stand from the chair, nodding in the general vicinity of the group as a whole. "Thank you, gentlemen." *I will have to get their names and research this Dan Jackson.* I stroll out of the room, letting the door close behind me. Heading back to the lobby area, I wave goodbye to the young woman and step into the elevator. My joy erupts in the confines of the metal box as it makes it descent back down to the twenty-second floor. Both fists alternately punch the air above my head as my hips shimmy from side to side. I shuffle out of the car as the doors open, and Lynn bombards my personal space.

"So … promoted?" I nod, showing a grin so wide my cheeks ache. "Yesss!" She squeals, clapping like a fanatic. "You were up there so long. I started to think you may be fired."

I laughed. "No, they were just explaining some things."

She hugs me tightly, nearly squeezing the life out of me. When she finally lets go, I head back to my office, dancing about on cloud nine. After locking my door, I collapse in my chair and smile out my window. *I did it!* My phone vibrates on my desk, sounding as if someone is drilling holes into the wood. Grabbing it, I see three more messages come through before I can even unlock it.

"Congrats, Zola! I knew you could do it," Kyla sends in the group message. Seems Lynn has already blabbed.

"I am getting cake and her 1800. Kyla, cook that Cajun shrimp pasta of yours she likes so much," Lynn adds.

"When?" Kyla inquires.

"TONIGHT, OF COURSE!"

Ugh! I swear Lynn does not know the meaning of early-morning work. She will be able to sleep in since her clinicals are on Tuesdays and Thursdays at eleven.

I contemplate letting Traymel and Travis know. This is a big deal for me, and I want to share it with them. After sending Travis the message first, followed by Traymel, I anticipate their responses. Traymel replies immediately with "CONGRATS" in all caps, followed by a few emojis, causing me to smile. Travis takes a little longer to reply, which at first upsets me. I let my short temper make up ideas until around lunchtime a text comes through. He explains he was in meetings all morning and left his phone in the car.

By the end of the day, I am still ecstatic about the promotion and ready to celebrate with my besties. Lynn has the right idea that we should rejoice. Getting this promotion has been a work in progress, and it feels great to see all that effort rewarded. A great deal of managers tends to forget to appreciate their employees when they are giving their all. They seem so quick to reprimand, and they praise only when the benefits are in their favor. A person following the job description and excelling in his or her duties should be given more appreciation than a pat on the back. Yes, it was nice at first, but as the years progressed, it became a little redundant and lacked true meaning.

When I arrive home, I see Kyla's Jeep already parked in the grass, leaving my spot in the driveway open. *How considerate! She knows I would cuss her out.* Heading inside, I stop abruptly on seeing the work they have put in. Decorations are strung about the living room, sunroom, and kitchen. There are banners, balloons, and confetti. Kyla is at the stove, and Lynn is listening to the stereo while sipping on some drink concoction she most likely experimented on. I tiptoe near them before screaming out loud, scaring the piss out of them. Hugging my waist, I bend over laughing hard until I am roughly pushed, left tumbling on the kitchen floor.

Lynn comes and sits on me, smacking me against my arm. "You stupid punk!"

I continually laugh, which then triggers Kyla into joining, and soon Lynn has no choice but to follow. We all, in that one spot of the kitchen, are laughing like drugged hyenas. It is several minutes before we can resume the festivities. I fix drinks, and we dig into the pasta. There is nothing like quality time with good people. This celebration has turned out to be relaxing and needed amid the troubles the three of us have been facing in our lives.

Thirteen

It's a busy week. After that awesome night with the girls, I wake up to a major headache and am late to work. *Late the day after being promoted. Like, who does this?* I am lucky my meeting with Mr. Mitchell is not scheduled until ten since he had a dentist appointment that morning. I am able to sneak in and be in my office by the time he does his rounds.

The meeting goes well. I learn all my job responsibilities, which are pretty much the same as before. The major difference is I am now in charge of eight marketing coordinators and analysts and need to remember and get acquainted with almost twenty clients, ensuring they are taken care of. Also, I must run stats to verify business is steadily growing each quarter. Being paid a salary, weekend work will be required as well as being bothered at home when I am off. A way employers can get you to work around the clock without having to go broke doing it. *Seems Mr. Mitchell really did do a lot of work after Mr. Jones quit besides constantly riding my ass.* This is going to be a lot tougher than I expected as I enjoy my time not on the clock.

The following day, I meet with a decorator who takes my choices on carpet color and wall design, as well as a sofa, desk, and chair. The other furniture is universal. I plan to have my office flair bold with a feminine touch. Being the only female partner, and African American at that, I want it to stand out compared to all the others. They just promoted the new age.

I make it home pretty late that night. Lynn is already in the sunroom, sprawled across the couch, doing homework on her laptop with books scattered around her. She is taking a summer course, so her final-year workload will not be so overwhelming. Checking the cabinets, I grab a pack of ramen. I also take a link of sausage from the fridge for a simple dinner. This is my favorite go-to, especially during those broke times. I turn on the TV and watch some news while I wait on my food. There is a picture of Michael in the corner of the screen as the anchor is talking away. I turn up the volume to hear better.

"It is sad to hear that our fellow mayor is going through such a tough time. His wife has not been doing well in her treatments these past few weeks. It seems her condition has taken a turn for the worse. This time is rough for his family, and we hope everyone will keep them in their prayers." The newscaster shares with a frown.

"Hey Lynn! You hear this?" I peek around the counter in the sunroom to see large multicolor headphones covering her ears as her head bobs away. I grab a wooden spoon out of the drawer next to me and throw it at her, successfully hitting her shoulder.

She slips the headphones off her ears and glares at me. "Really, bish?"

"Come listen to this; they are talking about your married man. His wife is not doing so good."

"Yeah, I know." She looks back at her computer. "I met her."

Say what? Turning the TV off, I get up from the stool and walk to the sunroom. I sit on the table next to her, shutting her laptop. "You cannot say something like that and not give me details. When? How? Why?"

She rolls her eyes. She lifts the laptop off her lap and places it on the floor between us. "You remember that head nurse that has it out for me?"

I nod before smacking both my palms on my thighs. "Speaking of! She filed a sexual harassment case on Lincoln."

"No way! That is ridiculous." Lynn swings her feet off the sofa and faces me. "Well, my last clinical was Thursday last week, and she worked that shift. She had me go clean up a patient who just so happened to be Michael's wife, who is surprisingly a beautiful woman. Zola, she seems so broken." She heaves an exasperated sigh. "You know, according to her, I was not even the only woman he cheated on her with. All those lies he spouted to me, telling me this was a one-time thing and I just did something for him, how I made him feel alive, and the way I gave him a different perspective on life." She rolls her eyes and shakes her head.

"Like, that woman opened her heart for Michael, and he just broke it, as if it meant nothing to him, and expected me to do the same thing. I wonder why she stayed around and allowed him to deprive her of future happiness."

"I mean, people do crazy things for the people they love." I think back on my sister, who is getting married to a man who does not deserve her for all the hurt he put her through for so many years.

Lynn looks me in the face with sadness, tears misting her eyes. "Well, now cancer has taken over, and she is willing to permit it to end a life she does not feel worth living. I feel bad for ever having a relationship with Michael. Even after finding out he was married, I continued to assist him in violating his vows. How do I even find a man like that attractive? Clearly it would never have worked out for us."

I frown. Here she is, once again beating herself up. Lynn has always felt she is a messed-up individual. She watched her mother letting herself go for all those years because of the hurt her father inflicted on them. She tried to fill the void with artificial happiness. She never had a good male model, and to her, marriage is a joke. *Which I can say I agree on.* Wanting to be with a sole person never was a desire of hers.

"It just scares me to end up in despair, which many women tend to find themselves in after heartbreak," she mumbles, wiping her eyes. "Even now, Kyla is having issues with Damien that are putting a strain on their marriage."

"I feel Kyla has her part in that strain." *She is still entertaining Lincoln.*

A ghost of a smile appears on Lynn's face. "However, I am starting to understand why women are agreeing to be drawn in. Johnathan has been making me feel something wonderful and slowly changing my opinion. The butterflies flutter inside of me, making my heart go haywire, when he is around. I feel joy when his arms are wrapped around me. I cannot contain my smile when he is mentioned. I count the seconds when I am away from him. Nevertheless, with all the emotions churning in me, my fear still looms in the back of my mind."

She returns to her homework while I sit down to eat my food, musing over her words. The way she feels for Johnathan is the same for me. However, Traymel and Travis both bring it out of me. I know that I still love Travis after all this time. I have yet to utter those words to him, even though he has mentioned it to me on several occasions. Once I open that door and fully let him in, the tides will turn and the pain will begin. I gave him a chance to hurt me in the past and I am not sure I am ready to take that risk again. Even with the things I am finding out about Traymel have me doubting that option as well. Love is not there now, but I feel something strong. I know I should not be pessimistic about the fact. Yet I see all the signs from others and the conclusions that come about. I mean, Kyla is supposed to be happily married with Damien, and look at the troubles she has found herself in just because she cannot seem to shake her response to Lincoln.

My first day as chief marketing officer creeps up on me fast. The promotion I earned is officially a reality, engrossing me in excitement. I wake up two hours before I have to report to work, not wanting to be late.

I dress in a sleek black knee-length pencil skirt with a long-sleeved mock neck white polka-dotted blouse and black booties, deciding against stockings because of the intense summer heat. I style my dreads in a low bun at the nape of my neck and adorn my ears with inch-long chain earrings. After adding mascara and eyeliner as my only makeup, I give myself a close inspection in my floor-length mirror. I want to give off the vibe of a boss yet still uphold being a woman.

I grab my phone and smart watch off my nightstand before stopping by the kitchen for a glass of milk and a store-brought croissant from the box on the island. Grabbing my new Michael Kors vanilla tote bag, I rush to my car to make it through the mayhem on Interstate 5 in a timely fashion.

I am thankful to find not one wreck slows my progress the entire way to Lilac Essences. As I make it to the garage, I see my assigned parking spot right by the elevator, among the other partners'. The smile I have been wearing since I woke up still beams upon my face. I slip out of my car and walk into the elevator with another person and hit the button with twenty-five on it proudly. I nod to the other woman who barely glances my way. The ride this time seems to drag, as the anticipation gets the best of me. I have no idea what to expect or what I am most likely to encounter.

When the elevator doors open, I step out into the familiar lobby and smile at the efficient secretary I met just the other week. As I round the glass barrier, I hear a muffled argument coming from Mr. Mitchell's office. Deciding it is best not to eavesdrop as I normally would, I continue in the direction of my new office.

Just then, a door opens, and I catch the tail end of a conversation. "That black bitch does not deserve it, and you know it."

Pausing in my stride, I glance back in the direction of Mr. Mitchell's office. On the threshold, walking out, is none other than my nemesis, Landon, who has had the audacity to call me out of my name. Our eyes connect when he looks up, and a scowl is plastered on his face. I cock my head slightly to the side and give him a sardonic smirk. I mouth "checkmate" clearly so he can understand. His scowl deepens as he storms my way. I turn my body, completely facing him by the time he is within a foot of me.

"You may have coerced Mr. Mitchell into giving you this promotion." I snort, rolling my eyes. "But I know your flaws, and I will make it my mission to destroy you." He steps even closer to me. I hold my ground, tilting my chin slightly upward, not allowing him to intimidate me. His hot breath hits my skin when he speaks. "Enjoy your moment now. It will be coming to an end ... real soon." He turns on his heel and heads toward the elevator.

Shrugging, I continue my path, excited to see the result of the decorations. Walking up to the oak door, I smile yet again at seeing my name engraved on a gold plate in the center of the door. My fingertips glide against it, proving it to be real, before I take a selfie. I turn the brass knob and push open the door, revealing my new domain. The thick black carpet covers the entire floor. A curved teal sofa sits diagonally against the far-right corner of the room, near the floor-length window that takes up half of the back wall. The view is of the ocean and is almost as wonderful as the city view from the SkyWay Room. My modern executive desk with a mahogany finish sits adjacent to the window but across from the sofa in the far-left corner. A row of black filing cabinets lines the wall next to my desk. The walls are painted in an off-white color and covered in paintings of African folklore scenes and abstract images.

Closing my door, I head to my desk and allow myself to sink into the deep cushion of my leather office chair. It even has a massage option. I lean back, propping my boots atop my desk, and release a sigh.

"This is *awesome!*" I whisper-shout to no one.

Just then the door opens, and I hurriedly drop my feet to the ground and stand as Mr. Mitchell walks in.

"How are you settling in?"

I look around the space again with awe. "I am just admiring everything."

"Well, I hate to rush you, but we have a board meeting in twenty minutes. There is one every Monday at nine forty-five sharp and Friday at three." He eyes the decor. "This is an unusual setup of colors."

"Yup! Feminine"—I gesture to the couch—"yet dominant." I sweep my hands out in front of me and to my sides, my palms facing the carpet.

"The meetings are held in the same room you visited before."

I nod.

Mr. Mitchell claps his hands in front of him and slowly rubs them together. "I will let you get to it."

After his exit, I set my tote in the bottom drawer of my desk and power up my computer. After grabbing a notebook and pen from the drawer, I head over for the board meeting with the boys' club. I am sure they are excited to have a woman on their level—a black one at that. Keeping my shoulders back and my head held high, I stroll into the room. Again, the chatter comes to a halt as four pair of eyes swing my way. *Hopefully this does not become a norm.* Smiling, I head to the vacant chair and the meeting commences.

Monday meetings are long, tedious, and exhausting. We discuss what needs to be accomplish during the week, improvements that need to be implemented, and new ideas to grow us into a bigger corporation.

The board consists of five members. Mr. Mitchell is CEO. I am the chief marketing officer. A Mr. Wade Manson is senior security. The chief financial officer is Mr. Eric Francis. Lastly is Mr. Paul Washington, the director of hospitality. We all work as a command center for a community of different organizations working together as a unit to grow a greater company. I knew the other floors in the building contained other businesses, but I assumed we were all different entities. In just this hour of conversation, I am learning so much more.

Fourteen

A loud beep sounds through the airport before a voice comes through the speakers. "Flight 1248 nonstop to Miami at Gate C2 is now boarding. The A group may now line up in numerical order."

I stretch in my chair, standing to my feet. The girls and I traveled home once again this year to meet up with Nicole and her best friend Katy for the bachelorette trip I planned. It is a three-day Bahamas cruise on the Royal Caribbean. Nicole has never been out of the country, and I heard the Bahamas is a nice place to visit. This will be a new experience for all of us.

My family threw me a party for my big promotion last night. We are always celebrating big events with one another. Unfortunately, we got a little carried away and almost missed our flight this morning. Now we are all struggling to stay focused and looking rough.

"Is that us?" asks my sister, removing the earbuds from her ears.

"Yeah, we are in the priority group," Kyla responds.

We gather our belongings and stand in line with a few others. The airport is bustling with people trying to board their flights. The summer months always have a larger influx of travelers, with kids being out of school and with the more enjoyable weather that brings folks out and about.

Looking around the terminal, I inquire, "Is Lynn still in the bathroom?"

"Yes. She better hurry up or she gonna be left," Nicole says, moving up the line.

We stand in a group by the TSA agent as she scans our boarding passes and allows us down the ramp. This trip could not have come at a better time. We all needed to let loose and have fun as a release from the obstacles we constantly must overcome in life. This is going to be a trip of fun, adventure, lots of alcohol, and celebration with the girls.

We are dressed in a bridal party attire, with Nicole in a white romper—"Bride to Be" ironed on in gold across the chest—and a clip-on veil. The rest of us are sporting purple shirts with "Bridal Gang" printed on the back in bold black lettering, with our statuses on the front.

"Dang, y'all could have waited for me," Lynn chastises us as she boards the plane, huffing and puffing.

She takes her seat between Kyla and me in the emergency exit. My sister and Katy are in front of us. Katy is a skinny, dark-complected female who stands about five feet six inches and has a small Afro. She decided three years ago to stop perming her hair and embrace her natural look.

"You shouldn't go to the bathroom at the last minute," I respond, rolling my eyes.

"Um, not in control of nature," she quips, buckling her seatbelt. "Anyway, where are the *drinks?*"

"I believe we have to actually get in the air before they start serving," says Kyla, scrolling through her Instagram.

"Y'all are really crazy." Katy giggles, putting her bag in the compartment above us.

Nicole leans toward her friend. "Which is why I try to stay away from them."

The blonde woman who I assume is the head flight attendant moves toward the front of the aisle, grabbing the phone from the wall. The plane begins to back up from the ramp as she speaks through the phone, which projects her voice through the speakers throughout the aircraft. "The cabin door is now closed. All larger electronics must be turned off and stowed away. Any smaller electronics must be in airplane mode. Please divert your attention to your flight attendants as we go through a brief safety presentation."

Stretching out my legs, I lean back in my chair and close my eyes, tuning her out. I have flown enough times to know this presentation by heart. My thoughts drift to Traymel. We have been on three dates so far, and I am liking him more and more. His compassionate side makes me feel special and wanted.

On the last phone conversation, two nights before this cruise, he finally told me the story of his ex-fiancée. I had already heard the gist from Wesley but thought it was wise not to bring it up. He would tell me when he is ready, which it seems he finally was.

Her name is Melody, and they were scheduled to marry in the fall after dating for three years. Traymel caught her banging her best friend in their bed after coming home early one day from work. He had planned to surprise her since she complained he worked so much. She turned out to be a lesbian and only dated him to deny her attraction to other women. Talk about cutthroat. Why agree to marry? He was really broken up about it. I heard the hurt in his voice. Being with me is giving him a reason to move on because he deserves better.

It all led up to him asking me to be his girlfriend. Talk about a shocker! I told him to give me time to process and decide. Dipping my pen in company ink has never been my cup of tea and been overthinking what could happen if this does not work out. Going through the awkwardness and strain is not worth the few minutes of fun. My career is my passion. I just received a major promotion and am currently under the microscope to prove my worth. Being at the top is important to me.

I have always been the downfall in my relationships, cutting them off before they can grow into something more. I would rather embrace being alone than having to worry about being hurt. Being single allows me to make the rules, and the decisions are based on my wants. I can go to sleep and wake up without a nagging conscience of how someone will feel about my actions. What Traymel and I have is fun and new—no need to muck it up with feelings. Well, it may be a little late for that. Wesley told me Traymel is still harboring feelings for Melody, and I have no intention of being anyone's rebound.

Nevertheless, even with the girls' protestations, my heart itself is still somewhat attached to Travis, who is now reconnecting with me. Those old feelings are rekindling, and the pull is becoming harder to fight. I want us to be friends, yet sexual thoughts do constantly slip in. It does not help with Travis teasing me on our video chats or flirting with me via texts. I feel that Traymel and I should not take that step unless I am ready. There is much at stake.

"Zola, you hear this?" Lynn asks, sipping on her mimosa.

"Huh?" I confusedly respond, snapping out of my head. Glancing out the small window, I see a vast blue sky filled with clouds slowly floating about with no direction. *Boy, I do not even remember takeoff.*

"Seems she is daydreaming." Kyla retorts, engrossed in her paperwork. Of course she would bring work on a vacation.

I side-eye her before bringing my attention to Lynn. "What was I supposed to hear?" I unbuckle my seatbelt and slip my right leg underneath me.

"Your sister doesn't know the meaning of an all-girls trip." Lynn leans over the back of my sister's seat. "I swear your head is stuck up Ethan's ass."

Nicole whips her head up to her. "Shut the hell up, Lynn!"

Confusion is evident in my features. "Did I miss something?"

Kyla groans, looking up at me again. "The boys are on the cruise too," she notifies me. "Seems Nikki invited Ethan, and he is bringing the groomsmen."

"Say *what?*" I turn toward the seat my sister is in, incredulity in my eyes. How was he even able to pull that off? I did not tell Nicole where we were going until two weeks ago. *Now I understand why Travis was not at the party last night.* "Why would you do that? I thought Ethan didn't like boats."

"He doesn't. Lynn did not let me finish before she started bugging out." Nicole stands, kneels in her seat, and faces us. She sends Lynn a glare before bringing her eyes to me. "The boys are not coming on the cruise. They will be meeting up with us in the Bahamas. They are flying straight there."

I smack my lips. "Of course, Ethan had to find a way to keep an eye on you."

"Really, Zola?" Nicole responds, sounding irritated.

"Please have a seat and buckle your seatbelts; we will begin our descent shortly," states the same flight attendant from earlier. We all settle down, and I go back to peering out the window.

If Ethan is bringing his groomsmen, it means I will have to be around Travis. Physically. We are on better terms, but FaceTiming is different from face-to-face interaction. The last time we were in the vicinity of each other, things got a little heated, and I was still angry with him. Not to mention that Travis has made it clear he wants to rekindle things with me, taking us beyond friends. *Ugh! I just want some relaxing time without all the stress.* Travis will surely be up in my bubble, distracting me from figuring out the answer I need for Traymel's question.

I jolt in my seat when the tires of the plane slam against the concrete of the runway and begin slowing down as men in orange vests guide us to our ramp. The seatbelt light clicks off, and all the passengers rise from their seats at once, spilling into the aisle, gathering their belongings from the chairs and overhead bins, and patiently waiting for their turns to deplane.

Once I step out of the long tunnel, my eyes sweep across the large airport, an expansive maze before us. People of all shapes and sizes bustle about. Some are rushing to their gates, while others stand in line for food during their layovers. It seems everyone in America has come to Miami today. The girls and I wind our way through the thick crowd, using the signs hanging from the ceiling to direct us to baggage claim to retrieve our luggage.

"Is the shuttle picking us up from here?" asks Nicole.

We walk to our turnstile just as it activates. Bags upon bags shoot out of the slot from the tunnel that travels from wherever the bags are taken.

"Yes! I told them to meet us at noon, which gives us ten minutes before they arrive," I confirm, checking my watch. Kyla hands me my bag.

Jumping up and down, Katy pronounces, "I am so ready for this trip."

"I am ready for the men," Lynn adds, eyeing the group of hotties passing by with their belongings.

I swear, sometimes I forget she is in a committed relationship now.

The shuttle will bring us straight to the loading docks of the ship. They start letting people board at 2:00 p.m., but I want to make sure we do not feel rushed getting there or get stuck in that ridiculous long line. The airport is forty-five minutes away, and I am sure Miami has horrible lunch hour traffic on this beautiful Thursday afternoon.

When we reach our destination, our luggage is tagged and loaded on a ramp to go through security and be brought to the rooms later. Passing up the preboarding photo ops, we head to the already growing line to check in. Surprisingly, it moves quickly. The large single line splits into three smaller ones just down the hall, leading to different stations for a better preboarding process. The workers look weirdly chipper to be having to go through this. I feel this job would be a hassle, considering the need to deal with the complaining, unprepared, or just plain rude people.

After checking in, we head down the catwalk onto the ship. The glass-enclosed walkway, suspended in the air, gives us a full view of the enormous ship waiting to take us on our adventure. It consists of twelve levels. The first four are reserved for the housing of the workers that pretty much live on the ship for months at a time. Floors five to seven contain the entertainment rooms and dining halls. The remaining top levels are where the patrons stay for the duration of the cruise. I see folks running about on the docks below, checking last-minute details to confirm everything is in order.

No one is allowed past the main floor, so we gather at a table by the bar and order drinks to pass the time. We wait almost two hours before everyone is released and able to head to the rooms. Kyla is beginning to get agitated. She seems to be in dire need of a nap.

Our rooms are located on the tenth floor and connected by a door. My sister and her friend are in one, and my trio is in the other. Both rooms have a balcony and two full beds. Since Lynn is the shortest, she has the bed that falls from the wall above the couch, which an attendant on our floor pulls down every night and folds up every morning.

I claim the bed by the balcony. This is a norm because I have a weird feeling about being in the bed nearest to the door. I feel that if anyone breaks in, the person in that bed dies first, giving me time to get away. It is a horrible thing to think.

Setting my purse on the bed, I walk through the sliding door and onto the balcony to admire the view. Waves crash against the bottom of the boat. A crisp breeze from the ocean ruffles through my dreads as the sun bakes my skin. Other patrons stand on their balconies.

"Whores! Put your suits on and let's hit the deck. I want to see the hot guys!" screams Lynn from the bathroom.

"Aren't you in, like, a committed relationship?" I chime.

She emerges from the bathroom, already in her bathing suit. "I said *look*, not touch." She pauses with a smirk. "Well ... inappropriately."

Glancing toward the balcony next to us, I see my sister is sitting in one of the chairs. "Nikki, we are going to the deck."

"We will meet you up there. Katy's suitcase hasn't arrived yet."

I head back into the room to sort through my own suitcase to find a bathing suit to wear. Deciding on the red tube top one-piece, I take over the bathroom to change. It is time for the craziness to begin.

Fifteen

"Zola, get up! We arrive in an hour," Lynn informs me as she walks out of the bathroom.

I put a pillow over my face and loudly groan, kicking the heels of my feet against the mattress. My head is pounding after all the drinking we did last night at the club. I failed to stay hydrated in between the countless of drinks and shots I consumed, drowning my problems in the large amounts of liquor. We partied until almost three in the morning, overtaking the dance floor as the majority of the attention fell on us. Today we stop in the Bahamas and will be meeting up with the guys. I am still trying to prepare myself to see Travis.

Ethan deciding it was a great idea for his bachelor party to be in the Bahamas the same weekend Nicole's bachelorette party is on a cruise there further proves his need of control over her. If he were not afraid of boats, I am sure they would have been on this exact cruise. And she is stupid enough to have agreed for us to spend time with them while there.

Ever since Ethan convinced my sister to take him back for good after all the crap he pulled, he has tended to keep her on a short leash, afraid of losing her. I'm not sure whether she has noticed his extremes or just does not care about them.

Rolling out of the bed, I notice the door to the bathroom is open and the light is out. Lynn is in the room with the other two, but Kyla is nowhere to be found. She is always and early bird. *Guess that is why she stays napping.*

I grab a quick shower and handle my necessities. I then don a gold-linked chain and powder-blue halter triangle bikini. Next, I wrap myself in a gray mesh sarong, giving a teasing view of my swimsuit through the holes. My dreads are perched in a high ponytail on the right side of my head, the ends brushing against my shoulder. Black gladiator sandals strap up my legs, stopping at gold buckles just below the knee. I slip on large square sunglasses to help block out the sun rays at the beach. Just as I am applying sunscreen, the sound of the horn from the ship fills the room, signaling to the passengers that we have arrived and are free to disembark.

"I am so ready to meet me a Bahamas man!" Katy exclaims, walking into our room, followed by Lynn. They have become really cool during this whole wedding business.

"I am right there with you, girl." Lynn agrees.

"You'd best not! Johnathan will cut up," Kyla says as she enters the room, dressed in her white cutout knot-front bandeau one-piece with blue jean shorts. "He has shown to have a jealous streak." She is right. He has had some spasmodic moments.

Lynn plops on the bed next to me, sipping on some wine. "J. J. will be okay!"

There were other cruise lines at the port, causing thousands of people to unload at once, ready to explore. Today the weather is beautiful—that perfect fall temperature where it is neither too hot nor too cold. We gather our belongings and follow the throng of people making their way to the ship's exit, heading down the ramp with Lynn's loudmouth yapping away to Kyla. The crowd parts in different directions to group up for excursions, shop at the stores on the docks, or spend time on the beach.

It is not long before the men come into view. What a sight! They are specimens sculpted to perfection. I must give it to Ethan and Nicole on their bridal party selections, which are made up of only gorgeous people. Folks all around us are eyeing both groups with lust and envy as we stroll toward each other.

Even so, Travis is the one that captures my attention the most, causing my mouth to feel as dry as the sands of the scorching Sahara Desert. A simple pair of red nylon swim trunks and a black V-neck fit the muscle panes of his body. The all-black Converse shoes and aviator glasses complete the look.

His unmoving gaze on me attests that I am not the only one mesmerized by the other. I sway my hips a little more as we close the distance, sticking my chest out so my plump breasts stand at attention. Our eyes drink up the sight of one another. The Duoing we have been doing does not compare to having him here in front of me. My dirty thoughts try to run wild. *This is what I was afraid of.*

"Babbyyyyy!" Nicole croons as she runs the remaining few feet to Ethan before hopping into his arms. He twirls her around, dropping light kisses across her face.

"Gross! Y'all are going to make me sick," says Jason, Ethan's best friend from college and one of the groomsmen, making a gagging expression.

"That I can agree with," Lynn comments, looping her arm in his. "I like you. Let's go get us a drink and move away from this mushiness." Laughing, Jason allows himself to be dragged to the restaurant and bar area. The group follows suit.

"Hey, Zola, looking good as always," Keith, another friend of Ethan, divulges as he comes and walks beside me. Travis stands on the other side.

I roll my eyes. "Keith, still not going to happen." He has been crushing on me since I graduated college. I met him at my graduation party. He is cute in a Will Smith way but just does nothing for me.

Jamal, Travis's brother, bursts out laughing as he places his arm around Keith's neck, pulling him away from me. "Boy, I mean she showed you no mercy."

I click my tongue before peeking up at Travis. "Glad you informed me you were coming to the Bahamas." Sarcasm drips from my words.

"Wanted to surprise you," he shares with a grin.

I exaggeratedly roll my neck like one of those bobbleheads that people used to keep on their cars' dashboards back in the day. "Sure, you did! Enjoying your stay?"

He bumps his shoulder against mine. "Better now that you are here."

"Travis! Where are you going with that weak-ass pickup line?" Kyla jeers as she comes up next to him. She grabs my hand and pulls me away, leaving him to bring up the rear.

We order three rounds of shots and each grab a to-go drink before heading down to the beach. The shore is packed, so it takes us a minute to find a spot for us to chill out. Jason and Keith go back to the truck the boys rented and grab some blankets and chairs so we can all settle down.

The women strip to their swimsuits before rushing off into the surf to splash and take pictures.

I can tell Travis is enthralled by me. Every time I peek his way, his eyes are on me, constantly roving over my body, causing tingles across my skin. I quickly avert my eyes away each time. These few scraps of material covering only the important parts from prying eyes leave nothing to the imagination. He is so fixated he does not notice the boys have gotten up to play football until the ball hits him in the head after Jamal throws it at him.

The guys ended up having a game against another group of men situated further down the beach. After they win, they regroup with us as we sunbathe on our towels. Travis comes and lies down next to me, rubbing his sweating body against my torso. In an instant, I spring up from my towel and punch his arm.

"Really, jackass? That's disgusting." I push my sunglasses up on my head and glare at him. "I was actually starting to dry off."

"Oh, good!" He leans over and rubs his sweaty head against my chest before looking into my eyes with a mischievous smile. My head tilts back, and I let out a giggle before standing up.

"Where are you going?"

I toss my sunglasses and phone on the towel. "Back in the water to rinse your sweat off."

He gets up from the sand without using his hands. "Good idea!"

Before I realize what is happening, he picks me up by my thighs and throws me over his shoulder. He jogs toward the water with me pounding on his back. My butt is exposed to everyone. Ignoring my pleas, he makes it a little way into the water before tossing me in the surf. I come up for air, giving him a pointed look. Pushing through the water, I lunge at him, knocking him underneath the surface.

He shrugs me off before swimming farther out with me following him close. When we reach the deeper part, he stops midswim and turns toward me. Caught off guard, I bump into his chest. Strong arms wrap around my waist like bands of steel and drag me into the water's depths.

In a moment of fear, my legs unconsciously encircle his waist, with my arms around his neck, and I hold on for dear life. It is a survival move. We return to the surface after a few minutes, both gasping for air into our constricted lungs.

I wipe the water from my eyes with the back of one of my hands before looking at him. "You stupid muta—"

My rant is cut off as his lips firmly press against mine. I stiffen against him. He tightens his hold around my body and pulls me closer, leaving no space between us. My breasts flatten against his broad chest as his rock-hard member nestles in the gap between my thighs through our wet bottoms. *God, he feels so good against me.* It almost feels as if nothing is separating our nearly naked bodies. I release a gasp, which he uses as an advantage to slip his tongue into the warm heat of my mouth. It sweeps every crevice thoroughly as his hands rub languidly against my back. I moan as my heartbeat picks up pace.

I suddenly break away, blushing. I uncoil my arms and legs from around him, putting some distance between us. While treading water, I squint at the shore to where our friends are located before looking back at him.

"Travis." I bite my lip. "I don't know what you want from me."

He reaches out, but I dodge him. "I want what we had before."

Fuck! Don't say that. "That is not possible anymore."

"Why not?"

I exhale a breath, and Traymel flickers in my mind. "Because … because I have moved on." *I think.*

"Your body does not seem to agree."

"My body is stupid, and I am just really horny." I smack my forehead, looking up at the sky. "I cannot believe I just told you that."

"I am horny too." He smiles, coming closer to me. "Horny for you."

My eyes bulge. Turning in the direction of the shore, I start swimming away. The sound of his laughter precedes him as he follows. We make it there just as everyone is packing up the gear. Nicole gives me a weird look as we walk up.

"There you two go. Only fools would go that far out in the water," Jamal remarks, grabbing ahold of the chairs. "We are heading to the house for some grilling before the girls have to return to the boat."

After trekking to the parking lot, we all hop into an all-black Yukon and head to the beach house they are staying at. I opt not to sit next to Travis, who left a spot available. Shoving Lynn in before me, I settle in between Kyla and Katy. I am determined to try my hardest to keep my distance from him for the rest of the day.

When we arrive, it is no surprise when Ethan and Nicole make a beeline to Ethan's room. They could not keep their hands off each other the entire time at the beach. Nicole even gave him a hand job, not caring whether anyone noticed, which unfortunately I did.

"Guess that means I am stuck grilling," Remarks Jason as he looks to the spot where Ethan once stood. "Keith, bring the meat out."

"I'll keep you company," Lynn croons with a coy smile, leaning close to Jason.

"No, you are going to help me make sides," declares Kyla, dragging Lynn into the kitchen with her.

"I am going to shower." My eyes dance between Jamal and Jason. "Which bathroom can I use?"

Travis comes up behind me, placing his hand on my lower back, right against the exposed skin above the elastic band of my bottoms. "You can take mine," he murmurs before one of the others can respond. Goosebumps appear at his touch.

I reluctantly nod and head toward the stairs. *There goes avoiding him.* He leads me up to his room. My eyes appreciate the view of his bare back flexing at his movements. I lick my lips as ideas waltz about my mind. My restraint is yet again slipping. That earth-shattering kiss in the water, accompanying my celibate way over the past several months, clouds me with desire. I need to quench this insatiable craving. Once inside, he points in the direction of the bathroom and closes the room door behind him. I sigh in relief, glad he did not stay.

I walk to the bathroom, reach inside the glass-enclosed shower, turning on the water, and strip naked. I rinse my suit out in the sink and hang it from the hook on the back of the door. I grab one of the bodywashes on the counter and a clean towel, and I slip into the warm spray of the shower. I sing off-key to "Pour It Up" by Rihanna as I rinse my hair.

A few minutes later, the sound of the shower door opening grabs my attention. Before I can turn around, tatted arms wrap around my slippery waist. Something hard and long pressed against the crevice of my butt cheeks. I squeal and thrash my arms in fright, causing me to slip on the wet tile bottom of the shower floor. The grip upon me tightens, steadying my balance.

Looking over my shoulder, I lock eyes with my intruder. There is an amused glint in those beautiful brown eyes. "What the fuck, Travis?" I wiggle out of his grasp, pushing against his chest. My body is yet again firing up with the need of him.

A boyish grin tugs at his lips. "Not happy to see me?"

"Um, really!" I push my wet hair out of my face and frown, masking the lust that I feel with him so close, so attainable. "Is there a reason you are naked in *my* shower?"

"You are horny." He steps closer. "I am horny." He places his hands on my hips, pulling me closer again, and drops light kisses on my nose and cheeks. "So why not solve the problem."

A low whimper comes from my lips as one of his hands glides down my stomach. His teeth nip at my neck, followed by his velvet tongue traveling across my feverish skin, eliciting sensations deep below. My tongue is thick in my mouth as his finger finds my treasure.

"We so should not be doing this," I barely whisper.

Travis slowly strokes my seam. "Let's not think about it and just embrace this." He roughly shoves my back against the far wall under the shower head as the warm water rolls down our feverish bodies. He lifts me up by my buttocks, and my legs instinctively wrap around his taut hips for the second time today. Steam is misting around us.

I give one last weak attempt to stop what is about to happen. "Tra—"

He cuts me off with a raspy voice, the sound scraping against his throat. "Zola, shut up!"

Without a moment of hesitation, he thrusts inside my swollen core, catching my yelp of surprise with his firm lips, kissing me with unfathomable urgency. He smacks my wet ass before gripping it in his palms, squeezing tight.

Soon my daze becomes hazy, my lungs begging to be given air. He finally grants us oxygen, moving his lips down the column of my neck. At a spot right above the area where my neck and shoulder join, he laves the delicate skin with his tongue prior to latching his lips on it and sucking hard, leaving his mark. When I clench around his girth, his control slips, and he picks up the pace to pound into me hard. My boobs jiggle before his eyes from the impact.

"Fuck! Fuck! *Fuck!*" I shout, my head thrown back against the wall behind me.

Remembering the others, I bite down hard on my bottom lip, trying to quiet my moans. My eyes flutter close as I grip his waist tighter with my thighs, rolling my hips to meet his repetitive thrusts.

Before long, my chin rests atop his shoulder, my nails digging into his back as I hit my peak. The weightless explosion steals my breath. Waves of sensation ripple through me. He stills after one last thrust, slipping out of me before releasing his own estacsy. As we slowly catch our breaths, he rests his forehead against my breasts, finding comfort against me under the spray of water.

I cannot believe I got another taste of him after all these years. It is so much better than my inexperience. My thirst is still not quenched—only building the desire. My hips rock slightly, wanting another round.

A door closing in the hallway snaps me out of my daze. The realization of what I have just done crashes down on me like a crumbling building in an earthquake. *I just had rough shower sex. With Travis. We are in a house full of our friends on vacation. What am I doing?* I unwrap my legs from his waist and push against his chest for distance. He peers into my eyes before I break contact and look down.

"I just can't ... I mean ... Ugh," I stutter before dragging my fingers through my hair. "Could you just go?"

Travis grabs my chin, tilting my face to his. I shake his hand off. Opening the shower door, I shove him out. He stares at me with his mouth agape while I slam the door in his face. I inhale through my nose, trying to calm my nerves.

I see him stand there for a minute, probably contemplating coming back inside. However, he leaves the bathroom. Picking up the bodywash, I resume my shower, telling myself I did not just enjoy that.

Once I finish, I step out and dry off. After squeezing the excess water out of my bathing suit, I slip back on the top but forgo the bottoms. I walk into the bedroom, rummage through his bag, steal a pair of black basketball shorts, and slip on my sandals. When I return to the kitchen, Lynn looks at me with a knowing gaze.

"Had fun?" she teases, eating a cherry from her drink.

"Um"—I quirk an eyebrow at her—"from showering?"

"Yeah!" She snorts. "With company."

I roll my eyes, not giving her the confirmation she is looking for, and make myself a drink. I think about Travis inside me, stoking this yearning fire that seems to burn in his presence. This just made my life complicated in a way I never thought I would experience again once I swore off relationships.

Leaning against the counter, I sip on my drink, staring out the window to the backyard. Travis, wearing only his trunks, mans the grill. The sun is shining upon him like a halo. As though he feels my gaze, his eyes sweep to me, triggering me to jump and quickly turn my head.

Lynn roars in laughter at my reaction. "I sense a walk down memory lane."

It is about thirty minutes before everyone is at the table, ready to eat and drink. The bride and groom are the last to arrive, and they attend only because of Nicole's love of food and Jamal's threatening her through the bedroom door that it will all be gone. Travis and I have avoided speaking since the shower, but now we sit across the table from each other. I feel his unwavering gaze on me. And I refuse to acknowledge it, trying to seem engrossed in the conversations around me.

"Zola, what is on your neck?" quizzes Nicole, squinting her eyes in my direction.

I smack my hand over the exact mark she speaks of, remembering the feel of his lips there. Finally peering at Travis from under my lashes, I say, "Um, what are you talking about?"

"Seriously?" She smacks her lips. "Clearly you know what I am talking about with that guilty-ass expression."

"Nikki! Big sis had some fun in her shower earlier," Lynn snickers, bluntly staring at Travis.

"OMG, Lynn! Seriously!" I exclaim, covering my face with the other hand, blushing.

Nicole slams her hands on the table. "Which one of you fuckers messed with my sister?"

An audible gasp leaves my lips. "Why are we talking about me like I am not a grown woman?" I push my plate away. "It is not a hickey and not up for discussion, so let's just drop it." I down the rest of my drink before standing from my chair. "It is time to go back to the boat anyway before we get left." I brusquely leave the dining room.

"Bae, leave it alone!" Ethan shouts as I walk out the front door.

I wait outside for the others to join me. We pile back up in the SUV, and Ethan drives us back to the docks. It is a much more comfortable ride now that the boys are missing. I lean my head against the window as Nikki glares at me through the side mirror. I roll my eyes. My attention shifts to the passing scenery as thoughts filter through my mind. If I am to become Traymel's girlfriend, I will miss out on rekindling things with Travis. *Do I even want that?*

Sixteen

It was a rough week after the cruise. The girls badgered me once we got on the boat about what happened between Travis and me. Partially lying, I told them he sneaked into the shower and we just made out, leaving off the detail of my having awakened from my period of no sex. Nicole was, of course, upset to hear this. However, I could tell Lynn knew the truth by her silence. She was not a part of the scolding I received from Kyla and Nicole.

Last I checked, this is my life and I do not need anyone's approval. I am not surprised at my having allowed him in that way. We have overcome the majority of our past drama. We still argue like crazy, but that is true with all of the people in my life. I just feel I should have had more control over the situation and fought the temptation. *Why is it so difficult to do these days?*

The idea of me and Travis having shower sex would have been a great joke if someone had mentioned it to me before it happened. With our rekindling friendship over these months, the growing feelings continue. Unfortunately, I still feel slightly hurt because of how things ended with us.

Yet when we were in the ocean hanging out, it awoke that long-forgotten wanton need that he can always bring out of me. I made a judgement based on my sexual urges, caring not about the future but only the present. That experience felt well worth it: the magical burst of sensual tingles, my toes curling from my explosion. This was similar yet was a milestone more. I embraced this feeling one other time, a long time ago.

Nevertheless, my feelings about it are all jumbled up, and then there is the confusion of where it leaves me and Traymel. He wants me to be his girlfriend, and I am out in another country fucking my ex, enjoying a bliss that I have guarded from him. I have thoughts of not wanting to get caught up in feelings that seem to already have grown.

Butterflies caged in my stomach flit about whenever I am in the presence of either. They are like yin and yang, north and south; yet when I find my heart in the center of a sea of raging emotions, they both tug with exactness, making it difficult. I am unable to choose between them, wanting them both for different reasons and needing them both to soothe me.

So I do what I do best and block myself off from my problems, cutting my brain off from the confusion and uncertainty. I walk a path of darkness to hide from the truths, hypnotizing my senses to answer their carnal need of them both. I am preventing what I always dreaded since that first experience. I would have preferred being bitten by a rattlesnake to having the open wound that seems as if it will never patch itself completely. I avoid anything not related to business with Traymel, and I ignore all of Travis's calls and texts, shutting them out to avoid being dragged back into their aura of control.

Late nights have been my enemy these past few days. I restlessly toss and turn as thoughts of both men plague my mind. Lack of sleep is taking its toll on my body. Bags are forming beneath my eyes. A weakening body. Struggling to hold interest. I am normally not a heavy makeup wearer, but a few years back, Lynn introduced me to concealer, which I have lately been using on my dark circles. The wonders it works to make me look ready to take over, instead of portraying the truth—that I am spiraling down into a black hole.

Monday afternoon, a week after the cruise, Traymel corners me in the copy room and pleads for me to have another date with him Saturday. The sappy look on his face tugs at my heart. I feel as if I have wronged him, and now he is here, begging for me, showing me my importance to him by stepping out of his manhood for a moment.

After failing to come up with a plausible excuse for denial without admitting my guilt, I agree. He invites me to his home and for a meal he will cook. *A man that can work the kitchen.* The date appears to be serious and could lead to the next step. Knowing I have already once succumbed to a similar occurrence, this makes my thoughts work in overdrive once again. Should I put myself in that predicament knowing the likely outcome of what will happen in the situation? I am not the one with the guy problems. It is always about the sex without the feelings, to avoid complications such as the one I am currently experiencing. Why is this so hard to solve?

I have been on the fence about Travis. As many say, there is nothing like the first love. That connection can make a person feel as if her heart has just been jumpstarted and she is able to take her first breath, taste her first flavor, smell her first aroma, feel her first touch, and see her first image.

I quickly rush out the condo to my car, hopping over the three stairs to land firmly on the ground. I am late to a meeting with Wesley. The building inspectors are coming by next week to do a final inspection before they release the wing over to the hospital. I need the pictures and blueprint of the wing to use when promoting their work. Traymel is in Tennessee to restructure one of the buildings.

I head to Wesley's office once I arrive at the headquarters. My heels tap against the marble with a repetitive clicking sound. After nodding at a few familiar faces, I glance at the wall clock above his secretary's desk and see that it is three minutes past the hour.

"Wesley, sorry I am late. The traffic is really not my friend," I announce as I burst into his office. My long strides cover the distance to his seated form. I come up short when I notice a man sitting in one of the chairs in front of his desk. Shoulder-length dreads the color of fire are tied in a ponytail at the nape of the man's neck. *Those look familiar.* "Oh gosh, you are in a meeting. I thought you wanted to meet at nine."

The man turns in his chair at the sound of my voice, looking up at me. The shock mirrored on both our faces could be considered picture worthy. Our eyes connect, recognizing each other with no delay. It turns out the man is Travis. I am caught in a daze as I catch sight of him for the first time since that afternoon. He is still as handsome as before.

Gathering my composure, I avert my eyes, swallowing hard to bring moisture to the Sahara Desert in my parched mouth. Wesley leans forward in his chair, his hands perched on his thighs. His eyes focus as if he has 20-20 vision, and he watches our interaction similar to the way one might watch a movie, not wanting to miss a single detail.

"Zola?" Travis gasps, coming to his senses.

"Travis." My eyes dart back in Wesley's direction. "What is he doing here?"

Travis responds instead. "Mr. Dreer needed to go over some paperwork in person, and since my father is still out of the country, I made the trip."

I turn back his way, upset by his presence. "Why didn't you let me know you were coming?"

"Um, if you recall," he says, dropping his foot to the ground from atop his knee and turning completely my way, "you have not been answering any of my calls or texts since the cruise."

The cruise. That trip that we enjoyed is an experience now imprinted in my brain on constant repeat, torturing me with more possibilities. I glance away guiltily after his comment. "Wesley, I'll be in my office until you finish your meeting," I state before walking back out through his open door.

I massage my temples as I sit at my desk at LTW Construct headquarters. I was not expecting Travis to be in San Diego, let along this building. I know he is going to reach out to me in person before returning home to talk about what happened. It is just not something I have the energy to deal with right now. I wish I had been strong enough to stop that day before I complicated the situation. Travis should not still have this pull on me after all these years. I feel like prey, captured in his silken web of some immense emotion.

"Zola." A hesitant voice fills my ears. The deep baritone sound makes me yearn for him.

I shut my eyes and loudly groan. *Of course he would come and find me when his meeting was over.* I contemplated leaving when I walked out of Wesley's office earlier, but I did not want to deal with the traffic when coming back later.

Glancing up at Travis, my small hazel eyes squint to the point of barely being open, conveying my annoyance at seeing him standing in front of my desk. "Can we not talk about this here?"

He puts most of his weight on his left leg, and a gust of air issues from his flaring nostrils. *I'm sensing anger.* "Well, I can't seem to get you to talk to me over the phone."

"Travis, I just need to think." I slowly drag my hand down my face, wishing he would just leave.

"That is your problem, Lala," he says, calling me by my nickname he gave me when we were much younger. *There he goes again, pulling at my strings.* He grips the edge of my desk, leaning over. "You overthink shit."

I cock my head to one side with a touch of attitude in my movement. I arch an eyebrow high. "Really, Travis! I am not in the mood."

"Well, too bad!" He leans closer with a cold stare. "I am not leaving until you give me something."

I shoot from my chair and slam my hands on the desk, leaning in his face. "What the fuck you want me to say?" My temper is rising at this point. An intense staredown takes place, with each of us daring the other to submit.

Losing the battle, I sigh and turn toward the window. "I am confused," I start. "What happened in that shower shouldn't have, yet it did. And it felt the best not only because of the feeling"—I glimpse over my shoulder and pointedly look at him—"but because it was with you."

He pushes up from the desk. "I enjoyed it too, and it *should* have happened, which is why it did. It will happen again."

I return to my gaze out the window, not wanting to look at him and get lost in those pools of brown. "No, because we are the past and I am moving on," I lie, hoping to push him away.

Travis ambles over to me, places his hands on my shoulders, and begins to lightly massage the tense muscles. "Stop fighting your feelings for me." Hot puffs of air tickle my ear as he speaks.

Great! I have heard that line before. Why do the men in my life lately assume I have feelings for them that I am fighting? Just because I am jumbled does not mean I am fighting anything. The feelings that exist are apparent to me, just not accepted. My problem is trying to sort them out.

"Zola, I don't want to push you … but … being with you that day proved to me how much I want and need you in my life. I am not willing to let you give up on us because of my stupidity in the past." Travis slides his hands from my shoulders to the middle of my back before retreating.

The atmosphere is thick with tension. I stand completely still, my eyes shut tight. My body is yearning for his touch to return. His clothes rustle as he heads to the door, stopping short of it.

"I'll stop by the house tonight so we can talk further. Text me your address. I fly out in the morning, and I want this problem of ours solved

and done with before I leave." *Is he being commanding? This is new …
and hot.* "Having sex should have brought us closer, not put distance into
the friendship we have been rebuilding." The door swings open and then
closes, and I am left alone yet again.

I release a pent-up breath I did not realize I was holding until now. A
headache is building in my head once again. I turn to the empty office,
staring at the closed door, remembering his words. I know that the sex did,
in fact, bring us closer, which is why I need to push him that much farther
away. It unlocked that sealed door to the forbidden—a door that took all
my effort to walk away from. Now I find myself standing upon the same
threshold, my fingers itching closer to the knob.

My cell vibrates against the wood of my desk, dancing in a circle as the
screen illuminates with the white reflection of its inner lights. It is Wesley
messaging to let me know he is ready to meet. *Talk about timing.* I was
expecting a message earlier, after his meeting with Travis ended. I find it
weird that Wesley asked me to meet him at the exact time he scheduled
another meeting for. He is the one I would consider the most organized
and punctual out of the three. *Guess it slipped his mind.*

I grab my phone and text Travis my address before striding to Wesley's
office. *No need to beat around the bush. If Travis wants to find me, he will.*
He is a man to go after his desires. I am now in no rush to get through
this day and deal with the issue I will have waiting for me tonight. I need
to find the strength to not allow him to again distract me.

That afternoon, I find myself in a common normal occurrence—
sitting in traffic, wanting to scream at the brake lights of all the unmoving
cars before me. I swear there is never a time of day where the Pacific Coast
Highway is free of vehicles so one can fly freely at hazardous speeds with
no obstacles. What is different this afternoon than at any other time in
this same position is that moving at five miles per hour is not as annoying
as usual, considering I am in no rush to get home.

Travis did not tell me a specific time when he will come over, even
though I asked him many times throughout the day. Instead he left me
on read, raising my anticipation of his intentions. Maybe I will be lucky
enough to miss his visit. He will in turn probably just wait outside my door
until I arrive, aware I must return.

After shuffling through options, I still do not know what to say to explain why this is such a big puzzle for me. I understand that the smart thing is to leave the past heartbreak alone and focus on building something new with Traymel. However, Travis and I already know the pros and cons of each other, and maybe this go-round will be a lot smoother and less stressful then starting anew. *Both men are putting me on a time limit to decide. If they only knew I am juggling two different offers. Travis is right! I do overthink.*

Once I arrive home, I grab the mail from the mailboxes before pulling into one of the spots for my condo. Relief washes over me when I do not spot Travis waiting. This gives me more time to fester. After getting inside, I walk to the kitchen for something to drink, where I notice a note on the counter from Lynn about her sleeping at Jonathan's tonight. *Great! I am going to be alone with Travis. Got to make sure I do not slip up and sleep with him again. There is still that date Saturday with Traymel, and I do not need another moment of carnal activity with my past tainting my conscience.*

I take a quick shower and change into something more comfortable. The doorbell rings as I lotion my legs. I still my hands. My head feels as if I have been sucked into a soundproof room, with only the noise of the continuous ringing of my ears present as blood rushes to my head. Sighing, I stand to my feet, pulling down my night shorts as I head toward the front door on wobbly knees. Looking through the peephole, I confirm Travis has finally arrived.

I open the door, not bothering to acknowledge his presence. I then walk away to the kitchen to pour a glass of wine. I am going to need this liquid courage. He walks in and closes the door, the ominous click sounding out, locking us in this apartment together. Alone. Detectable tension sizzles in the atmosphere. He follows me into the kitchen, and his eyes rake up my body as I lean against the counter. He pauses a long time on my chest, where my darkening buds are pouting for attention through my thin tank top.

"Can you not undress me with your eyes," I grumble, taking a gulp of my wine. *Looks like this is going to require the whole bottle.*

"I can't help it when you come to the door dressed like that. Those shorts barely cover your ass, and you don't have a bra on, so I can see your nipples through that." His hand waves about in the air, gesturing to my attire as he points out its skimpiness. "By the way, I love that you got them pierced." He walks closer toward me.

I take a step back, matching his foot movement in the opposite direction, completing our own tango step before my side connects with the edge of the island. I round the island, using it as a barrier to separate us before quickly heading into the sunroom. I finish the wine and set the glass on the coffee table.

"So what do you want to talk about?" I ask, settling on the sofa.

He strides over and sits next to me. He removes my clasped hands from my lap and holds them in his, rubbing his thumbs lightly against their backs. I try to pull away from his grasp, but his hold tightens. We sit like this for a few minutes, his head bent forward, dreads hanging past his face.

Dramatically sighing, Travis looks up at me, a meaningful expression etched upon his face. "Zola, I love you." There is a quick pause as my eyes widen. I let that phrase settle in my mind. "You are the air I breathe and the starlight in my dark skies. I have wanted you since the day of your senior prom. That moment, I realized little LaLa had grown into an intelligent and beautiful woman that I wanted for myself, to enjoy every bit of. Taking your virginity that night scared me, and I made a childish move. I constantly beat myself up for it, wishing I could turn back the hands of time."

Tears coat my eyes at his words. *Don't cry! Don't cry!* He brings our joined hands to his lips, where he gives them a fleeting kiss so light. If I had not seen it with my own eyes, I would have never known. "Being with Bianca was a mistake, and it only happened to aid me in getting over you. I was actually relieved when she cheated." He chuckles. "Ending something before it became the second biggest mistake of my life. The first? Letting you go."

Leaning forward, Travis presses his forehead against mine. He looks deep into my eyes as my heart beats rapidly. "I am sorry that it took me so long to realize my mistake, and I will spend an eternity to make it up to you. If only you would give me the chance. You are special to me, and I just can't live without you again."

I blankly stare at him speechless, tears now running down my cheeks. *Did he just say all that? He poured his heart out to me, getting on a ledge and just jumping. I waited years for him to tell me he felt the same for me as I did for him. I allowed myself to believe it would not happen—that I would never be good enough for him to have as his one and only.*

119

I do not know how to take this news. *Do I even still love him? Yes, I ache for him, but is it at the level from the past: that endless obsession for an unreachable want—the level that will match his. We have been apart for years and only recently reconnected. I am sure I am not ready to open my heart again for either him or Traymel. The hurt back then was too great.* I close my eyes and steady my heart rate, calming myself.

Travis leans forward, pressing his lips to each of my cheeks in turn, kissing away wet streaks left by my tears. Even with what he told me, I am still jumbled regarding which decision is best.

Love should not be this tough. Love is that warm, fuzzy sensation that fills your beating heart with positive emotions that overcome the senses—an unwinding path of desire and admiration for the one most important to you, where smiles of joy happen without effort, leaving your cheeks aching from laughter, and your eyes dry from tears. The butterflies caged inside that persistently flutter about, wanting to freeze time to experience it on a continuous loop.

I open my eyes and stare straight into his, getting lost in their depths. *Is that what I feel for him?* I bring my hands up under his dreads, cupping his rough cheeks in my palms. My thumbs grace over the growing hairs of his five o'clock shadow. Inching nearer, I press my lips lightly against his, savoring the touch. Travis sits there, unmoving, waiting for my next move.

Once again, my body is immersed in an orbit of heat. Yet chills shoot down my spine. *What is this?* It is nothing like what I felt in school, this eruption of sensations.

Moving to my knees on the sofa's edge, I swing one leg over his lap, climbing atop him while deepening the kiss. My dreads are now draping in our faces. Using this angle to control our unquenchable desire of each other. His tongue strokes mine as muffled moans echo from us both. My hips involuntarily grind against his clad lap, his penis hardening against me, fitting perfectly in my nook. His arms are like bands of steel around my thin waist, crushing me against his rippled chest. My fingers tunnel through his dreads, gripping his scalp.

He stands up in a swift motion, me still in his arms, and walks to the back of the condo. For a second, he breaks our kiss, looking at the closed doors before him. I point in the general direction of mine, not turning my body. Walking inside, we topple among the pillows accenting the bed. Our

120

clothes are thrown in various directions in our haste. *This is almost like a memory from a past beginning.*

Travis nestles his glory between my thighs, rubbing against my swollen lips. My hair is spread out behind my head, making me appear to be an angel with a blue halo. Our eyes lock in silent approval of what is to happen next. Not wasting another moment, he sheaths himself in my already dripping center. An audible gasp parts my lips.

Shifting my hips, I try to accommodate his intrusion. Leaning over, he catches one of my pierced nipples in his mouth and begins tonguing the jeweled delight. He stretches me to maximum capacity with slow and languid strokes, causing me to whimper by pulling out to the tip before thrusting fully back in. My muscles clench around him, urging him to pick up his speed.

"This is not just sex for me, Zola," he whispers against my lips before biting the bottom one. "I want you to yearn and enjoy every second. Beg me for this feeling—sparks of pleasure to cover every inch of your beautiful body. Me being different from all the others."

This slow torture is getting the best of me. Every time I feel a climax coming, he ceases movement, drawing the hunger out longer, leaving me with this bubble of fireworks resting heavily between my thighs, needing to erupt. I writhe beneath him, gripping the comforter in my fists as my head frantically rocks from side to side against the pillows, yearning for the completion only he can grant me. I raise my hips to slam against his. My hands slip between our torsos, twisting his nipples.

A rumble fills his chest. One of his arms slips under me, pulling me up from the bed and setting me on his lap. My back is arched, my breasts naked and lifted in the air for his sight. His knees are against the bed, holding us up. Immediately the gentleness from before dissipates as he roughly thrusts inside me, bouncing my body atop him. I feel his mouth everywhere, marking me as he lays claim to my body. *His body.* It is a tribute to what he has—not as his commodity, but as his treasure.

I have never had sex like this. It is not just a means to an end, but a start of a beginning. My nails rake down his back before digging into his skin, leaving ten crescent marks of power.. Expletives and screams, as loud as my lungs will allow, echo through the room, finally tipping over the edge. *I know my neighbors are mad.* The bubble bursts. Sparkles from the fireworks cloud my vision through hooded eyes. My body rides the waves of its pleasure, leaving me unable to fully catch my breath.

Soon I feel the stilling of his body. Heavy pants of air brush across my face. Travis releases his own grunts of ecstasy, giving me everything he has to offer. He then carefully lays me back against the blanket. My body, soothed and malleable, lies beneath him. He bends down to run his tongue over my lips before murmuring, "Belong to me."

Seventeen

"I am so glad it is my last semester of nursing school. I should be done in December, and come the new year; I can start my career at the Scripps MD Anderson Cancer Center." Lynn states, pulling the cookies out of the oven. She has been interning over the summer and has made a good impression that they already offered her a job once she graduates.

The girls and I have finally found some time to have a group hangout amid our busy schedules and life dramas. We forgo the happy hour and decide to stay indoors during the raging storm wreaking havoc outside. Dressing in pajamas, we ordered Chinese, made chocolate-chip cookies, and are now settling down to indulge in large amounts of wine while catching up on the happenings in each other's worlds. I am grateful to be able to spend time with them and take a break.

Again I succumbed to Travis's charms. After that mind-blowing sex, I fell asleep in his arms only to awake to an empty bed. He left a note on my nightstand informing me he had to catch an early flight home and will contact me later. *Home.* I used to call it that also, but now I have built a life here. That was Thrusday morning, and I have not heard from him since. I am not actually complaining, since now I am even more confused than I was prior. I do not know what to say to that ball of feelings he dropped on my plate, putting me in a spot to accept him as more. There is no way we can return to just friends now. My emotions are everywhere and nowhere.

"I am still surprised you made it this far. School is not your thing," Kyla jeers, biting into a hot cookie.

"It is not." Lynn agrees. "However, having Jonathan there makes it that much more doable."

"I bet!" Kyla giggles for a second before her eyes become blank and a dark cloud moves over her.

I glance at Lynn, who also notices Kyla's sudden mood change. "Kyla. Are you okay?"

She takes a large gulp form her glass, savoring the sweetness of the liquid in her mouth before swallowing it. "I am meeting up with Lincoln tomorrow night."

Lynn spits out the wine in her mouth, misting the air before her. "Say what?"

I lean back in the recliner, crossing my legs beneath me. "I thought you said you were going to move on from him … that your marriage was more important."

"Wait. Wait, wait." Lynn wipes her mouth on her shirt, sitting up from her lounging position. "Clearly I am missing something."

"You still never told her." I click my tongue. "Lynn! Kyla had an affair with Lincoln a few months back."

"*No freaking way!*" Lynn shouts, her eyes ricocheting between Kyla and me. "And you heffas kept this secret from me this *whole time*." Hurt appears on her face.

"I actually just recently found out, after the boys came to that happy hour and she met them."

"Bish! That was like five months ago." *Damn! She has a point.*

"It's my fault, Lynn." Kyla rubs her middle finger along the rim of her glass, absently looking into the yellow-white liquid. "If she'd never overheard my conversation with Lincoln, she would still be in the dark. I had no intention of telling either of you."

"But why?" I ask after I swallow my sip.

"Because I believed that the more people that knew, the higher the possibility Damien would find out. I feel horrible about my unfaithfulness. And I am still communicating with Lincoln after all these months. It started as a revenge plot after learning who he was at Newtopia. Now I look forward to our conversations—our game of cat and mouse."

I finally ask the question that has been nagging at me. "Are you falling for Lincoln?"

"I'm married, La! I love my husband." Tears begin to fall, wetting her cheeks.

I lean forward, my elbows resting on my knees, pushing the issue. "You didn't answer my question. I already know all that."

She bites her lips before finishing off her glass and then refilling it, stalling for time to maybe decide on an answer. That she did not negatively respond instantly speaks volumes, confirming my suspicions. "Poor sha! This is bad. Your heart is torn. Your twin is making you doubt what you already know is best for you."

Her face scrunches in confusion. "My twin?" Then realization dawns. The lightbulb goes off within seconds. "We are dealing with brothers." She snorts, wiping her drying tears with a tissue.

"Yes!" I agree. "I have a date with Traymel tomorrow also."

"Well hell! I will be spending the night at Jonathan's tomorrow as well." Lynn adds, grabbing a cookie from the tray on the coffee table. "Seems we are all with our ..." She pauses, side-eyeing Kyla. "Correction. With *a* man tomorrow night. It is crazy that I am the only one who is committed to one person now."

I snort. "That it is." Lynn throws her half-eaten cookie at me. "Seriously? Are you three years old!"

We continue our talk of our men well into the night, letting the wine clear out any inhibitions and speaking what is truly on our hearts. Lynn and I trudge to our beds, completely drunk off our asses, leaving Kyla passed out on the couch after covering her with a spare blanket. I barely make it in my room before I crash atop my bed, falling asleep instantly.

The following morning, I awake with only a slight hangover. I made sure to stay hydrated most of the night. I stretch across my bed, making a noise like a dying animal. After brushing my teeth and relieving my bladder, I pad into the common area, noticing Lynn and Kyla still asleep. I go to the kitchen and gather ingredients from the fridge to cook breakfast for the crew.

Again my thoughts drift as I move about. This time they center around my work. My career has finally overtaken that milestone, and now I can reap the benefits. Being the only woman on the board will prove to be challenging yet not impossible.

I was unable to rub my promotion in Landon's face, since he never returned to work after our scene in the hallway on the first day of my promotion. He sent his sister to come clean out his desk and give his letter of resignation to Mr. Mitchell. When her eyes fell on me leaving the copy room as she waited for the elevator, they were cold and accusing. *Boy, if looks could kill.* It seemed weird, considering I did not know who she was until Lynn told me later that afternoon. I guess Landon had a lot to say about me outside the workplace. Her animosity toward me felt so personal for someone getting only one side of the story.

I had been given two blessings within the first three weeks of achieving my goal, bringing total bliss into my work life: the major promotion and now never having to work with my nemesis again. I am sure he left because of my advancement. After years of shade and verbal attacks, I beat him at his own game and stole the title that was always rightfully mine—a feat he was doubtful I would achieve.

I remember my young childhood days, when I would play Mario Kart on my Super Nintendo and constantly get stuck on the Rainbow Road course. No matter how much I would repeat it, even choosing different characters for various advantages, I never could finish the three laps with all my lives intact, until the one fateful night of complete determination when I was able to cross that finish line with Yoshi. The pure joy that I felt at finally overcoming that obstacle is the same as I feel now about proving Landon wrong, becoming partner, and building my career.

"Yass, food." Lynn mumbles sleepily, joining me in the kitchen just as I am turning off the grits.

"Of course your greedy ass awakes just as I am finishing up." I coat the biscuits in the oven with some honey butter, letting it bake inside. "Kyla! Wake your ass up!"

"Shut up!" Kyla's arms stretch out in front of her. "I been up." She sits up on the sofa, her hair a mess. Her tangled strands are sticking out in various directions like the snakes Medusa has atop her head. She grabs the remote and turns on the TV, probably to watch the news. She is big on keeping up with current events. It is because of her that Lynn and I even know what is going on in the world half the time.

"Breaking news!" the newscaster states. "It has been confirmed that Susan Jones, wife of Mayor Michael Jones, has lost her fight in the battle of lung cancer. She passed late last night. The family has taken a real blow and will kindly accept prayers from all the citizens of San Diego."

"OMG! I just met her a few weeks ago. She had stopped caring about getting better, but I was hoping it was just a phase," Lynn comments, moving into the sunroom to get a better view of the TV. "I am sure Michael is pretty broken up about this. I know I cut off the sexual relationship, but he is still important to me. I will have to find time this weekend to stop by his house to give my condolences."

It is sad to know that his wife indeed received her wish. It's a tragic loss for the city of San Diego. I have never met her but have seen Michael on several occasions and feel bad for what he is going through. This is a heartache no one should have to endure, yet death is inevitable—a permanent and irreversible ending that we will all experience in the future. Some tend to embrace it, whereas others fight. Many wait decades until that day, whereas others are taken from us too soon.

"That is so sad," Kyla murmurs, removing the blanket from herself before standing up and heading to the kitchen. She makes her way to the coffeemaker she brought for the condo. Lynn and I have no taste for it, but her addiction does not allow her to start the day without at least a cup.

We enjoy breakfast before going our separate ways—Lynn to spend her weekend with her boyfriend, and Kyla to go back home to spend time with her family before meeting up with Lincoln to discuss some condition. She does not give us many details. I hope she knows what she is doing, allowing herself to be in that lion's den, vulnerable.

I know from experience how the presence of a man that means more to you than you admit to yourself can cloud your judgement at a moment's notice, leaving you regretting the aftermath. She is sure that Damien is her endgame. So, to make sure that endgame happens, she needs to keep herself away from temptation.

I am anticipating my date with Traymel tonight, trying to keep a clear mind. I hope to see how I feel with him and whether something more suitable for us can grow. Now knowing what is at stake for Travis and me, the girls believe Traymel is the better choice. My mind needs to come up with a conclusion and free me from this torturous loop I find myself in.

I watch TikTok skits as I sit in my hairdresser's chair, getting my dreads retwisted. I'm grateful she was available at such a short notice. I try to do them at least once a month because of the rate my hair grows. A white envelope flashes across the top of my screen, indicating a message. Opening it, I see it is from Travis.

"Bae, I miss you. This week has been rough!"

I smirk. *Sure, ya do, stranger.*

"My father returns next week, and I must get everything in order before he arrives."

I guess.

"Trust me! That night has been in my head on repeat. I can't wait to taste you again."

I roll my eyes, locking my phone and not responding. *The audacity of him to assume we would sleep together again.* I never gave him the impression that anything changed. He poured his heart out. I just did what I did best and used my body as a distraction—a way to forget for a moment the difficult topic of discussion. I take a deep breath. Yearning runs through me as that night filters through my mind. I think of his touches, his expertise, his control. *Stop it, Zola! I am going to see Traymel tonight. No thinking about Travis allowed!*

After I leave the salon, I head to the grocery store to pick up a few items before heading home. After unloading the groceries in the kitchen, I head to the sunroom and plop on the sofa, gazing out the large window. Thoughts of Travis once again slip in, giving me a mental picture of that experience.

A loud banging on the front door ruffles my nerves. *Are the cops paying us a visit?* Picking myself up, I tentatively make my way to the door. Glancing through the peephole, I see the bald head of a man bent over. His right palm is pressed against the wood as he leans into it. Opening the door, I spot a ragged Michael on the threshold.

"Where is Lynn?" he gruffly asks, his breath reeking of alcohol and his clothes rumpled and dirty. He resembles a person that has been living on the streets for days—a sad sight as the mayor.

"Um ..." I glance behind him, looking for his bodyguard, who is absent. "Not here."

His palm connects with the doorframe with a solid thud. "Is she with that boyfriend of hers?" His eyes search behind my head as if Lynn is standing somewhere in the shadows.

"Probably so." I step back a little wearily. "Michael, have you been drinking?"

"*Of course I have!*" he screams, lines creasing his forehead. "My wife is dead, and the love of my life left me. My life is a ruin!" His glassy eyes squint at me, blaming me for his misfortune.

I frown, remembering the news this morning. *No wonder he is a wreck.* "I am sorry to hear about your wife."

"I don't care about that woman." He rubs his bald head, sadness in his eyes. "I want Lynn!"

Wow! Even with the death of his wife, he is still obsessed with Lynn. I hope that he lets that go. She has moved on with Jonathan. "Maybe you should try calling her," I suggest, hoping we are not attracting any attention. This is just what I need these days—the mayor making a ruckus on my doorstep in the middle of the afternoon.

"Call her? Or I could go find her at that man's house." He turns and heads back to his car. "She is my woman!" *I feel he should not be driving, but then again, not my problem.*

I shake my head as I close the door. I rush to the sunroom for my phone and send Lynn a quick text to be on the lookout for her drunken married man. With Michael's resources, I am sure he already knows the whereabouts of Lynn, and she is in a world of trouble with the can of worms that is about to be opened. I head to my room for a quick nap.

About an hour later, I shower and get ready for my date. He stays by the beach in Kyla's area, so I have a way to go and do not want to be late. I have a habit of that. Searching through my closet, I settle on a Barcelona red asymmetrical halter dress with strappy black heels. I place my hair in a massive bun at the nape of my neck and adorn my ears with some dangling black earrings. Glossing my lashes with mascara, I glance at my bed clock to see I am right on time to leave.

My phone buzzes with a text from my sister. She and Ethan just got into a fight. *That is not surprising.* This is a normal occurrence for them. It must have been a bad one for her to be contacting me. Surely responding will have me late, as she will want to expound on all the details. I will wait to contact her in the morning. They will most likely have made up by then.

I gather my things and head out the door, and I turn on classical music to calm my nerves as I drive to Traymel's. I am afraid and curious of what might transpire tonight, noting the outcome of being with Travis. Traymel has given me time to know his stance, and I am still no closer to deciding.

I shoot him a text, letting him know I am downstairs, ready to be buzzed into the building. I walk inside and take the elevator up to his floor. He is standing outside his door, waiting for my arrival. As I cover the space, my eyes analyze him from head to toe. I chuckle at the fact he is comfortable enough with his sexuality to wear light colors. He is dressed in khaki slacks that are tapered to his hips, along with a light pink button-down dress shirt. The top two buttons are undone, giving a peek of his bare chest.

"You look amazing!" he boasts, his eyes checking me out.

I wink, a big grin spreading across my face. "Thanks! Loving the pink."

"Had to let out my softer side tonight so you will take pity on me with all your defenses."

Rolling my eyes, I walk in through the door he holds open and take in is home. It is beautifully decorated and homey, with black leather sitting furniture, and accents of gold and red decor throughout the living space. Off to the side, a large kitchen with a black marble bar top separates it from an entertainment area. I can see doors off of the living room, which I assume leads to the balcony. A small hall veers off to the right to his bedroom. The white walls are covered in framed pictures.

"Your place is nice," I compliment, looking his way.

He cocks an eyebrow at me from the stove. "I bet you was expecting something else."

My eyes sweep the area again. I did expect it to be barer and blander—a bachelor pad lacking warmth. I feel there has been some input from a female. *His ex-fiancee, perhaps.* That thought slightly fouls my mood. "Your assumptions may be right."

I amble out to the balcony as the cool late-night breeze filters over me, my dress lightly flowing around my legs in the wind. The view of the ocean in the distance is wonderful. A full moon is setting against the edge where the sky and the water seem to meet. I pull out my phone to take a picture of the beautiful sight.

A message from Kyla in our group message appears with a link to a video with over five thousand shares and even more comments. It shows an older man paused in the middle of speaking, looking the worse for wear. *Is that Mayor Jones?* I click the play button, shocked speechless as I listen to the words. Michael is still drunk and emotional from this afternoon. I realize he must have not gotten in contact with Lynn, or their conversation did not go well. I expect him to be shaken up about his wife dying last night. Instead he is professing his undying love for Lynn. *This is not good!*

I try calling her and get no answer. It is a plus that he uses only her first name in the video, meaning people will likely not know exactly who he is speaking of. They will want to find out, though. She will have to stay clear for a while. It is distasteful of him to be crying over another woman when his wife just died. His tears should be for her, not the woman who ditched him.

Traymel comes up behind me, confining me within his arms. "Your dinner is served, mi lady," he whispers in my ear.

I lean my head back against his chest for a second, forgetting the video and enjoying the feeling of being in his arms. His nose nuzzles the area below my ear, and a shiver jolts through my body. I smile before turning out of his embrace, slapping his arm. I head inside, with him following after closing the door.

He leads me to a table covered in a linen cloth, set for two. A bottle of an expensive brand of wine in an ice bucket, open and breathing, sits in the center. Two large candles in a chrome holder flicker on either side. A single red rose lies beside one of the plates.

Pulling out my chair and sitting down, I hold my dress against me. Traymel pushes me in before sitting in his own chair. A shrimp and crab cream pasta over a bed of linguine noodles causes my mouth to water. I lean over and inhale the steam rising from the dish. "OMG! Shrimp." Gushing, I spread a napkin across my lap.

He smiles, pouring wine into each of our glasses. "You told me how you love seafood, and my specialty is pasta, so *voilà!*"

"It looks good!" I take a bite and savor the burst of spice and flavor that erupts in my mouth. My eyes flutter closed, and I moan at my awakening taste buds. A creamy sauce with perfect consistency coats the noodles. The seafood is cooked to the correct tenderness.

"You keep moaning like that and I will have to take you to the bedroom," he discloses, his eyes hooded as he grips the silverware with unneeded force.

I blush as I lick my lips. "What makes you think I want to go to the bedroom with you?" I take a bite of shrimp and slowly chew. "I am only here for the food."

He stares at my lips for a second before responding. "Believe that if you want."

We chat about topics unrelated to work and learn even more about each other. After the food is completed, we venture to the living room with the remaining wine and our glasses. Sipping in silence on the couch, we watch each other. Again I feel those sparks I felt when near Travis. I hate that I want them both.

Many would gossip about my next move, calling me a whore or saying I have no self-respect or decent standards. Well, I have already admitted that I *love* sex. I have also endured a long drought. And right now, I want Traymel. I have fantasized for the longest time about how it would be with him and what hidden secrets are beneath his suits. *What better moment!* I have not committed to either of them yet, so I am not obligated to have a sense of morals. Besides, I can not make a decision between the two of them. not knowning what its like with Traymel between the sheets.

I remove the glass from his hand and place it along with mine on the table. Taking the initiative, I grab the front of his shirt in my small fist and roughly yank him toward me. Our lips connect. His tongue swiftly penetrates my marginally parted lips. As it sweeps throughout my mouth, I lean back, pulling him atop of me. His weight presses me into the cushions as his rather large hardening length lies against my thigh. One of my hands snakes down, gripping it, urging him to take us to the next level. My need for him is overwhelming.

He stands and unbuttons his shirt, dropping it on the ground before picking me up bride-style and carrying me to the bedroom. My fingertips feather across his bare chest. He places me atop the bed and lies between my legs. Large hands settle against my breasts, restricted by only the fabric of my dress. He rubs circles around them, flicking his thumbs against the tips. His hands move down my sides until they reach the hem of my dress, and there they inch it up to my stomach.

He scoots farther down my body, and his nose moves to the crevice of my thighs, inhaling my arousal. My panties soak with anticipation. Taking the waistband of my thong in his teeth, he pulls the flimsy fabric down to my thighs. Switching to his hand, he drags it the rest of the way and tosses it to the floor. He then puts my legs, where they bend at the knees, on his shoulders.

He returns his lips to my core. I feel him lick from front to back slowly—lightly. It is a mere touch to show his presence but to still tempt me for what is yet to come. My thighs close in on his head just as he probes my wet heat with continual sensual strokes. My eyes close with heaviness as I clench the sheets in my hands, biting back a moan. Traymel licks and sucks me as my pleasure rises to its peak, ready to go over the edge. When my breathing begins to quicken, he stops and slips off the bed.

"Where are you going?" I ask, puzzled, sitting up on my elbows. I have not even come yet, and my lips below are aching.

Ignoring me, Traymel takes his pants and boxers off in one swift move, and his massive cock springs free. *Whoa! He is packing.* He climbs back onto the bed and kisses me deeply. I taste my juices still lingering against his lips. His lips leave mine, and he pulls my dress off over my head before returning to lick down my neck. I moan as my hips rise off the bed to meet his for friction. The warm member hangs between us. As his tongue travels through the valley of my breasts --I slightly stiffen-- remembering the few marks from Travis that litter my chest. If Traymel is aware, he makes no comment. He takes a jeweled tip in his mouth, laving it with his tongue. *Men really enjoy nipple piercings.*

Finally he slips inside, stretching me. Our sweaty bodies fuse together as one. "Fuuuuck!" I holler out, my eyes rolling into my head and my nails digging into the skin of his arms. He begins to slowly stroke inside me as my heartbeat once again picks up. *This slow tortue is a common trait between both men.* This man is keeping me on the edge, slipping in and out with a sensual flow as smooth as a bow gliding along the strings of a violin in a classical tune. Our lovemaking is a melody of our bodies. Blissful sensations explode within me as I go crashing over the top with the high note of our song.

Before I can get my bearings, he flips me over onto my stomach and begins to pound inside from behind, hitting at a different angle. His smack on my ass rings throughout the silent room, which is filled only with our moans of pleasure. As I come to completion a second time, his fingers squeeze my hips and he hits his own release, uniting us as one.

Eighteen

Drip
Drip.
Drip.
What in the world?
Drip.
Drip.
I heave an exasperated sigh.
Drip.

I so do not want to wake already after the night I have experienced. To remain here, unmoving. Envisioning every touch, every whisper, and every yearning is causing my body to warm up and ease this chill.

Wait, why do I feel cold?
Drip.
Drip.
Drip.

Slowly cracking my left eye, I see a faint light seeping in from the shroud of darkness. Stretching my sore muscles, my arms rub against the cold ground. Bolting upward, stars collecting in my eyes, I take a deep breath, trying to overcome the dizziness of the sudden movement. A dank smell permeates my nostrils, causing me to cough. Taking in my surroundings, I am perplexed at what I see.

I am sitting in a ten-by-ten concrete room. Thick steel bars take up one wall. There is a light dimly illuminating a dark hallway that seems never-ending. A rustic toilet sits in the far corner with a puddle of water forming at its base.

Well, found the source of that annoying noise.

Other than that, the room is bare. There is not even a window for some fresh air. I stand up and dust my hands off on my clothes. *Wait, who dressed me!* I am wearing tights and a Dallas Cowboys sweatshirt that clearly belongs to a man, judging by how it engulfs me.

"Well, someone roots for a shit team," I mutter to myself. "Why am I making jokes right now, in this situation?" I snort, burning my nose. "Great! Now I'm also talking to myself. Well, as long as I don't respond."

Am I dreaming? Slapping myself in the face, I discover that in fact, this is my reality.

How did I get here? Why am I here?

I begin pacing the confined space. My head feels stuffy, as if I am coming down with a cold. I can barely focus as a dull headache thunders in the back of my head. Massaging my temples, I take a second to run through my thoughts. The last recollection I can muster is that of falling asleep in his arms. *Speaking of which, where is he?*

A shadow appears in the corner of my vision. I glance to my side into some eyes through the bars. I squint, making out a man leaning against the wall in the hallway. A smirk slowly pulls against his lips. I cannot stifle the gasp I release from my parted lips. We stare at each other for what seems like forever, neither of us breaking eye contact while gauging the other's reaction. He breaks the silence with the high pitch of his voice.

"You're awake!"

"The fuck!" My jaw hits the floor. *Him?* "Why am I here?"

To say I am confused would be an understatement. I'm in a prison-like cage, God knows where. I wonder how he even got me here. I am trying to keep myself from freaking out until I determine the severity of the situation. He went through the trouble of bringing me here for a reason. *At least I believe it was him.*

"Because you are in the way," he concludes, as if that is a clear explanation. Missing out on the main detail. I wonder what I could have possibly done to get him to act like this. As he walks further into the light,

I see that a maniacal expression covers his face. This is a version of him I never could have imagined.

"In the way of what?" I cautiously ask.

He raises his arms in the air as if he has just called upon the heavens. "My happy ending," he declares.

I bring my palm to my forehead with a loud smack. I close my eyes, as the previous thud in my head is now a full-blown banging against my temples. This man is just not getting to the point of the matter, and it is irritating the hell out of me. Despite the predicament I find myself in, anger is lingering beneath the surface. *My cursed short temper.* I guess I am supposed to understand what exactly is going on, but I do not.

I try to run through my mind for possibilities, but again I am simply muddled. There is nothing I can come up with that might have gotten me on his bad side. I really thought he was one of the few people in my life these days that I did not have an issue with. *Again, I am wrong.*

"Wesley!" I give an exasperated sigh, looking at my captor. "I really have no idea what you are talking about. Can you explain?"

He groans, crossing his arms atop his protruding stomach. "Traymel wants you … and … I want him."

My eyes take on a quizzical look. "Want him?" Before I jump to conclusions, I will wait for him to clarify.

"I have been in love with Mel since our childhood days, which I am sure you can understand since you have the same thing with Travis." He pauses, taking a step closer to the bars. "Traymel always made me feel welcome and brought me out of my shell. Unfortunately, my heart had to mess it up for me, and I fell for him in high school. He, on the other hand, only saw me as his best friend."

His arms drop from his chest. "No matter how many times the females in his life messed him over, I was there for him in those moments, hoping for more and never getting it. I am tired of it!" His right-hand balls in a fist and slams against his left palm. "I was finally ready to proclaim my love. But who waltzed into that boardroom with her flair?" His eyes glower at me. A muscle twitches in his jaw. "None other than Ms. Zola Saunders."

"I did no—"

"I saw the way he watched you through the entire presentation," he continues, not allowing me to say my piece, blaming me for something

I had no control over. "How you both interacted the many times that followed." He scoffs. "Then he came and asked me one afternoon about being nervous taking you on a date, and I knew I could not allow that to happen."

"I tried bringing Travis into the picture to tempt you away, but you still found a way into *my* man's bed," he professes, grasping the bars in his beefy hands. "I have deterred many women in his life, and you are no different."

I stare at him speechlessly. *Did he just say he is in love with Traymel? Wow! Did not see that coming. So I am in this makeshift cell because Traymel and I decided to move to the next step. Is he serious? Wesley is truly off his rocker. I have not even decided if I even want to be with Traymel. Yet he is jumping to assumptions because we had sex.*

I once again pace around the cell, trying to grasp the situation. Wesley stands there and watches me like a hawk—as if I can get out of here without assistance. It seems I am not the only woman in Traymel's life that he has manipulated a void between. If only he knew the thoughts running through my mind on a daily basis, being on the fence between two guys.

I pause in my wandering as a thought comes to my head, and I quickly whip in his direction abruptly enough for my neck to crack, yet the slight pain that accompanies the movement is not more important than the idea that is causing my heart to still.

"What do you mean you brought Travis into the picture?" I query, stepping in his direction, slightly nervous. "Does he know about Traymel and me?" Fear grips me as my stomach churns in protest.

"How should I know? I brought him to San Diego that day so you both would run into each other and rekindle that lost love," he complains, his face red with anger. "Unfortunately, it seems he did not do a good job of keeping your attention."

I knew it was weird that he double-booked a meeting. Our interaction was coerced. I snort. "You are delusional."

If only he knew what went down that night and that I am still second-guessing my possible relationship with Traymel, his first love. It's crazy he has played me this whole time. He befriended me to find my weakness and exploited it for his own good. I was so busy trying to avoid the twins that I completely missed that Wesley was being fake. I guess Nicole was right about me being gullible. I have always prided myself in having a sense of control.

"What do you plan on doing with me here?" I inquire, rubbing my hands up my arms, the chill still in the air.

"Well, I haven't gotten that far," he states, turning his back on me and rubbing his hands together. "I just need you out of the picture until I can persuade Mel to be with me." *That will take forever.*

"Where is Traymel?" I remember he was the last person I was with. "How did you even get me out of the house without him knowing?" *Maybe he is in on this?* I recall that Lincoln has been known to be sketchy. *It may run in the family.*

He faces me again. "I have a key to Traymel's condo for emergencies, and when I learned that he was cooking for you, I went over to see how the date went." His eyes rake my body as he sneers. "Of course, the bed-hopping Zola had finally put her claws into him and clouded his judgment with her feminine charms. So I injected you both with a sedative and brought you here." *And we never heard him come in.*

I rush to the bars, gripping them in my fists. "Where is here, exactly?" I ask as I once again scan the area, hoping for a clue I may have missed.

"Underneath the De La Prole Hotel."

My mouth gapes. "That expensive hotel off Boardwalk Boulevard?" He nods. "Why would they have this under their building? There are no rules against this?"

"They do not know it is here." He shrugs. "This was one of LTW Construct's first projects. The manager is friends with the twins' dad and is an established hotel chain owner in the northeast and wanted to try business on the west coast. This one has the most unique design compared to the others." He smiles, stroking his goatee. "We thought it would be cool to build this. It was not really supposed to be used, but the occasion arose."

"What about Mel?" I ask again, my voice quavering.

"Left him sleeping in the bed. He will wake up with a mild headache, as I am sure you are aware of." He slides a bag through the bars. "This is some food and water to hold you over until I return."

"Wesley, you can't keep me here." I plead, a sob threatening. "This is ridiculous! I will leave Traymel alone; just let me go."

His head falls back as he laughs. "Do you find me a fool? The minute

I let you go, you will go to the cops. I gave you a chance to leave Mel alone, and you did not. Now enjoy imprisonment." Dropping the bag to the ground, he walks down the hallway, closing the door at the end and leaving me alone.

I pull against the bars in frustration. I feel as if I am in some twisted Netflix movie or a thriller novel. *I am never going to get out of here.* Kyla and Lynn would never expect Wesley to be capable of this, and only the boys know about this place—and that is only if they remember. *Will anyone even believe I was kidnapped?*

Glancing at the bag, I decide to eat to keep my strength up. There are two turkey and swiss sandwiches, a banana, three apples, an inch-square chocolate brownie wrapped in Saran Wrap, and five water bottles. Deciding to ration my food now since I have no idea when he will return, I eat half of one of the sandwiches with the banana and a bottle of water. Looking around my surroundings again, I only now notice there is no bed. He left me with only a thin sleeping bag on the ground. *Just great!* I sit on it Indian style and blankly stare in front of me. *I guess now I wait. Maybe he will come to his senses and let me go.*

I understand that Wesley is caught up with this childhood love of Traymel that he has not shaken, but I don't see how he came up with the bright idea to lock me up, putting me through this ordeal for such a simple reason. Here I am, fighting with my own love life, yet I would not go to such drastic extremes. *Why would he not just make me look bad? Try to run me over. Hell, destroy my career since it has just begun. My job!*

I have an important meeting with the board Monday, and I am here. After a month of taking the reins, I must give an update on the progress of my department. I have been doing well by not arriving late, to set an example. I've memorized all the names of my staff and the major clients. My late nights have been filled with overflowing paperwork to ensure my success.

Hours later, I awake with a jolt. My body trembles in the cold air. The sad excuse for the blanket is wrapped around my legs. I rub my eyes with the back of my hand while rotating my head to work the stiffness from my neck. I am surprised I fell asleep. I do not know what time it is, considering I am underground and surrounded by concrete.

Standing to my feet, I reach for the ceiling, my bones cracking. As I head over to the bag for another snack, I notice a sleeping bag with a pillow and three cylindrical white pills in a small cup. Relieved to have something warmer and comfier, I lay out the sleeping bag and place the pillow on top. The pills could be Tylenol, but I cannot be 100 percent certain. I am currently in a hostage position, and my captor drugging me would not be all that surprising. My headache is now back to a light thudding.

After eating the other half of the sandwich and finishing another water, I lie beneath the thick material of the sleeping bag, sighing. Sleep is no longer deadening my senses. Instead I am again lost in my thoughts—lost to find myself in this current situation.

My fingers glide over my newest tattoo, the butterfly. I smile at the memory of being with my friends as we celebrated all we have been through. We have always found ways out of our messes. Now I am caged, missing the freedom that I took advantage of everyday. Tears prickle at my eyes as I fight a sob. I seem to be unable to find a way out of this mess.

Days pass—from what I can assume, as I have lost track of time. My food supply has diminished, and I am nursing the last bottle of water. My clothes are dirty, and I smell horrible. I have moved the sleeping bag to the corner of the cell opposite the toilet that just so happens to be unable to flush, hoping for relief from the rancid odor. My tears have long dried up, and now I am left with only a numb feeling. *Am I going to die here?*

Nineteen

I lie on my back, staring absently at the ceiling. This position, along with walking the length of the cell in circles, has been the only thing that has helped the time go by and prevented me from going insane. My thoughts are no longer of my friends, as they have turned into morbid scenes. I am questioning whether anyone is looking for me or whether anyone cares that I have been kidnapped. Perhaps they believe I ran away. I keep up hope that Lynn and Kyla know I would not do something like that. We have all been so engrossed in our own lives and problems that they may think it became too much for me and I needed a mental break. I did always take random trips home in the middle of the week during college when my grades were not too great.

The door at the end of the hall opens. I sit up to see who my visitor is after all this time, hoping someone else besides Wesley will find me here. With my luck, that is not the case. It is only my captor who comes sauntering to the bars.

"Gosh, Zola!" Wesley says, scrunching up his face. "It reeks in here."

"Says the person who left me here for days with a broken toilet!" I snap, standing to my feet. "I need a bath. Real food. Let me out, Wesley."

"It has only been five days. And I agree, you need a bath." He drops a duffel bag on the floor at his feet. "Unfortunately, that is not possible at the moment. Because of that nosy friend of yours, I have to move up my plans." Bending over, he digs through the contents, coming up with something white in his hands. "Take off that sweatshirt and put this on."

My eyes sweep to his hand before moving back to his face. "My nosy friend?"

He groans in annoyance. "Lynn. She went to the cops! They now have your picture posted around town and put an APB on your car. I assumed cops did not worry about kidnappings of adults. I thought surely everyone would just believe you would run away." He tosses whatever is in his hand at me, causing me to recoil from it. "It is just a shirt. Hurry up! We have to move while they are changing shifts."

Maybe there will be a chance I can get away. I pick up the shirt and turn my back, slipping out of the sweatshirt and pulling on the tank. Turning back to him, I see a rope and a roll of duct tape on the ground next to the bag. He is holding a pair of handcuffs in his hands.

"Come closer, with your hands held out," he instructs.

I smirk as I close the distance between us. It is funny that he assumes I will do anything he says willingly. Closing my fists, I raise my arms for him. When he reaches for me, I grab his arm and pull, slamming his face against the bars.

"Bitch!" he shouts, grabbing his nose, which is bleeding profusely. "You will pay for that." He digs through the bag, coming up with a towel he places over his face, leaning his head back.

"You're supposed to lean forward, jackass." I roll my eyes and resume sitting on the sleeping bag. "Unless you are letting me free, I am not going anywhere with you." I cross my arms across my chest, sending him a murderous glare. I feel so much better now.

"I do not have time for this." He pulls out some keys from his pocket, opens the door to the cell, and steps inside.

Jumping to my feet, I rush him, hoping to get the upper hand. Regrettably, I do not notice the stun gun behind his back until it is too late. It connects with my chest, and volts shoot through my body as I shake violently. I collapse to the ground, unimaginable pain and tremors overcoming me. Wesley flips me over to my stomach, handcuffing my hands behind my back. Drool coats my lips as I try to catch my breath from the aftermath. Wesley places a strip of duct tape over my lips.

As he hauls me to my feet, I struggle in his grasp for balance. "Pull a stunt like that again and I will raise the voltage." He yanks hard on my arm, pulling me toward the door of the cell.

As we make our way down the hallway, dizziness becomes an issue for me. My vision begins to blur, and I stumble, falling against the wall. "I don't feel so good." I acknowledge, closing my eyes to stop the spinning room.

We take a few more steps before I am pushed to sit down in a wheelchair. Then he wheels me up to an elevator on the other side of the door. It stops at the parking garage beneath the hotel. He steps out, pushing me before him to his Expedition, which so happens to be parked next to my car. *How did that get here?*

"Get in!" he orders, opening the back door.

Not wanting to experience being shocked again, I slowly stand as best I can with my hands cuffed behind my back. Just as I am up to my feet, I am shoved from behind, and I fall face-first onto the seat. Wesley lifts my legs inside before slamming the door. Leaving the wheelchair, he hops into the driver's seat.

"Don't … make …a … sound," he threatens as he pulls out of the parking spot.

I wiggle to a sitting position. We drive through the garage's maze until we reach a ramp that leads to the exit. The sun is shining bright. I feel it has been forever since I have been in the fresh air. Five days seems like a long time underground. It is an experience I would love to never have to endure again. Just as we reach the street, I see a group of people standing outside the hotel's entrance. I try to scream for their attention, forgetting the tape across my lips. Instead, all I can hear is muffled grunts and shrills. Wesley slams on his brakes, reaches behind him, and smacks me across the side of my face, his ring cutting me near my eye. I take the hint and remain silent the rest of the way.

It is about a fifteen-minute ride until we pull up to a spacious one-story house in a quaint neighborhood. Kids are running along the sidewalks. He pulls the Expedition into the garage and closes the door. A gasp escapes my lips when he takes a gun out of the glove box. Tucking it into his waistband, he steps out. He walks to the door leading into the house, slipping a key into the lock before going inside. I sit there wondering whether I should follow him or stay put. A point was made clear when I saw he was in possession of a firearm. Nothing I can do at the moment will win out.

He soon returns, changed into more laid-back clothing. Opening the back door, he motions for me to step out. I stare back, not moving. Rolling his eyes, he grabs my ankle and pulls me to the edge of the seat before yanking me out by the arm. I trip over my feet as he drags me inside the house. I see a glimpse of a large kitchen and dining room table. We proceed into the living room. All the lights are turned off with the blinds closed, leaving the room in complete darkness other than the glow of the lit fireplace.

He places me in a chair positioned off to the side of the fireplace, next to some rather large house plants. Bending to his knees, he ties my ankles to the legs of the chair with some rope.

"All right. You take a nap now so I can get some things together before our guest arrives," Wesley states, pouring some liquid on a towel. *Nap? I am far from tired.* The next thing I know, he places the towel over my nose. I inhale the strong stench of the liquid as my eyes get heavy. *Of course, chloroform!* I have only seen it used in the movies. Within seconds, I am out.

"Zola, wake up!" I feel someone gently slapping my cheek, trying to see whether I am conscious.

"You won't wake her now. She is currently drugged," I hear Wesley inform the person.

I fight to open my eyes, straining, inhaling a deep breath of air not tainted with that chemical. Slowly I crack my eyes open, millimeter by millimeter, and I begin rapidly blinking to gain my senses.

In front of me is a squatting Traymel. A sorrowful expression shows on his face in the light from the still burning fire behind him. I try to say something, yet nothing comes out but a mumble. *The tape.* Traymel, noticing my issue, slowly peels the tape from my lips, leaving a light burning sensation on my skin.

"Traymel?" I whisper, still a little out of it, trying to get my bearings.

"Well, well. Welcome to the party, Ms. Saunders," Wesley says as he comes up behind Traymel, a wicked smirk across his face. His nose is bandaged from his run-in with the bars earlier.

"Wesley, what is going on?" Traymel asks in horror. "Why is she tied to the chair?"

"Ugh! Can we get to her after we eat?" Wesley asks nonchalantly, as though having someone tied up in his living room is a common occurrence. "Let me check on the chicken."

"No, Wes! Are you fucking crazy?" Traymel shouts, turning his way, causing me to jump from the loud noise. He stands to his feet. "I am going to untie her and get her to the hospital. She is not looking so good."

"Do not touch her, Mel." Wesley hisses, holding up a large knife in his hands.

Traymel glimpses down at the knife, holding up his hands as he speaks calmly, trying to defuse the situation. "Wes, tell me why Zola is tied up in your house?" His gaze returns to his friend. "Are you the one that kidnapped her?"

"Yes!" I quickly confirm before Wesley tries to come up with an excuse. The word scratches against my dry throat. *So no one believed I ran away. That's a relief!*

Dropping the hand holding the knife to his side, Wesley glares at me. "I was trying to have this conversation after we ate and spent some time together. She was supposed to be the big finale." He gestures to me with his free hand, exhaling. "Have a seat so we can discuss everything."

Traymel looks my way as my eyes are pleading for him to free me. I squirm against the restraints. Instead he walks to one of the sofas and sits on the edge, keeping his eyes trained on Wesley. My lips tilt in a small frown. I am baffled as to why he is letting me just sit here tied up. Surely he can overtake Wesley with just his size and strength. *Maybe I am not that important to him.*

"I guess I can start from the obvious. I did kidnap Zola that night she came over to your place."

Arching an eyebrow, Traymel interrupts him. "The *night?* She slept over and didn't leave until morning."

Wesley sneers. "No! I went into your apartment and sedated both of you before taking her from your clutches." His free hand balls into a fist as he walks closer to where I am still tied up. "My heart was pained, seeing you both naked in an embrace, content. It should have been me wrapped in your arms."

He continues his short stride until he is standing right in front of me, his eyes full of hatred—the same hatred I have seen since I woke up in that cell. He sees me as nothing but an obstacle to achieving a greater goal.

Wesley leans forward at the hips, raising his hand toward me. My eyes bulge as I catch sight of the knife, its sharp tip inches from my midsection. My heart rate accelerates. I suck in my stomach to give myself some distance from the cold metal. The action does not go unnoticed, as a smirk graces his lips.

"I should have been there since the beginning, before all those useless … idiotic … women infiltrated your life, breaking your heart." His teeth clench. I let out a deep breath when he turns from me to face Traymel again. "I had to get rid of her just like the rest. However, women these days are harder to manipulate the older they get." He shrugs. "So it got a little extreme."

I am still curious how he dealt with the other girls. I know my luck with men is not the greatest, but to be kidnapped and on the brink of losing my life …I mean, I am not even dating the guy. Right when I finally was starting to get my life back on track.

I peer over at Traymel. Shock is evident across his features as he listens to his best friend reveal his darkness. Wesley fooled us all into thinking he was an upbeat and positive person who hardly ever got upset. Instances would just roll off his shoulders without him showing any emotion or any indication that they bothered him—a trait many people lack. Emotions can be a strong force, causing people to act out of character in difficult situations and giving them courage to do what needs to be done. It seems Wesley just kept those daunting emotions hidden inside, letting them simmer until they erupted.

"She was supposed to rot in that cell until I confessed my love and you chose me as your happy ever after. I would—"

"Rot in that cell!" I blurt, interjecting. "For fucking your friend?" My anger surfaces as I remember those five long days underground in that place. Freezing against the hard concrete. Rationing small amounts of unsustainable food. Breathing in those rotten smells. Waiting for my freedom. Praying that he would soon come to his senses. Unfortunately, that was not the case. If it was not for Lynn, I would still be in that undesirable situation. *Not that my current predicament is any better.*

Wesley continues as if I have not even spoken. "I would have made you forget you ever met her. Our love is true and could be magical." He moves toward Traymel and squats right in front of him. "Just think about it, Mel. We already have a strong bond that we created throughout our childhood. First love shall always prevail."

Various facial expressions flash across Mel's features: first disbelief, secondly confusion, thirdly shock, and lastly sadness. "You love me? Like, more than friends?" he asks incredulously.

"Don't seem so surprised," Wesley retorts, his fist tightening on the handle of the knife.

"I am not trying to make light of the situation. I'm just confused at what I have just learned. I am sorry to say, but I do not feel the same." Traymel's head hangs low, his knees spread open. "You are like a brother to me, and I respect and love you in a nonintimate way."

Wesley closes his eyes and takes a deep breath before standing to his feet. "That is unfortunate. I was really hoping this would end in a different way."

It took me a second to understand his meaning before he lunged at Traymel the knife aimed at his chest. I suck in a breath, surprised at Wesley turning against his beloved. Traymel rolls off the sofa at the last second and begins to crawl away. Wesley jumps onto his back, knocking them to the floor, bringing the knife near Traymel's neck.

"I don't want to fight you, Mel," Wesley huffs in his ear, perspiration forming atop his forehead.

"Then don't!" Traymel's elbow connects with Wesley's side, catching him off guard. He uses the moment of hesitation to move from under him, the knife slicing his cheek in the process. *Finally he is using force and getting the upper hand.* Falling on his back, Mel leans up, using his right fist to uppercut Wesley in the jaw with full force. Wesley's head snaps to the side, and the knife slips from his hand and clatters to the floor. Blood and sweat mix together on Traymel's face as he stands to his feet.

I hop up and down in the chair, still trying to wiggle my body from the restraints. The movement catches the attention of Traymel, who looks up before heading in my direction. Wesley charges him, crashing them atop the coffee table, which breaks on impact. A gasp escapes my lips as a sickening crack of bone echoes in the room.

Wesley takes advantage of being on top, and rain punches down on Traymel as he holds his arms out in front him, blocking the majority of the hits. Traymel then knees Wesley in the chest before delivering a right hook to his temple, knocking him into the couch.

Traymel swipes his hand across his face and crawls in my direction. Reaching me, he begins undoing the knot at my feet. I look over his head, meeting Wesley's cold eyes, which stare back at me with such contempt as he struggles to his feet, knife in hand. Mine instantly widen as Wesley once again lunges toward us.

I open my mouth to utter a warning to Traymel of his impending doom. However, I am too late. As if sensing the motion behind him, Traymel turns just as Wesley is upon him, the forgotten knife piercing his flesh. Time seems to still as I watch the next few minutes in slow motion: The blade digging deeper from the force of Wesley's movement. Traymel's hand automatically reaching for the point of impact as he locks eyes with Wesley's tearful ones.

"M-Mel! I love you," Wesley wails, dropping his hand from the knife embedded in his chest near his heart. "Why did you make me do this?"

Traymel falls to his back, staring at the ceiling, as his breathing becomes labored. My screams shrill in the room as he slowly fades away.

Twenty

My screams soon turn into dry sobs as I stare at Traymel's unconscious form lying on the floor. Blood is leaking from the wound in his chest, which is slowly rising from staggered breaths. *Did Wesley really stab his best friend—the one he claims to have loved since they were younger?*

"Mel, wake up," cries Wesley as he leans over Traymel, shaking his form. "Wake up!"

"You *monster!* I cannot believe you really stabbed him!" I yell, resuming my efforts to free myself from the chair. "Don't just sit there; call the EMS."

"Shut up, you bitch!" he bellows through clenched teeth. "This is your fault! If you would have just kept your legs closed, we would not be in this predicament."

"My fault? You kidnapped me!" I shake my head. "You are one crazy person."

He stands to his feet and closes the distance between us. "I am *not crazy!*" The back of his hand connects with my face, busting my lip on contact. The metallic taste of blood trickles in my mouth. The chair teeters from the force. He turns his back on me, and his hands rake through his hair as he begins pacing. "This is not how this was all supposed to go. My whole plan just keeps backfiring."

I glance at Traymel. "Wes, please! Call 911. He still has a chance to live."

"Yeah, so I can go to jail!" He pulls at his strands. "I need to come up with a plan that does not involve me getting caught with everything that is going on." He stops his pacing and begins snapping his fingers. "How will Mel ever forgive me and give us a chance?"

I roll my eyes. He still believes he can have a life with him. I do not understand what was going through his mind when he came up with this hare-brained idea. Wesley is clearly off his rocker.

A loud whirling noise blares from the kitchen as smoke begins to float into the living room. *Is something on fire?* Wesley takes off toward the kitchen. I put my last efforts into pulling my feet from the binds holding me to the chair. The cuffs rub against my already raw wrists as I twist them every which way. Just as I get one foot out, the chair rocks to the side before losing balance and crashing me to the floor. I sit up, my hands still cuffed behind my back.

It seems there is a growing fire in the back of the house. The smoke alarm in the living room joins the one from the kitchen as more smoke pours into the area, tainting what little clean air we have. Wesley still has yet to return.

I peer toward Traymel who still has not moved. The smoke clog my airways, sending me in a frenzy of coughing. I duck further against the floor as my eyes burn from the vapors. Luckily, I hear approaching sirens in the distance. I pray to myself that Traymel is still okay and keeps fighting until help has arrive. I fight a wave of dizziness from the inhalation as firemen rush into the room. *Yes, we are saved!*

A persistent beeping noise awakes me. My body feels stiff as I shift against an uncomfortable bed. As I open my eyes, the bright light causes me to quickly snap them back closed. I groan, raising my hand over my face to block out the brightness. Trying again, I slowly open one eye until it adjusts, followed by the other. A long tube is taped to the back of my hand and running under my bed. The noise is coming from a heart monitor beside my head.

I place my hand back in my lap, looking around. This is clearly a hospital room, as evidenced by the bland white walls, the small TV hanging in the corner of the room, my being connected to a hundred machines as though I might die at any moment—and let us not forget the unfashionable gown. I have had my share of hospital visits—not for myself, but for my brother, who seemingly had a death wish when he was younger. I hesitantly sit up in the bed just as Lynn walks into the room.

"Zola! You are awake." She rushes over and engulfs me in a hug. "I just knew something was up when you disappeared."

"Ahh!" I squeak, wincing in her arms as my face presses into her boobs. "Traymel! Is he okay?"

"He is currently in surgery." She lets go, frowning. "The knife missed his heart, which is a blessing."

"And Wesley?" I wiggle to find a comfortable position. "This isn't motorized?"

"He wasn't there when the firemen arrived." She leans over, picking up a remote hanging beside the bed.

I adjust the head until I am completely sitting up, and I sigh in relief. That other position was bothering my neck. "Wasn't there? How is that possible?"

She clasps both of her hands over mine. Completely ignoring my question, she asks, "What happened? Where have you been the last few days?"

Before I can respond, the hospital door swings open again, and in walk Lamar and Nicole. "La! You ever scare us like that again, I will personally pummel you for everyone," Lamar states, walking over to tightly hug me, cutting off my airflow.

"Let her breathe, jackass," Nicole says before smacking him upside his head. I giggle at my crazy siblings. "Zola, how are you feeling? What happened?"

"Ms. Saunders, glad to see you are awake," announces the doctor who joins us in the room, again interrupting my explanation. "I just need to check your vitals. There is a cop outside waiting to take your statement. You had a mild case of smoke inhalation and dehydration upon arrival, but after some rest and fluids you should be okay. I will be able to release you soon."

I nod as he scribbles on his clipboard before exiting the room. A cop enters shortly after his departure to ask me questions. I relate the series of events to everyone in the room, getting it out of the way at once. The cop assures me that he will put an APB out for Wesley and that he will be held accountable for his crimes.

Once he leaves, I am bombarded with more questions by everyone until all the details have been covered to their satisfaction. Lamar threatens to kill Wesley on sight if he gets to him before the cops. *My overprotective brother.*

Lincoln comes to check on me and informs us that Traymel's surgery went well with few complications and that he has been placed in a medically-induced coma to recover. That is when I notice that Kyla is missing.

"Lynn, where is Kyla?" I inquire, changing into some clothes she brought from home. It is after midnight once I am released.

"She didn't answer when I called to let her know you had been located. I sent her a text."

We all pile into Lynn's car and head to the condo. As we pull up, I notice someone sitting on our steps. Lamar assists me out of the car, and we all walk toward the person. Familiar knotted brown hair falls from the woman's bent head, which lies atop her knees.

"Kyla?" I ask with apprehension.

She glances up at us with a tear-streaked face and puffy eyes.

Nicole comes up behind me. "Gurl, what is wrong with you?"

"Damien"—she hiccups through her sobs—"Damien walked out on me."

Lynn rushes to her side and pulls her into a hug. "Did you tell him about Lincoln?"

Nicole arches an eyebrow. "Lincoln? Did I miss something?"

"It seems this conversation is between you girls," suggests Lamar. "I'll go make us some dinner while y'all catch up on everything." He takes Lynn's keys from her.

"Aw, Marly! Ain't you just the sweetest," I taunt as I squeeze his cheek. He rolls his eyes as he helps me the rest of the way in the house and leaves us all to chat in the sunroom.

"Zola! I am sorry I did not make it to the hospital. Are you okay?" Kyla remarks, wiping her nose with a tissue from the box in front of her.

"I am fine, sha, and we will get on that topic later. Tell me about this whole Damien situation," I say, leaning toward her to catch every word.

Kyla takes a deep breath and goes into detail. She explains about sleeping with Lincoln again after meeting him at the same hotel I was kept underneath. *Seems the others do frequent the place.* He had a rooftop date awaiting her because she owed him for him not outing her to her husband one day at the mall last month.

She once again blames the indiscretion on alcohol and confusion. She will need to accept the truth sooner or later if she wants to get through this situation. Lincoln took matters in his own hands, setting up a meeting with Damien at his office and spilling the beans regarding all the sordid details of his relationship with his wife. I knew that if he heard it from someone else—especially the other party of his wife's affair, he would flip.

My heart is heavy on hearing that my friend went through this ordeal by herself. I determine that when I see Lincoln again, I will beat the living daylights out of him. How dare he intervene in my friend's marriage? I understand her role, but it took two to tango. He did not need to handle it in that way. Once she is finishes, she is again in tears as Lynn holds her in her arms, rocking her like a baby.

"Did Damien ask for a divorce?" Nicole asks, looking as though she is watching a soap opera.

"H-h-he just said he can't deal with this right now," stutters Kyla, still in Lynn's embrace.

"Well, just give him some time, Ky," I suggest. "Let the idea of this settle in, and hopefully he will not let this come between you. It is a bigger blow hearing it from Lincoln than you. I am sure he felt like a fool, and that's not good for a man's ego." I can remember the many times Lamar got upset if one of his women tried to play him—even if he was the one in the wrong.

"I want to strangle Lincoln right now!" Kyla proclaims, swiping at her teary eyes.

"Whew! To say y'all always be on my case with Ethan," Nicole remarks, playing with her nails. "The men problems between y'all ain't no better."

"Really, Nikki?" I side-eye my sister.

"What? I am just stating the facts," She replies innocently, shrugging her shoulders.

"Food is ready, ladies," announces Lamar as he strides into the room.

"Good! I am too hungry right now." Nicole stands from the couch and heads to the kitchen.

Lynn squeezes Kyla's shoulder before standing up and following my sister. I stand and take Kyla's hand and pull her to her feet. We engulf each other in a hug that is much needed considering today has been rough for us both.

"Now, what is this I hear about you being kidnapped?" Kyla asks as we break apart from each other.

"Guhhhh!" My arm links with hers, and we head into the kitchen after the others as I tell her my story of the love triangle I unexpectedly found myself in, hitting the major points.

Our meal of burgers and fries turns into many laughs among our crew as we all try not to think about all the troubles we have faced in these past few months. We're all trying to move forward on the paths we now find ourselves on, enjoying a brief but welcome break in not having to worry what may come next. We are not even contemplating the choices that were made to put us in our predicaments.

Twenty-One

We all crash and sleep late into the morning hours. It is not until late the following afternoon that I wake up in my own bed. A wide smile is spread across my lips. After being in that makeshift cage for five days and undergoing the hospital visit, it is a wonderful feeling to be home, safe and around my family and friends. Staring at my ceiling, I thank the Lord for allowing me to get out of that ordeal in one piece.

Ring! Ring! Ring!

I reach over to my nightstand to grab my phone. Last night the cops delivered my car, which was still parked in the parking garage of that hotel. My phone was turned off and hidden in the glove box.

Seeing Travis's name on the screen, I smile. "Hey, Yooh!"

"Baby, are you all right?" His voice quavers with weariness on the line. "Lamar informed me on some of the details last night. I can fly out there tonight."

"Travis, that is not necessary." I lie on my back, cradling the phone against my cheek. "I will be back home in a month, and I assure you I am fine. It was just a scary experience I want to forget and move on from."

He sighs on the other end. "Are you sure you still want to be in the wedding?"

"Of course!" I exclaim. "My only sister is getting married, and I will not miss that."

"If you are *sure* you are okay … I will wait to see you next month. My dad is back in the country, but work is still stressful. He is even more adamant these days about retiring. That traveling spoiled him." He chuckles. The sound warms my heart. "I miss you so much! How I want to feel your soft lips against mine."

I roll my eyes as a light blush graces my cheeks. There are still some undecided feelings I need to figure out with the men in my life, especially since my involvement with one put my life at risk. *Will I let it put an end to what Traymel and I were building?* "I miss you too. Let me call you later; there is some business I need to attend to."

"You'd better not be going to work today," he reprimands. I am sure he is scowling as we speak.

"Work pays bills, so if I was, that's none of your concern," I retort, sitting up. "However, to smooth your ruffled nerves, no, I am not going to work."

"Good!" He says. I snicker. "I will talk to you later."

I hang up, rolling out of bed and heading to my bathroom to get ready. After I am dressed in jeans and a simple tee, I head downstairs to see my siblings chatting in the living room.

"Well, runt, we need to get out of here to make it to our flight on time," Lamar says, standing at my appearance. He advances on me before taking me in his arms and lifting me off the floor. "You stay out of all this craziness. I will ship you back home if anything else happens."

"Ugh! I am a grown woman, Marly," I remark, squeezing his neck tightly. "I can take care of myself. And put me down."

"Yes, you did a good job taking care of yourself a couple of days ago," Nicole mocks, standing to her feet. I cut my eyes at her over our brother's shoulder, causing her to burst out in laughter.

"Thanks for being on my side."

She pokes her tongue at me. "Come on, sis, and drop us off. I am not tryna pay for no Uber."

Rolling my eyes, I pinch Lamar's ears to get him to put me down. It sucks that they must leave already. I enjoy having them around. They put me in a state of peace. I had forgotten about my problems as I spent time with them last night.

I grab my keys, and we all pile into my car. Lynn must be at school. After I drop them off at the airport and we do a last round of hugs, I decide to head over to the hospital to check on the condition of Traymel.

He is currently in the ICU, still under the influence of the drugs keeping him in his coma. Wesley luckily missed his heart, but he did pierce a lung, which caused a large amount of internal bleeding. He is currently not permitted visitors other than family. *Guess I can wait until he is released.*

As I stroll back to my car, my phone rings in my pocket. I pull it out, and an unrecognized number flashes on my screen. Ignoring the call, I slip into the driver's seat, tossing my phone on the passenger side. As I start the engine, the phone vibrates. The same number appears on my car's dashboard. Checking my watch, I read the message: "Death will knock at your door sooner than you think."

The sound inside my car fades as a roaring fills my ears. A feeling of suffocation overcomes my senses. I stare vacantly as I reread the message over and over, wishing it would disappear so I would not have to endure this state of shock.

A knock on my window startles me, and I whip my head at the person leaning outside the glass. An older man in a security uniform points down at the floorboards. Only then do I notice that I am still in park, with my foot completely depressing the gas pedal in front of the hospital.

Quickly removing it, I shyly wave at the man before pulling off from the curb. Ignoring his shouts to gain my attention, I race to the highway, gaining distance from an unknown force. I am sure that was Wesley that texted me and he somehow knows I was there to see Traymel. I would not be surprised if he were somewhere lurking in the shadows. A chill runs through me.

Deciding it is best not to be alone, I take a detour to Kyla's house, hoping that is where she is. As I pull up in the driveway, I see her vehicle along with Lincoln's. *Oh no! Not again, Kyla.*

After parking behind her car and next to his truck, I hop out and head to the front door. As I reach to ring the doorbell, I pause when I hear sounds of shouting through the door. It sounds as if they are arguing. I press my ear firmly against the wood to hear the conversation a little better.

"It has all been a mistake, Lincoln, and I need you to accept it and move on."

Something crashes to the floor. "I'm not accepting anything, because you want me just as much as I want you."

"Damien is my husband!"

I nod against the door. *You tell him!*

He chuckles. "The husband you cheated on with me on multiple occasions. The husband that no longer lives here. The husband that cannot make you feel the way I do."

"*Get the hell out!*" she screeches loudly enough for the block to hear.

"I will leave for now"—his voice moves closer to the door—"but you'd better get it together."

"Don't you threaten me, Mr. Crane."

"That isn't a threat." The door opens, causing me to lose my position and almost topple to the ground. "It is a promise." Lincoln turns to the door before stopping midstep when he catches sight of me.

"Zola!" exclaims Kyla behind him. "What are you doing here? Are you okay?"

"Um, I—" I glance at Lincoln. "Why are you here? Haven't you done enough damage?"

He arches an eyebrow.

Kyla barrels past him and engulfs me in a hug. "Come in, La. Lincoln was just leaving."

Lincolns glares at her. "Kyla, we will finish this conversation." He nods my way before moving to his truck, hopping in, and driving off.

I follow Kyla into the house after she walks back in toward the kitchen. That ugly animal-print vase Damien got her a few years ago is in pieces in the doorway of the living room. *Good riddance!* She grabs two glasses and pours us both some wine.

"So I have to know what that was about, because it seemed intense," I observe. She exhales before handing me my glass and taking a sip from her own.

"I called him in a fit of anger this morning when I couldn't fall asleep, crying and cursing him out before hanging up in his face and finally blocking him." She takes another sip. "He took it upon himself to show up on my doorstep and then barged his way in." Kyla looks up at me, her eyes red and puffy from her nonstop crying. I can see she is trying her hardest to fight back another wave of tears. "Zola, I really want my husband back."

I place my glass on the counter and reach for her, pulling her into my arms. Soon I join her with my own tears, having my own battle over that mystery text, knowing that my freedom was taken from me the minute

Wesley kidnapped me and that I will forever be on the lookout until he is captured and locked away. He is on a mission to destroy me, and he is determined to be with Traymel. We rock from side to side in our misery, finding strength in each other.

I spend the rest of the week holed up in my room, in a dark abyss of emotions, not settling on one thought. My family constantly calls and texts me about my well-being, begging me to come home for a while and take a break from my busy life.

Lynn brings me food throughout the day, though I have no appetite to eat. The thought makes my stomach unsettle—something I would be troubled by if my mind were not already occupied with everything else.

Traymel is out of the ICU and will be released tomorrow. He has been contacting me nonstop, but I just do not have the energy to speak to him. That involvement was not his doing, and he was a victim as well. However, I am not in the right state of mind to discuss the nightmare I endured. I sent my well wishes via Lynn when she delivered flowers from the company as a gesture to show we appreciate our clients and are there for them in their times of trouble.

Mr. Mitchell informed me that my job is secure and that I can return whenever need be. Many have suggested I attend counseling to cope with the ordeal, but talking to a stranger about my troubles is not something I am comfortable doing. I would just feel like an idiot spouting my insecurities to a complete stranger while paying him or her hundreds of dollars to listen and direct me to find my own answer. *I mean, since I will ultimately learn the answer, why not just wait for it to appear on its own?* My best bet is to get back in the spin of things and lose myself in the struggles of daily life. I cannot stay cooped up for long; being alone is not serving my sanity well.

Monday morning, I return to work bright and early. Lynn was adamant about driving me, and I allowed her to lessen her worry. She believes I am a ticking time bomb that will detonate at any moment.

After that day with Kyla, I have not shed another tear about the incident. I also have not received any more threatening messages. Wesley was spotted at the hospital two days ago but was able to shake the people chasing him. He has left the city limits for now.

"Zola, these just came for you," mentions my assistant, Rachel, as she walks into my office. Being a part of the board, I have been granted my own personal assistant. It is weird having someone else run errands and do paperwork for me.

In her hands is a bundle of balloons. A large black-and-gold one with large writing on it that reads "Welcome Back" is surrounded by an array of regular black, gold, and red ones. I smirk at the display.

Setting the weight on my desk, she hands me a card. "Most people would send flowers; balloons are a first," she notes, eyeing the colorful display.

I glance at the card. "Because anyone who knows me knows I do not like flowers." Sure enough, they were sent by Travis. He was upset last night about my unyielding decision to return to work today. Our conversation ended in us arguing and me hanging up on him and blocking his contact. I guess he is trying to apologize.

"Well, you are a strange woman." She sets some files on my table. "Your meeting with the board is in twenty minutes, and then a lunch appointment with DrakeShades. Nelson has dropped the ball twice on their advertising package, and they are ready to pull out their account."

I groan in frustration. "I was hoping he would have shaped up on my little vacation."

Rachel eyes me skeptically. "I am sure what you just experienced wouldn't be considered a vacation." I shrug. "Again, strange woman."

I laugh. "Have Nelson meet with me this afternoon. He'd better cross his fingers I fix this today, or he will be clearing out his desk."

She nods, walking out.

This is exactly what I need—problems I can control and handle. I should have dragged myself out of that room and ignored everyone's suggestion to take a break. Sitting still has never been my forte.

Twenty-Two

Traymel swings open the door when I knock, causing a gasp to catch in my throat. A bare chest blocks my line of sight. I remember those wide panes that my fingertips explored that magnificent night—as smooth as a baby's bottom. His nipples harden from the cold air filtering from his apartment. A scar from that horrific night, slowing fading on his left pectoral. Sweats hang low on his hips, exposing his deep V-line. A patch of hair swirls around his belly button … on a path to something greater.

His bulging eyes show he did not expect me to be standing there holding his takeout. I had to put in some effort to convince the delivery guy to let me take the food. He was hell-bent on making sure he saw it to its exact location, as though he would be terminated otherwise. *Like, dude, it is not that serious.*

He cocks an eyebrow at me. "You drive for DoorDash on the side?"

"No." I try to laugh, but instead the noise I make is a disgruntled grunt. "I met your driver at the entrance and took the liberty of bringing it to you since I was already on my way up."

"And he just believed you?"

"I am very convincing." I wink at him, hiding the fact it took some work. "Are you going to lemme in?" I ask, not sure how he feels about me ignoring him the past two weeks.

His eyes rake up my body as he takes me in. I am in rough shape after being kidnapped by his best friend and still trying to get a grip on things. I'm wearing some baggy olive joggers that stop midcalf, with a yellow tank top that loosely fits against my torso. My dreads are in my signature messy bun atop my head. I am sure the dark circles under my eyes evince my lack of sleep.

He steps to the side, taking the takeout from my hands. "Are you hungry? I am sure I can spare some." I close the door behind me before heading to the living room.

The wonderful smell wafts around me. I inhale a deep breath as my stomach lightly grumbles—but not in a good way. It makes me feel kind of sick. This is the norm these days. I have not eaten much lately because of all the stress. Weight is slowly disappearing from my curves.

Today my appetite was completely nonexistent since I was mustering up the courage to have this conversation. "That is okay! This is a quick visit," I answer, still standing in the foyer. I rub my hands together, my eyes darting around the room. Visions of that night that led to my nightmare seep into my thoughts.

Sitting on the couch, he opens the container and smiles in delight. He pops some fries in his mouth. "Um, okay. Would you like to sit?" Grabbing ahold of the mammoth burger, he takes a bite. His perfect white teeth pierce through the delightful bread, beef, veggies, and sauce—something that normally has me drooling but instead brings about a dry throat.

I shake my head, calming my nerves. "I think we need to call it quits." I quickly blurt out as he pauses from chewing and glimpses at me. "I have been confused over the past few months, and with everything that has happened ..." I drift off, licking my lips. "I just feel I should begin focusing on me and building my career. I am done with the men problems." I come to an end with a little more determination this time, knowing this is something I must do. It's what is best, no matter how much it may hurt.

Setting the burger down, he wipes his hands on a napkin as he finishes the food in his mouth. "So you aren't giving us a chance?" His gray eyes are pleading. "You know I suffered at Wesley's hands too."

I sigh, trying not to crack under the hurt I witness, not wanting to believe my words. "It is not just the Wesley situation."

"You sure?" He shifts in my direction, his eyes drilling into me. "Because all was good up until that point. Since then, you have ignored all my calls or texts. Hell, you didn't even stop to check up on me."

"I did come by the day after I was released, but only family was allowed."

My fist connects with my chest as I defend myself. "Lynn told me you were recovering, and I was still a little spooked about the kidnapping." I leave out the information about the text. I have yet to mention that to anyone. My chin drops as my head hangs low. "I just needed time to think."

"And the conclusion you came to was for us to stop dating," he hisses, slamming his hand on the coffee table.

I jump at the sound. "Technically we never started." My previous trepidation is now replaced by anger. *I have a right to think what I do.* "We were just in a phase of fun, and I was still conflicted with Travis." My eyes bulge and I bite my bottom lip as I realize I have slipped and said something I should not have said.

"Travis? As in Travis Sinclair?" His voice rises.

Crap!

"The son of one of the owners of ACME?"

I do not respond, trying to think of something to say to get myself out of this situation.

"What does he have to do with this?"

"He … he is my … Um." I stutter, looking around the room to avoid eye contact. It seems I may just have to tell him the truth. *Well, some of it.* "He's my first love, and we kind of connected when I went home for Jazz Fest."

"*What!*" Traymel roars as he shoots to his feet, anger apparent in his eyes. I step back, eyeing his tense stance. A vein pulses in his forehead. He strides toward me with controlled steps. "You have been screwing another man while you were with me?"

"We are not exclusive." I place my hands on my hips, appalled by his attitude. I do not recall us becoming official, allowing him to have some claim on me. He knows about my reservations regarding relationships. "I told you from the beginning I wanted to take things slow, and I gave you no promises."

He rubs his hands across his face, his nostrils flaring. I can sense him getting angrier by the moment, feeling some type of betrayal. He was trying to grow something special with me, and I was just not ready for that next step. *I should have never gone down this path. I should have ignored it at my first sign of hesitation.* The kidnapping finally gave me a clear view on everything that troubled me. I was given time to decide my next step.

"Wow! Wesley was right." He gestures toward me with a wave of his hand. "Another Melody in the making. You really are a slut."

I gasp a second before my palm connects with his cheek in a resounding slap. My palm faintly stings from the impact. "How dare you! To think I was ready to be with you and leave Travis," I express with glassy eyes.

Traymel looks at me with astonishment. "You can't be serious? You just broke up with me not even a second ago," he snaps.

Turning on my kicks, I head for the door, my fists clenching at my sides. Pain from the hurt of what he said boils in my chest. I do have feelings for him. Breaking it off was a difficult decision, but I did what is best for me.

"I guess Wesley got his wish!" I say, throwing the speech over my shoulder. "Thanks for opening my eyes to who you really are." I open the door and storm out before slamming it behind me. I hear something crash to the floor as I walk down the hall to the elevator.

Twenty-Three

It has been a whirlwind of craziness since we landed back in the city of New Orleans—our home. The beginning of our budding friendship bloomed into something genuine and lifelong—a friendship with a real bond of trust and support from someone other than blood relations. I could not be happier for the two girls I have by my side right now. I know our story will have many more chapters that will be written in the future.

"When is this rehearsal dinner?" Kyla asks as she walks into the room.

"In three hours," I reply with a yawn, just waking up from my nap by my friends talking.

"Look who is finally up. You been extra lazy this week. You still hurt over Traymel?" Lynn probes, plopping down onto the bed beside me.

I roll my eyes. "Did you forget? I am the one who broke up with Traymel." I place my right hand against my chest as I sit up. "Well, actually 'called it quits,' since we were technically not dating."

"Just make sure you keep that same attitude when you see Travis tonight," counters Lynn.

Kyla shakes her head at us and steps out onto the balcony. We decided to get an AirBNB for the wedding, since most of my family is down and occupying all the free rooms at Mom's house. Nicole moved in with Ethan three weeks ago, and Lamar still stays in his one-bedroom bachelor pad.

I join her outside as she looks down at the people bustling about along the streets, getting ready for the chaos that the weekend always brings to the city's center of New Orleans. During Halloween, you tend to see a variety of random things as folks dress up to celebrate the holiday.

A couple catches my eye as they make out in the shadows between a club and a daquiri shop. The man's hand slips under her skimpy dress and a second later, she moans against his lips.

"I guess he found his prize," Kyla comments, also watching the scene.

I hope they do not really plan to get it on in broad daylight. They say we Nawlins folks do crazy things, but even we have class. Well, most of us do. Lynn joins us. standing next to me. She catches sight of the couple, who have now started fucking against the wall. The woman's legs are wrapped around his waist as he pounds inside, his hands flat against the wall on both sides of her head. She is pulling at his strands.

"Are they serious?" she scoffs.

Kyla nods and shrugs as we continue to watch the show. It makes me think back to my wild days. Even I have never thought to do something so uninhibited.

"Didn't you have a few outside rendezvous in your younger days?" she asks, still gazing at the show. A smirk lifts the corners of her lips.

Lynn turns her way and gasps. "First off, I am still young, boo. Second, I didn't get caught." Looking back at the couple, she yells, "Get a room, you horny fools!"

The man jumps and looks up in our direction. The woman quickly unwraps her legs from his waist, and she scurries off along the street, pulling her dress down. He flips us off before chasing after his catch of the day, having a hard time pulling his pants up as he runs. We burst out laughing.

"Well, that was entertaining. I'm going to check on Jonathan to see if he is settled in and maybe get me some of that action like those two." Lynn says with a huge grin on her face.

"Ugh really! I do not need to know about your bedroom activities," Kyla asserts as we walk back into the room.

"Well, I didn't actually share the activities, but if you must know, I am going to bend over slowly and grab my ankles until my pu—"

"OMG, shut up, Lynn!" Kyla exclaims, putting her hand over Lynn's mouth to stop her revealing rant.

Lynn giggles before heading across the hall to the room she will share with Jonathan. Kyla and I are sharing this room since unfortunately we do not have plus-ones for the wedding. Since Lincoln blabbed about her infidelity, Damien moved out to live with one of his frat brothers. He has not asked for a divorce yet but also has not spoken much to her since their big blowup. I have been acting as the middleman when it comes to Jamar so he does not have to be bothered with her. She has tried many times to get him to talk and forgive her. However, he claims he needs space and time to think about whether their marriage is even worth fighting for.

I am trying to figure out how I plan to deal with Travis at the wedding, since I have once again been avoiding him. I am also still in a restless state because of the awkwardness Traymel and I have been having to deal with at work.

Kyla flops on her bed as the tears begin to collect in her eyes once again. I know she misses her husband so much and knows she did him wrong. I pray he does not allow this to be the end of them, but it is hard to tell. Trust is delicate. It requires ideal conditions to thrive. With this stunt, she has broken his faith in her, and she genuinely wants to win it back. Lincoln has been a nonstop pain in her ass though. He just cannot accept the fact that she does not want to build a life with him. Even I am a little skeptical about what she really wants her endgame to be.

"I have no idea what Lincoln thought he would accomplish by blowing up my marriage, but I for damn sure will not be running into his arms after the chaos he caused. I even put a restraining order against him, hoping it would diminish his advances."

She swipes at her eyes, staring up at the ceiling. "And I thought I had feelings for him. It was just my sexual infatuation because of all the problems Damien and I were dealing with. Lincoln was like a breath of fresh air that ended up being nothing but stagnant."

I do not understand how cheating is such a common factor in today's age. Why waste so much time building up a life with someone who is supposed to be important to you just to throw it all away? Probably because those women are too weak to fight the temptation.

Her cheek lies against the blanket as she looks in my direction when I sit on the bed next to hers. "I truly regret staying late at the bar that fateful night that allowed Lincoln to come into my life. I know I should have said something to Damien earlier." She stands from the bed to head to the bathroom. "I am going to take a long, hot shower."

On opening the door, we hear the moans from Lynn's room. *At least she had the decency to close the door.* One time in college when the three of us shared an apartment, Kyla and I came home after a class and caught Lynn banging the history professor. It was a sight that scarred us for months. However, the plus was that he gave us all passing grades that semester. I felt it was to silence us from ratting out his fornication with a student even though he had a wife and three kids at home.

I close the door to block out the noise and go back on the balcony. Looking up into a clear blue sky, I inhale a deep breath, letting my thoughts cease for just a moment. A noise rumbles in my stomach before a stabbing pain pierces me in my pelvic area. A wave of nausea passes over my taste buds.

Dashing through the room, I rush to the thankfully unlock bathroom, interrupting Kyla's shower. She peeks out from the curtain to see me throwing up our breakfast from that morning in the toilet.

"Gurl, are you sick?" she asks over my gagging.

I sit on the floor and wipe the back of my hand across my mouth, breathing in through my nose. "Bruh! I am just stressing over everything with the promotion at work, overcoming that Wesley and Traymel drama, dodging Travis's overbearingness, and then dealing with my sister and this wedding." My head lolls back against the wall. "It is taking a toll."

"Well, if you say so." She looks at me for second before returning to her shower.

I stand to my feet a minute later, close the toilet lid so she can flush it when she is done with her shower, and wash my hands and mouth. Ever since the kidnapping, I have been keeping myself busy to avoid dealing with all the fucked-up situations around me.

With the new promotion, life has changed for me in Lilac Essences. And then there is my decision on cutting out my bed-hopping days, no matter how much I miss the presence of both my men, to focus on my self-growth.

After locking myself away, I am relieved to be out and about. I'm happy with what I am embracing these days. I grab one of the bottles of wine I brought with me from the fridge and pour myself a glass. Yet I am unable to take a sip because my insides churn at the smell.

I set the glass back on the dresser, hoping I do not get sick again. Now that I think of it, I cannot even remember the last time I drank. That's unfortunate for me, considering alcohol has always been my go-to when I am in need to calm my nerves.

It was a hassle with the four of us trying to get ready for the rehearsal dinner with one bathroom. Kyla was glad she got her shower out of the way early. I should have followed suit before the lovebirds made a presence. Of course, Lynn and Jonathan decided to share a shower and, I quote, "speed the process along."

I am so glad we are getting ready for the wedding at the venue. Lamar picks us up from the house to brings us to the hotel for the dinner. Kyla sits in the front with him, leaving me in the back with the annoying duo. It will never not surprise me to see Lynn in a relationship. Because of all that happened with her mom with her father, she has always been against it. I am glad she gave Jonathan a chance. He is a good fit for her.

"You and Damien are still on the outs I see," speculates Lamar to Kyla.

"How did ... You know what, never mind." She looks over her shoulder to glare at me as I pretend to peer out the window. She cannot blame me for sharing with my family. She knows how nosy they can be.

"Don't blame her. It was actually Nikki who told me, and here you are for the wedding and no husband." *Way to go, Marly. Blame it on the sister who is not here. Wait! I am sure she will just believe I blabbed to Nicole, which, again, I did.*

"Yes, it does feel weird." She frowns, looking back out the windshield. "I haven't spoken to him in days."

"I never thought that the Goody Two-shoes Kyla would be unfaithful." I see him smirk in her direction as I return to eavesdropping on their conversation.

She punches his arm. "Shut up! It was a bad judgment call on my end. Hopefully he will forgive me in the end."

"Well, if he doesn't ... I can." He rubs one of his hands on the back of his neck. I peer at him when he stops midsentence, waiting for him to continue. "I can be here for you." *Ewww! Lamar still has the hots for my bestie.*

"Aww, thanks for that, Mar." She flutters her eyelashes at him. "I can use all the friends I can get." *Burn, Kyla! Love it!*

"I am sure he is not just trying to be your friend, stupid," I chime in, making my bad habit known. Kyla snaps her head in my direction before gawking at Lamar, who is slightly blushing. I do not know why she is trying to act as if she did not notice it.

"Mind ya business, Runt," he grouses.

"That is so cute! Lamar still has feelings for Kyla after all this time," teases Lynn from her place snuggled in Jonathan's arms. I thought she was sleeping this whole time. Her eavesdropping game is better than mine.

"Really, bruh!" Lamar states, looking at us both through the rearview mirror with a false scowl. "This is a conversation between Kyla and me."

I lean over the console and look up at my brother. "Next time don't have it in a car filled with other people." Lynn and Jonathan start laughing, and Kyla soon joins in too. I stick my tongue out at him as he quickly glances from the road at me.

We arrive at the hotel soon after. With me being the maid of honor, my mother whisks me away to help her with last-minute preparations. This is another bafflement of mine. How do I pay to help someone else celebrate, be her little maid, try my damndest to make her happy, and be the center of her wrath when something is not going her way?

Nicole has been a *major* bridezilla, and I am so excited that this whole shindig will be over come this weekend and we can move on from this. I will never be anyone else's maid of honor in the future. Kyla was not even this bad. I have wanted to strangle Nicole about a hundred times. For a minute there, I did not believe she was going to make it to her special day.

Once everyone is settled, the dinner is chaos. Both mothers are arguing up a storm, as are some of the other relatives. *Why do these people have to make a ruckus in this establishment?* Nicole bursts into tears, angry at their behavior, before throwing one of the wine bottles across the room. It crashes into pieces on its contact with the wall. Our cousin Troy had to duck down in his chair to not be hit. She storms out. Ethan is trying to calm down his mom while Lamar drags ours out. Mom had the upper hand on Mrs. Reid. She was our family's backbone after her husband died of a brain anneyrsum. My family is not one to test. I follow behind my sister, texting Kyla I will be coming back late.

Twenty-Four

"Zola! Hurry up! You have been in there forever." Cries Lynn as she bangs on the bathroom door.

I take a deep breath as I stare into the fogged mirror at my reflection. With my constant lethargy and the throwing up, there may be a possibility that it is caused by a different factor. I keep telling myself that stress is all it is, but now that my period is two weeks late, I am starting to worry.

I brought two different brands of tests after the rehearsal dinner. Because of the way she has been watching my actions when she assumes I am not looking, I feel Kyla may be on to me. I am surprised she has not just bluntly asked me whether I am pregnant.

After talking with my sister the other night to help her overcome her jitters and finally marry the man she has wanted since high school, I decide to overcome my own fear of maybe becoming a mother. I pee on both sticks and hide them under my boxer shorts on the counter. Yet even after hyping myself up in the shower, I still do not have the courage to check the results.

Maybe I can get one of the girls to do it. No! That would just turn into another discussion that I am also not ready for. I have no idea who the father is. Because of my stupidity and confused heart, I slipped up and slept with both Travis and Traymel in the same week with no protection.

Condom use has always been my number-one rule of thumb when it comes to my sex escapades. *Now look at me! I am nearing thirty and still getting caught up in childish scenarios. How do I even go about telling them if I do happen to be pregnant? "Um, sorry, one of you may be a father, but we will not know until a few months from now.* Talk about the awkwardness and additional stress.

This is my sister's wedding day, and I do not want to cloud her happiness with this. I have waited this long; I can wait a little longer. Wrapping the sticks up in the shorts without looking at the results, I paste a smile on my face and open the door to a red-faced Lynn.

"Finally!" She shoves pass me to the toilet. "I had to pee *so bad.*"

"Sorry, Lynn. Beauty of this magnitude takes time."

She rolls her eyes as I step out to give her privacy, which does not really matter at this point since she is already on the toilet. I swear, true friendship opens weird doors.

I walk into the bedroom, where Kyla is sitting on the bed, frowning at her phone while fully dressed. "I swear you have always been an early riser." She shrugs as she stands and stretches.

I put on sweats and a sports bra to head to the venue since we are getting ready there. I stash the sticks in my purse for me to look at them later, after all the festivities. Fifteen minutes later, my mother arrives to pick us up to bring us to meet up with Nicole and Katy.

Today we are all smiles with Nicole and are proud of her as she takes on the next chapter of her life—even if it is with Ethan. Once we are all escorted to the bridal chamber, the craziness erupts yet again. There are three hairdressers, one makeup artist, and a nail technician waiting to get everyone ready for the ceremony in a few hours. Mimosas are poured and passed around as we chat and laugh and just take in everything. I am trying to play it off by not drinking, but when Lynn calls me out, I down a glass to get her off my back, fighting the nausea. *Hopefully there is no baby cooking in this oven.* Aunt Linda is moving about, taking nonstop pictures and videos for us to have memories of this joyous occasion. Nicole seems to be in better spirits today.

"I want to make a toast!" cheers Lynn as she stands in the middle of the floor.

"Ugh! Not you, Lynn. Nobody got time for your crazy talk," grumbles Nikki as she sits under the hair dryer while her nails are being painted.

"Come on, Nikki," remarks Katy. "Lynn is hilarious."

"Thank you! You and I are going to be great friends after this wedding."

Nicole rolls her eyes, and Kyla giggles. "Anyway! I just want to say, Nikki, I am genuinely happy for you. I had my doubts about this wedding. Love is not something I have witnessed often, always believing it is reserved for the highest bidder—a feeling that rarely comes around and sometimes is mistaken for something that is not genuine. Nevertheless, you and Ethan proved everyone wrong. All your family and friends are here to watch and celebrate this momentous occasion. May you have many, many prosperous years ahead and married life be everything you anticipated."

"Wow, Lynn! I didn't think you had that in you," comments my mother.

"It's the liquor, Ms. Anne." Everyone in the room erupts in laughter and cheers.

About two hours later, we are ready to roll. Nicole's wedding dress is gorgeous. It is an off-white satin empire waist with a sweetheart neckline—a masterpiece. There is a long chiffon train sewed into the waist area.

I watch as my mother helps put her veil on. Pure joy is radiating from her pores. She seems to have found true happiness and confidence in her decision. I am proud to see my baby sister take this next step in her life. These are the rare instances that make me reconsider whether marriage is a path for myself and whether I am meant to find my soulmate to live eternity with. Walking over to them, I give her a hug right as Lamar walks in. He is walking her down the aisle since our father is not in the picture.

"My three favorite women all in one place," he gushes as he takes us all in a bear-hug.

"I swear, Mar, if you mess up my makeup," Nicole chastises him.

Mom and I walk out the room and she goes to find a seat up front as I join the other bridesmaids to prepare for the wedding march. Even though it is a Halloween wedding, Nikki chose lilac and gray as her wedding colors.

The bridesmaids are wearing lilac chiffon dresses with mermaid scoop necklines, whereas the groomsmen have on gray tuxedos and lilac ties. As maid of honor, I have a satin lilac-ombre one-shoulder A-line gown.

The venue is decorated in array of gray and lilac flowers with streamers and a red carpet down the middle. The glass ceiling is polished to perfection to allow the sunlight to shine in, causing the crystal fixtures to sparkle.

The music begins, and the walk proceeds. I enter right before the bride, along with the best man, which happens to be Travis. I have not seen him since his visit to San Diego, and I have been dodging his calls since I decided to spend some time on myself. He was not able to make it to the rehearsal dinner since he got caught up with work. As he holds out his arm for mine, our eyes connect, and a smile breaks across his face. I see a bit a puffiness under his eyes, indicating he did not get much sleep last night.

"Beautiful as always!" he whispers as we begin our stride down the carpet. I give a soft smile.

The bridal chorus begins once we have taken our spot, and I watch my siblings make their way toward us. The mesmerizing look of love on Ethan's face as Nicole closes the distance between them would make any woman jealous.

I had hoped that I would be in her shoes one day in life, but that is a wish for another lifetime these days. Even with all the bumps and twists they have been through together; it was all worth it in the end. As they recite their vows and proclaim their love to everyone in attendance, a warm feeling fills me at how wonderful this all turned out.

When Nicole turns and hands me the bouquet so she can exchange rings, I catch Travis staring at me with a similar look to the one his half-brother gave my sister earlier. I quickly cast my eyes away to calm my beating heart.

The preacher then calls for the "kiss the bride" moment, and the crowd erupts in cheers as rice is thrown over the retreating newlyweds. The bridal party follow in procession behind them so we can take pictures in all our wedding getups before changing for the reception.

Once I am back in the changing room upstairs, digging through my bag, I come across my purse and remember I still need to cross that last hurdle. I glance around to see the others occupy with pictures and drinks. Closing my eyes and taking a deep breath, I pull out the sticks. Mustering an ounce of fearlessness, I open my eyes and see the results. I stare in shock as tears well up in my eyes. All the doubts are put to rest as they both display positive readings. I am truly pregnant. *Who is the father to be? Who do I wish it is? Where does my heart lie?*

Twenty-Five

I swipe through the pictures on my phone. The girls and I were rocking those dresses. Talk about a beautiful wedding! Looking up, my eyes sweep over the reception. The love from family and friends emits a vibrant aura in the air. Smiles that are not forced grace the faces of all the guests. Laughter that is genuine fall upon my ears like a lilting melody. No need for a mask of an illusion when you are happy around the people that mean the most to you.

Catching sight of my friends at the chocolate fountain, I head towards them, looping my arms with theirs as I squeeze between. "My lovelies! Are we acting like kids with the melty goodness?"

"It's just too delectable to ignore," Kyla remarks as she sticks her finger under the waterfall, coating it in the chocolate fondue.

"And you supposed to be the workout guru," Lynn mentions.

"Hey! I have my weaknesses too." She pops her finger in her mouth and moans in pleasure.

I lean away from Kyla with a smirk. "Guh, you sound like you having an orgasm over there."

She shrugs.

"Well, ladies, it is time for Jonathan and me to hit the road for our mini road trip back to Cali," Lynn informs before sticking a chocolate-covered cookie in her mouth, smacking her lips in delight.

I chortle. "Have fun, you red she-devil. And have *lots of sex!*"

"You know they will," quips Kyla. Lynn sticks her tongue at her.

I drop my arms from theirs. "Lynn, when you come back, I have some *major* news to tell the both of you," I announce with a shy smile. I am still trying to come to grips on my own accord with the news.

"Tell us now," Lynn whines, but I shake my head. "Well, why would you get my hopes up like that just to shoot them down?" She scrunches her nose in thought. "Is it about Traymel? Travis? Maybe preggo?"

I use all my strength to mask my expression of surprise that she guessed it so easily. I really want them to wait until I at least talk to the guys. "You will wait, nosy Rosie," I remark, laughing.

She crosses her arms and pouts. "So not fair!"

"Be safe on that road, girl, and send me pictures of some awesome sights," Kyla says.

We do a big group hug before Lynn and I skip off to give her final congratulations to the bride and groom. Kyla heads in the direction of Lamar. I have seen them around each other all night. I hope she is not letting her despair get her in another sticky situation.

Lynn goes to fix herself a plate from the buffet line for the road. Noticing the crowd growing on the dance floor, I go investigate the commotion. My mom and brother are dancing the cha cha slide, both drunk off their butts. Grabbing Kyla's arm from her antisocial position in the shadows, I drag her on the floor as others join in.

"*Lynn, come on!*" I holler just as she is about to head upstairs.

She skips over laughing, jumping in the front of the crowd and shaking her butt to the music, completely ignoring the synchronized steps to the song. Travis takes his phone out of his pocket and videos the show. When the song comes to an end, I have him take one last group picture of us before Lynn leaves.

I head outside to the side of the building to check my phone. I am waiting for some approvals for two new contracts I have been working on. Even though this is vacation, I am still a partner and need to guarantee my career is at its tip-top level.

On my way back inside, I notice Lynn rushing over to meet Jonathan by the door with the bag from upstairs. He throws out a cigarette he was just smoking, pushing himself from the side of the rental.

"When did you start smoking?" I hear her inquire as she walks to the car.

"I do it occasionally. Have a lot on my mind," he says with a shrug of his shoulders.

I peer at him as she touches his arm. "You want to talk about it?" she whispers quietly, barely loudly enough for me to hear from this distance.

He yanks his arm away, his fist clenched. "Maybe later, once we get on the road."

He tosses her bag in the trunk as she hops into the passenger seat. He then walks to the driver's side before placing his hand on the hood and giving me a cold stare. I return the phone to my bra as I give him the same intense glare. *What is his problem?* He shakes his head before climbing in the car and driving out of the parking lot.

I watch the retreating headlights as the car turns onto the road before stopping suddenly. My forehead creases as I watch Jonathan reverse the vehicle and drive back into the parking lot, pulling over by a large tree off to the other side of the building. Curiosity getting the best of me, I begin to jog over to the car to make sure everything is okay. Jonathan has been acting strangely since the rehearsal dinner.

As I reach the car, Lynn is climbing out, screaming at him. "Why do you never talk to me about what is bothering you?"

The driver's door swings open, and he also steps out of the car in frustration. He takes a deep breath before heading to her side. He swipes through his phone before handing it to Lynn. She reluctantly takes it and glances at the screen, pressing against it.

I walk a little closer as I hear the muffled sounds of a video in the still, dark night. It is the video of Michael proclaiming his love to Lynn on Facebook Live for the whole world to see. It seems, by the angry glare on his face, he knows she is the woman Michael is speaking of.

She peeks back up at Jonathan, masking her emotions. He reaches over and scrolls further down the screen. Whatever she sees next has her face blanching. I am sure it is another incident dealing with Michael. Since I hear no noise, I assume this time it must be a picture.

"This isn't what it seems," she says with a quavering voice, looking up into Jonathan's dark eyes as she hands him back the phone. Tears are collecting in her eyes. All that joy that bubbled through her throughout the day vanishes at once.

"Wh-Where did these come from?" Lynn stutters, fighting back a sob catching in her throat. I come up behind her and pull her into my arms as tears begin to fall.

"It doesn't matter where they came from," Jonathan responds through gritted teeth. "The point of the matter is what they show. With a man you *claim* to be over." Anger and betrayal are apparent upon his features.

"It is not what you think." She gulps, mumbling against my chest. "There is an explanation."

He slams the phone against the gravel before stomping it into pieces, causing us both to jump. "There is always an explanation when it comes to you. You cannot lie your way out of this, Lynn. I thought I could trust you. I believed you left your whorish ways behind you."

"Bastard!" we shout in unison. Lynn pushes against me and stomps closer to him, raising her hand to slap him, but he catches her wrist in midair. She yanks her hand out of his death grip.

"You and this anger problem of yours. You let it cloud your judgment as you jump to outrageous conclusions. Those pictures caught only a glimpse of what was really going on in those situations. Yet instead of asking *me*"—she pauses for emphasis—"about it like a trusting boyfriend, you throw my past in my face." Her head bends down, looking at the ground. She is now full-blown ugly crying. "But clearly it doesn't matter. In the end, I still will never be good enough."

She spent all these months working to be a good and faithful girlfriend for him, cutting out her wandering ways—something she never bothered with in the past. *And it is not even appreciated.* She told me she is in love with him, and she was planning to tell him on this trip.

"Thanks for being another person in my life to show me that love doesn't really exist," she shrieks, swiping at her runny makeup across her botched cheeks.

He steps closer to her, taking her chin in his hand and yanking her head up to look him in the eyes. Dark clouds move in from a distance—a thunderous storm at bay. His other hand reaches out and caresses her cheek.

"Lynn, I love you so much it hurts. You are the only person I have met that can make me happy and angry at the same time. When I received those pictures a few days ago, I did not want to believe it. I thought we were growing something more."

He closes his eyes for a quick second, breathing through his nose. "Seeing your friend get married, I envision that for us in the future." His eyes open again, a dark look covering his features. "Then I remembered that video he posted, professing his love and missing all the years you spent together, and it clicked."

His lips form a thin line. "He was the one that you were always with when you kept friend-zoning me. Here I have been competing with a man I will never win against. I am sure that now that his wife is out of the picture, you can both finally be a legitimate couple. There will be nothing I can do to persuade you to stay with me." He pushes her away from him, causing her to stumble back across the rocks.

"There is nothing you need to do," she blubbers like a fool, trying to get him to believe in her. "I am in love with you, Jonathan. Not Michael. He is my past, and you were supposed to be my future."

He arches an eyebrow. "Were? Am I not anymore?"

Her eyes cast my way, pleading for some type of help. I step forward when she lightly shakes her head before returning her glassy gaze to him. "I have to think about it. I am not sure if I want to be the person you dump your negativity on when you want to fight about false facts." She pulls her bottom lip between her teeth.

Jealousy can drive a person mad.

"You are clearly unhappy and need to work on yourself. I am not looking to be your psychiatrist or even your anger outlet."

"I was hoping you wouldn't say that," he replies. When he steps closer and she steps back, I turn on my heel to run inside to get Lamar and Travis to come help with the situation.

Jonathan seems extremely angry, and I am not sure what he is capable of. I still to this day believe that mark on Lynn's jaw was a bruise and not a hickey. I consider that maybe Jonathan is not the good person we all believed.

"I think you should leave. I am no longer in the mood to go on this trip," I hear Lynn say as I make my way up the hill.

The words "soul mate" whisper through the air past my ear just before another sound that is more unnerving than the first—and far louder.

Bang!

I stop in my tracks, whipping my body around, my eyes frantically sweeping the scene before me.

I wish I had turned around and glanced over my shoulder sooner. Maybe I should have never left her side to begin with. I thought I was doing the right thing by going to get the guys to handle Jonathan. These questions will forever haunt my imagination, because maybe, just maybe, I could have been able to stop a tragedy from happening.

He ... shot her?

Johnathan stands in the same place I left him, his right arm raised at a ninety-degree angle from his body, holding a black handgun in his grip, the shadows from the trees making the determined expression on his face more sinister.

He ... shot ... her!

My gaze shifts to Lynn. A ghost of sadness features upon her beautiful face, her body turned in my direction. That mass of red curls, illuminated in the moonlight, is struggling to be seen through the black cloud moving effortlessly above Envy Center, shrouding this memorable occasion in darkness. Lynn must have been walking away from him, back to the family she knew she could count on.

Yet ... he shot her!

I fall to my knees, my arms unmoving against me, as my heart beats to a stop. The look of surprise and despair is engraved on my face as a void forms in my heart. My eyes open to their maximum. My mouth goes slack, causing it to instantly dry. There is a feeling of suffocation as the air around me stills. My lungs are slowly collapsing from the lack of impetus to breathe. I am alone. Pained. Broken. Frozen in a distraught state.

Her body appears to fall like a feather, slowly descending to the ground. Her brains are scattered across the lawn, her blood coating the grass beneath her. It feels as if I am stuck in a torturous beat of time that cannot be escaped but that I can only gradually endure. Her body lies on the grass, motionless.

Just like that, my bestie, my firecracker, a piece to my trio, my family not of blood ... shot by her boyfriend. Her lover. Her possible forever. On a day I should be filled with overwhelming joy, celebrating the happiness of my sister with all whom we love. All of it is now concluding on a heartbreaking note as I watch a person, just as important as Nicole taken from me, causing her to miss out on a life that she just begun to live.

Scattered droplets of rain begin to fall, hitting my skin in a repetitive cadence, mixing with the tears seeping from the corners of my eyes. The raging storm from the heavens drenches the ground, washing away the evidence of God's lost soul, soaking me as my clothes plaster against my body. A cold gust of wind swirls about, chilling me to the bone.

This can't be!

Lighting strikes the skies, snapping me out of my daze. I suck in a large intake of air, filling my lungs with the much-needed oxygen, initiating the blood flow to my heart as rapid beats pound against my tightening chest. A ringing roars in my ears, quieting the screams of others. Dizziness overcomes my senses as I drift off into a realm of darkness.

Made in the USA
Las Vegas, NV
06 September 2023

77147849R00111